D0279201

To Mum and Dad

Damage Land

New Scottish Gothic Fiction

Edited by Alan Bissett

Polygon

Polygon
An imprint of Edinburgh University Press Ltd
22 George Square, Edinburgh

Typeset in Galliard by Hewer Text Ltd, Edinburgh,
and printed and bound in Great Britain by
Creative Print and Design, Ebbw Vale, Wales

A CIP Record for this book is
available from the British Library

ISBN 0 7486 6284 7 (paperback)

The Publisher acknowledges subsidy from

towards the publication of this volume.

Contents

ACKNOWLEDGEMENTS

Thanks to Alison Bowden, Magi Gibson and Holly Roberts for advice and support, and all of the contributors for their efforts.

Acknowledgement is also due to Professor David Punter of Bristol University, not only for the excellent teaching and guidance, but whose article 'Heart Lands: Contemporary Scottish Gothic' in *Gothic Studies*, vol.1, no.1 (1999) can perhaps be regarded as the spirtual father of this book.

Grateful acknowledgement is made to the following sources for permission to reproduce material in this book previously published elsewhere. Every effort has been made to trace copyright holders, but if any have been inadvertently overlooked, the publisher will be pleased to make the necessary arrangement at the first opportunity.

Janice Galloway, 'Mons Meg' from *Pipelines* (Fruitmarket Gallery, 2000). © Janice Galloway.

Helen Lamb, 'Letters from a Well-Wisher' from *Chapman*, issue 94 (Chapman Publishing, 1999). © Helen Lamb.

Brian McCabe, 'The Host' from *New Writing Scotland 15: Some Sort of Embrace* (Association for Scottish Literary Studies, 1997). © Brian McCabe.

James Robertson, 'Mouse' from *New Writing Scotland 12: A Sort of Hot Scotland* (Association for Scottish Literary Studies, 1994). © James Robertson.

The quotation from James Kelman on p. viii is from 'Interview With James Kelman' by Kirsty McNeill in *Chapman*, issue 57.

The reference to Christopher Harvie on p. 2 regards his article 'The Devolution of the Intellectuals' in *New Statesman*, 90 (1975).

‘All you’ve got to do is follow some people around and look at their existence for 24 hours, and it will be horror. It will just be horror.’

James Kelman

'The Dead Can Sing':

An Introduction

The dead shall live. The living die,
And Music shall untune the sky.
Dilys Rose

As capitalism/technology accelerates, growing ever-more sleek and all-pervasive, a fresh, white, virginal century waits to be written on, and Scotland, meanwhile, blinks in the glare of the early years of its parliament, there is every reason to deny history.

But the dead have voices.

The dead can sing.

The Scottish psyche has been formed from being cast as underdog in the dialectic of power, from our being subsumed both in our own culture and in that of a stronger nation's. There is a place there where the two halves do not meet. Damage. A hairline crack, and what rough beasts emerge. Fantasy – at which Scotland has always excelled – is perhaps a method of re-imagining that lost part of our identity, loosing ourselves from the chains of the Empire, self-mythologising, creating a powerful and alternative nation in the collective imagination. Just as Walter Scott invoked the spirit of the dead, of a romanticised Scotland from the past to replace the whimpering, subjugated present of the nineteenth century, so too does Alasdair Gray, in one of the most imaginative outpourings of the modern day, react to Margaret Thatcher as latter-day Hammer of the Scots. In *Lanark*, the artist Duncan Thaw escapes a harsh and impoverished Glasgow into the fantastical world of Unthank. In Iain Banks's *The Bridge*, the hero slips into a coma to the titular edifice in his subconscious. We display a curious habit of 'dreaming' ourselves great rather than actually *being* great ('Flower of Scotland', maybe, as case-in-point).

Swathes have already been written about the contradictions involved in the Scottish character: caught between pride and servitude, Catholic and Protestant, the reality of urban labour and a dreamland of hills and heather, a low culture filled with tartan and lager and a high culture embarrassed by this, what Christopher Harvie calls the 'red' Scots (or Anglo-Scots) and the 'black' (those locked in the Kailyard). One only has to think of *Braveheart*, itself a classic case of the (Walter?) Scottish act of plucking a false greatness from the past to supplant the present (this time compounded by the fact of it being made in Ireland by an Australian backed with American money). Wallace has just defeated the English at the Battle of Stirling (Bridge), but the celebratory feast has descended into chaos about which noble has right to the throne. A stoic figure of disgust, Wallace exits, leaving Bruce to claim, 'From top to bottom, this country has no sense of itself. Its nobles share allegiance to England. Its clans war with each other.' In the end Wallace is betrayed by his own kind, the implication being that Scotland will never claim autonomy because it simply cannot agree with itself. That I recourse to a fictionalised account of history to illustrate my point, rather illustrates my point.

Scottish writers, for their part, have returned time and again to themes of disunity and schizophrenia. James Hogg's *The Private Memoirs and Confessions of a Justified Sinner* (1824), now perhaps (justifiably!) recognised as Scotland's greatest ever novel, features a young laird who encounters a malevolent double, a mental projection or Satan himself. The most famous

Scottish 'split personality' tale, Robert Louis Stevenson's *Dr Jekyll and Mr Hyde* (1886) is given a modern spin in Brian McCabe's doppelganger novel, *The Other McCoy*, or in McCabe's own story here, 'The Host', or in Ali Smith's 'The Hanging Woman' from her aptly named *Other Stories and Other Stories* book, or in Jackie Kay's disturbing contribution to this anthology, 'The Woman with Fork and Knife Disorder'. Everywhere, split, disharmonious voices. And what a tune.

If there is a literary genre, meanwhile, as difficult to place the finger on, it is Gothic. The Concise edition of *Oxford English Dictionary* defines it as:

> Adj. 1 of the Goths or their language. 2. In the style of architecture prevalent in W.Europe in the 12th–16th C., characterised by pointed arches. 3. (of a novel, etc.) in a style popular in the 18th–19th C. with supernatural or horrifying events. 4. Barbarous, uncouth. 5. Printing (of type) old-fashioned German, black letter, or sans serif.

While Martin Gray, in *A Dictionary of Literary Terms*, adds:

> Any work concentrating on the bizarre, the macabre or aberrant psychological states may be called Gothic. In this sense, Gothic elements are common in much nineteenth- and twentieth-century fiction.

So though generic Gothic can be located in specific time-periods, such as the twelfth–sixteenth or the eighteenth–nineteenth centuries, the term also proves endlessly mobile and endlessly anti-generic. According to Gray, Gothic novels – or at least 'elements' – may be more common in literature than one may first think. A great many writers not considered 'Gothic' by a general readership (and certainly not to be found in the Horror section of Waterstone's), nonetheless burgle the classic

Goths (such as Anne Radcliffe, Matthew 'Monk' Lewis, Mary Shelley and Edgar Allan Poe) for a certain psychological resonance, meaning Gothic is perhaps recognised more now as an X-ray of the frailties of and strains upon the human psyche – a most literary of forms – rather than the 'penny dreadful' entertainment it was considered by the Victorians. I think here of Franz Kafka, J. G. Ballard, Angela Carter, Williams Burroughs and Gibson, Sylvia Plath, Kurt Vonnegut, Margaret Atwood, Thomas Pynchon, Mervyn Peake, Flannery O' Connor, Toni Morrison, Donna Tartt, Phillip K. Dick, not to mention Stephen King and Thomas Harris, two great popular novelists who are writing more obviously in the mode. Even a glance at a list such as this is enough to confirm how the genre has mutated, of how many weird-looking cousins it has spawned since Horace Walpole penned the first Gothic novel proper, *The Castle of Otranto*, in 1764.

Perhaps, more than words or names, a random series of images could illuminate Gothic for us:

A dead body (usually female). Either torn apart or smoothly serene.

A snarling dog (probably rabid).

A frozen spiderweb. Holly. Blood?

An empty playground in the dead of night, littered with broken glass, wind starting to lift, the sound of children's voices (your imagination playing tricks?).

A medieval window (perhaps biblical figures?).

The apocalypse. Plague, fire or nuclear war. It doesn't matter which.

Gothic, to me at least, is not a genre, but a way of *seeing*. It is that which is going on beneath the world, that which we'd rather ignore, thankyouverymuch, if it's alright with you. The paranoid glance; the feeling of being followed; the bloom of adrenaline as a street-fight erupts from nowhere; being alert to these, heightened, frightened, as if reality, life, survival, everything that we take for granted, has come into sudden and shocking focus. Gothic is about breakdown, about terror, about the collapse of territory, structure, order, authority. Gothic does not believe in the unity of the self or in the safety of the flesh. Its bible is written in the margins, its church is buried underground, its hymns praise taboo and its choir is the dead.

Interestingly, almost all of Scotland's great modern novelists seem to have captured this in some form or another, including the nation's current big seller, Ian Rankin, in whose novels there is always a body, always a journey into the darkened world that skulks beneath the façade of the capital. Janice Galloway's heroine in *The Trick is to keep Breathing* is caught somewhere between Jane Eyre and Bertha Mason, a woman struggling to exist within the confines of society and whose mind is slowly unravelling. Iain Banks has contributed the gruesome carnival of *The Wasp Factory*. Irvine Welsh scrabbles in the muck of rape and soccer violence in the truly disturbing *Marabou Stork Nightmares.* Alan Warner writes in that awful gap between death and mourning in *Morvern Callar*, the corpse on page one lending an eerie undertow to the rest of the novel. James Kelman, meanwhile, at first glance, would seem to be following an anti-Gothic tradition, exploring the plight of the deprived in a manner exclusive of spectral effects. I would urge, however, re-reading of *How Late it was, how Late*, the protagonist of which, Sammy, spends the entire novel blind, lost, confused, desperate, clinging to the brink. As Sigmund Freud (perhaps outdated, but never mind) documented in 'The Uncanny', the most frightening objects are those which we encounter every day. That moment in which the familiar becomes unfamiliar is drawn out by Kelman, until we realise that the most terrible object is the one Sammy is meeting at every turn: the State. The doctor's surgery, the police, the very outside world become imbued with a sinister, almost Kafka-esque, and deeply Gothic threat. This is not even to mention John Burnside's *The Dumb House*, Michel Faber's *Under the Skin*, A. L. Kennedy's *So I am Glad* . . . I could go on (and indeed do; there's a list at the back of the book).

Gothic – so imbued with the spirit of heraldry and medievalism – has always acted as a way of re-examining the past, and the past is the place where Scotland, a country obsessed with re-examining itself, can view itself whole, vibrant, mythic. When myth becomes chanelled through the splintered prism of the present, however (as in Chris Dolan's story here), what emerges can only be something distorted and halfway monstrous. And while the Gothic has often been the conduit for collective fantasies and nightmares, there is something/someone/some *body* that haunts the fringes of the Scottish imagination: the anonymous 'they' perhaps of Janice Galloway's recurrent phrase, 'they never give you any warning'; perhaps Hogg's and Stevenson's demonic doubles; perhaps the whisper of history, pain, feudalism, legend, all or none of these things, but undoubtedly Scotland's is a fiction haunted by itself, one in a perpetual state of Gothicism. If we have any sort of mascot which reappears throughout our literature, it is Auld Nick, the Devil himself, Milton's rebel, who was also adopted by Byron, Blake and Shelley and other anti-establishment Romantics and, indeed, by the proletariat of the French Revolution.

It is perhaps this, however, more than anything, which aligns Scotland with the Gothic. The 'genre' is one which has always leaned conspicuously to the left, traditionally taken great delight in tearing to shreds the bourgeoisie, the Church, patriarchy, or any other bastion of power. The well-to-do families of *Dracula* (1897) and *The Exorcist* (1971) are ripped asunder by invading demons. In the Parisian riot scenes of Dickens's *A Tale of Two Cities* (1859) peasants gobble wine from the streets, foreshadowing the royal blood about to flow. The films *The Blair Witch Project* (1999) and *Deliverance* (1971) have the smart-arse middle classes out in the woods, at the mercy of those to whom they initially think themselves superior. The Gothic has always provided a political subtext beneath its slavering exterior, as much concerned with the body of the state as the state of the body. Indeed, as evidenced by J. G.

Ballard's *Crash* (1973), Chuck Palahniuk's *Fight Club* (1996) and Bret Easton Ellis's *American Psycho* (1991), the Gothic – the shocking return to the power of blood – may be the most valid artistic reaction to the massed ranks of consumerism.

Interestingly, perusing the British Gothic canon, one discovers, for the period, an unusually large proportion of women (Ann Radcliffe, Mary Shelley, Jane Austen, Charlotte Dacre, Charlotte Perkins Gilman, the Brontës) and Celts (Oscar Wilde, Charles Maturin, Stoker, LeFanu, Scott, Hogg, Stevenson). Somehow, being on the 'other' side of colonial or gender politics seems to mean an alternative sensibility, a negative aesthetic; like Milton's Satan, the demonised look back with demon eyes. This is why the title of the anthology is not in the past tense nor passive. Both Gothic culture and the new Scotland are about damage caused *by*, but also *to*, that which has policed it.

In the most democratic way, of course.

And so Scotland, 'barbarous, uncouth' Scotland, haunted by the past, growing in the shadows, is territory which I feel is long overdue for exploration, indeed, *celebration.* I allowed each writer the freedom to largely pursue his or her own vision of Gothic (since to pin the term down too much seemed a self-defeating and rather limiting exercise). The results are staggeringly varied – in tone, style, but most especially in content. Here is a veritable treasure trove of neuroses, mythologies, ghosts, psychopaths, cross-dressers, neo-Nazis, pimps, butchers, contract killers, dead bodies and bodily-growths. In **Michel Faber**'s story, we see a strangely reversed colonisation, as an English couple in the Highlands descend into savagery. **Toni Davidson** situates the 'split mind' theme in a twilight sex club, his protagonist torn between innocence and abandon. **Andrew Murray Scott** visits the terrain of Urban Gothic, in a tale of (partial) redemption set in a lavatorial cityscape. **Helen Lamb** is the closest relation to Hogg, as a shadowy agency offers epistolary advice. Both **Magi Gibson** and **Alison Armstrong**, in quite different ways, explore an obsession of modern Scottish Gothic, that of masculine insecurity. **Ali Smith** raises the spectre of that most real of evils, in a tale both feather-light and deeply menacing. **Christopher Whyte** retains the medieval roots of Gothic, ultimately probing the reader's mind. **Dilys Rose** is partly concerned with the pyschological effects of Thatcherism on the national and personal levels. **Jackie Kay**'s story is perhaps the scariest thing here, though one of everyday insanity. **Chris Dolan** takes the manufacturing of myths to an ebullient, apocalyptic extreme. **Linda Cracknell** starts with a vampiric kiss and ends in the only logical place. **John Burnside** pulls off a magic trick: his story about a bloody murder is also poetic and moving. **Laura Hird** writes about bodily degeneration, fusing the tale of a boy coping with AIDS to one about an innocent slaughter. **Sophie Cooke** is in Alan Warner territory: the existentialist horrors of youth culture. **Brian McCabe**'s story is frantic with paranoia, his narrator making an abominable acquaintance (with himself?). **Maggie O'Farrell**'s protagonist is haunted through Edinburgh by an ex-lover, things building to a momentous climax. **James Robertson** also deconstructs the Scottish hard man, the quiet skitter of tiny feet suddenly, monstrously chilling. **Raymond Soltysek** imbues pathos into a child's first brush with death. And **Janice Galloway**'s intriguing fairytale reveals a corpse beneath the capital, a darkness at the heart of the nation.

Savour, then, these trips through Damage Land, these eruptions of fear and alienation, because ultimately, and vitally, it is the real state of the nation, in all its troubled glory. Scotland needs the Gothic – like we need a strong voice of opposition, like we need the space to dream, like life needs death – because the dead have voices. The dead can sing. And to paraphrase Janice Galloway: 'How blessed in us they must surely be.'

Alan Bissett
Stirling, March 2001

The Host

Brian McCabe

So. How. Was. The. Film.

I was speaking in words but I didn't know what I was saying and my voice sounded thick and moronic and my mouth was dry and my heart was hammering and my skin felt like a cold chamois leather as I touched my face with my fingers – no doubt the way I would normally touch my face with my fingers if I was asking somebody about a film they'd been to see but nothing was normal because here in my room was a man with two heads.

For a horrible moment there was no response from anyone. Had the words come out of my mouth at all or had they come out sounding so strange that no one could make sense of them? Was it my drugs? Had I forgotten to take my drugs? No, I had taken them earlier. Had I got the dosage wrong? No, I distinctly remembered taking the correct dosage.

– Well, I thought it was not a bad film, but the book –

I felt a surge of gratitude to Jim. He had heard my question and he was answering it. He was talking about the film, thank God, so for the moment the attention of the room was not focused on me. Had nobody noticed that I was trembling and sweating and finding it difficult to speak?

I tried to pick up my glass and get it to my mouth. I couldn't help turning a little to check that the man who had been introduced to me as Douglas really did have two heads. I had seen the other head quite clearly when he'd come into the room and shaken my hand – lolling on his shoulder, as if it couldn't quite support itself. I'd had to look away as I'd said my pleased-to-meet-you.

It was there all right; I hadn't imagined it. In the dim light of my room it was difficult to see the crumpled features of the face, which was as pale as a cauliflower, but I could make out two screwed-up eyes, closed tightly under wispy, whitish eyebrows. I could see no clearly defined nose, but the lips were unmistakable – they looked dry and cracked and unnaturally old. Unnaturally old – that is the meaningless phrase that came into my mind. The face had set into an expression which was both sour and aloof. The way the lips curled down at one side and up at the other made me think of a kind of a bitter relish, as if the owner of the mouth might take pleasure in sarcasm. At the same time there was something dreadfully vulnerable in the face's frozen sneer and the way the head lolled against the back of the armchair Douglas was sitting in – to all appearances a dead appendage. And no-one seemed to have noticed it. Douglas himself appeared to be completely relaxed, as if utterly unaware of his encumbrance. He struck me as a congenial sort of guy, probably in his early thirties. Apart from his other head, his appearance was quite ordinary. He had longish brown hair and a neat beard. He looked mildly interested in the world and had a constant, rather vacant smile. He wore a dark-blue jacket, jeans and a casual, checked shirt.

But he had another head.

A red-haired woman I didn't know and whose name I hadn't taken in was disagreeing with Jim about the film and there were one or two comments interjected by the others – including Douglas. He didn't say much – as far as I could make out, he was agreeing with the general drift of the discussion about the film. He was quietly spoken, maybe even a bit shy, but it was the kind of shyness which hints at an inner confidence.

They were having this good-natured, not-too-serious sort of

debate about the merits of the film they'd been to see – for all the world as if nothing was out of the ordinary. I felt a moment of relief. The hammering of my heart was slowing down to a steady, heavy pounding. Although I'd raised my glass of wine to my lips, I still hadn't taken a drink. Now I gulped some of it down in the hope that it would steady my nerves.

Was I over-reacting? I was with friends, after all. Jim was a friend, a good friend, I had known him since schooldays. He often went my shopping for me, and that meant a lot to me. One or two of the others had been coming to see me for over a year now. There were strangers, but Jim often brought people back after a late-night film. It was supposed to do me good, help me cope with my agoraphobia, which he thought he understood. At least he understood that it wasn't just the fear of open spaces. He knew that it went hand-in-hand with claustrophobia. He understood that my fear was the fear of people. So he brought them round. It was supposed to encourage me to overcome it – or so I'd thought. Tonight he'd gone over the score. There were too many of them tonight. I couldn't see them clearly one by one as people, they were blurred into the same animal. I kept seeing movements of the feet and the hands but I didn't know whose they were. But although I saw them as one, at the same time I felt desperately outnumbered. It was difficult to hold on to my self.

Had Jim brought all these people round out of a spirit of charity or therapy? Maybe it was also convenient for him. Maybe he didn't want to take them all to his place. Here he was, acting for all the world as if he was doing me a favour by crowding out my house with the entire membership, I shouldn't wonder, of the local film club – one of whom had an extra head.

I glared at Jim, hoping to convey my displeasure with him in no uncertain terms, but he went on elaborating on some crucial discrepancy between the book and the film. He'd never brought this Douglas back before, I was certain of that, but people in the company seemed to know him, or if they didn't, they seemed to have accepted the fact that he had two heads with no trouble at all. Or maybe they were being polite. Maybe everyone in the room was doing his best not to look at it or talk about it, but inside they were panicking just as much as me. Or could it be that they were being quietly supportive? After all, an extra head, one which seemed to serve no purpose, must be a dreadful disability, and Douglas seemed to be coping with it incredibly well. Maybe later on, I thought – but only if Douglas brings the subject up and wants to talk about it – maybe then I'll ask him if he has ever thought about the possibility of having it surgically removed. Oh God – no! I couldn't possibly ask him that – what was I thinking of?

Douglas leaned forward to flick his ash into the ashtray on the coffee table. The head sprang forward to hang over his shoulder. With a start that set my pulse racing and almost made me yelp with fright, I noticed that one eye had opened a little and seemed to be peering at me as if from a great distance. When Douglas leaned back slowly – apparently he was listening to the post-mortem of the film with interest – the other head still hung forward, leaning one cheek on the collar of his jacket. I shuddered as I made out for the first time the tiny, creased nostrils. The head had, I was sure of it, taken a breath.

– So what do you think?

Jim had turned to put this question to me and everyone now looked to me, their host, for an opinion.

– Well . . . I mean obviously . . . not having seen it –

– But would you go to see it, on the basis of what we've said, or have we put you off going?

– Well, I wouldn't want to go to a cinema, but –

What was I doing? Trying to make light of my own condition? Or drawing attention to it, to spare Douglas the attention of the room? But then, no one was looking at him, everyone was looking at me, and I didn't know how to go on.

Jim smiled and said:

– You asked us what we thought of the film.

– No, you don't know what . . . I wasn't asking you what the film was *about*, what I *meant* was . . . what was it like to go and see a film, to sit in a place in the dark with . . . a crowd of other . . . I mean . . .

I trailed off, trying to use the glass and the wine as an excuse to interrupt myself. I truly could not go on, not only because I was talking nonsense but also because the image of a crowded, darkened cinema had come into my mind, with its rows of silhouetted heads. One or two people laughed, apparently under the impression that I was being deliberately obtuse out of a sense of mischief. Jim looked at me in a pointedly puzzled way. I spluttered on my wine. I made the most of it, pretending that it had gone down the wrong way and I was having a coughing fit. Someone sitting next to me obliged by thumping me on the back, but in the middle of it I began to wheeze with disbelief. The head had now opened both eyes and was looking around the room.

Douglas took the cigarette from his mouth and, without even looking at what he was doing, placed it carefully in the other head's mouth. The other head sucked on it with some difficulty, then Douglas removed the cigarette and went on smoking it himself. A thin jet of smoke came from the other head's mouth, which was as desiccated as a shelled walnut, then it gave a little cough. How can I explain how this little cough made me feel? It was like a baby's cough, alarming because it hints at an articulacy and a history no one would expect of it. The sound of it made me shudder inside, as if on the verge of tears. I had to suppress a heavy sob welling in my chest. But now it was doing something else: I watched the head's mouth in awe, as its dark, liverish tongue licked its cracked lips before speaking:

– That was very interesting.

The eyelids of both eyes had parted, but were still stuck together at the corners in a way that looked extremely uncomfortable. The eyes, deep blue in colour, looked enormous in the shrunken face. But it was the look in the eyes . . . How can I describe it? There was infinite depth and distance in it, as if it was still looking at something in another world it had just come from. Yes, that was it, the head was waking up. The eyelids blinked rapidly to unstick themselves completely and now the dark eyes looked directly at me.

– I don't mean what you were saying, but the way you were pretending to cough. Most people don't cough unless they have to, do they?

The voice was rather thin and chesty, with a squeaky quality that made it sound slightly comical. It was like the voice of a very old man, but it also sounded like the voice of a child, made harsh by some bronchial illness. The other head smiled with one corner of its mouth, then uttered another babyish cough.

I couldn't answer. I was aware of the babble of voices around us. Apparently Jim was being witty and people were laughing. No one was paying the slightest attention to me or the head which had just addressed me. They were having a good time, apparently, but I was breathing hard and trembling and my hands were sweating so much they felt gloved in oil as I tried to find something to say to this head, this other head growing out of a man's neck.

I looked to Jim to rescue me, but now he was engrossed in some kind of intellectual duel with the red-haired woman. Of course, it was transparent to me that they were flirting. If only that had been all that was going on in my room – but no, there had to be a man with another head that wanted to talk to me. Douglas himself showed no interest whatsoever in the head, even though it had woken up so conspicuously. He seemed completely preoccupied with stubbing his cigarette out, refilling his glass and following the conversation.

The crumpled face was waiting with an infinitely patient sadness. I had to say something:

– I'm sorry. It's just that I . . . don't know how . . . I've never met a person with . . .

– Two heads? Is that what you're driving at?

– Well . . . I suppose so.

The head, hanging at an angle so that it seemed to be peering around a corner, did its best to nod with resignation.

– It's more common than you think.

– What is?

– Two heads.

– Really? I had no idea.

– Lots of people have two heads. Ask him.

The other head indicated Douglas with a movement of its eyes and gave out a sharp little giggle. I glimpsed a row of neat, square teeth. Douglas raised the wine glass to his other head's lips, taking care not to spill it. This he managed to do without so much as glancing at the other head. Even so a drop of wine dribbled from the corner of the mouth. Douglas put the glass back down and took a tissue from his jacket pocket, with which he dabbed the other head's chin – though there was little in the way of what would normally be called a chin. All this he performed while staring straight ahead, apparently quite engrossed in the discussion about the film.

For a moment I saw Douglas and his other head as a music-hall double-act – the ventriloquist and his dummy. As if by telepathy, the other head looked at me and said:

– A gottle a geer.

It chuckled at its own joke and the sound of its gargling laughter made me want to cry again. I had to fight back the shuddering sobs which wracked me inside and threatened to burst out at any moment. I call the other head 'it' because that is how I thought of this extraordinary phenomenon, but now I was forced to confront the fact that 'it' was a thinking, feeling being – 'it' was, I had to admit, a person. Had the poor man been someone's other head all his life? It was an intolerable thought.

The small, puckered face smiled up at me.

– How old do you think I am?

My attempt at congenial laughter, as if we were engaged in the everyday social game of guess-how-old-I-am, left a lot to be desired. The small face with its vast, deep eyes watched me steadily as I brayed unconvincingly, waiting for my answer.

It was very difficult to tell how old he was. The eyes were as steady and watchful as a child's, yet they had a terribly knowing quality, as if they had seen the worst atrocities of humanity – the kind of thing most of us only read about in the newspapers. I could no longer meet their consuming gaze, and I studied Douglas – his main head and face, I mean, but also his clothes and his hands – before venturing:

– Well . . . younger than me – thirty? Thirty-one?

The other head snorted briefly and said:

– That's his age. What about mine?

– I have no idea when you . . . came about.

– Came about? Oh, you make the mistake of thinking I grew out of *him*. No, my friend, you have it all wrong . . .

I was alarmed by the way one of Douglas's hands suddenly stabbed a finger emphatically at his own chest.

– You see, *he* grew out of *me*.

The hand now flew up to the uppermost side of the other head's face and scratched a loose flap of skin – it must be, I realised, an earlobe – then it swooped to the coffee table and, in one fluid movement, lifted Douglas's glass of wine to the other head's mouth.

– My God, *you* did that!

The other head drained the glass, set it down carefully on the coffee table and smirked at me with pride, as if it had proven its point beyond question.

– My God. I see.

The head nodded to me then, and with a look of profound sadness said softly:

– *Now* you see.

And I did see. I saw Douglas in a completely new way, now that it was clear that his other head could control his body. His main head, his normal head – or the one I had taken to be 'main' and 'normal' – now looked gross, a bland and doltish growth which had brutally usurped the other head's place, pushing it aside and, for all I knew, drawing succour from it – like a fungus sapping the life of the tree from which it has swollen. His open, rather vacantly smiling expression now appeared to me as abhorrent as the sated leer of a callous parasite. The other head looked weak, drained of life, dying.

– Yes, he's taken over. I'm on the way out.

– That's terrible!

The other head smiled at me sadly.

– Oh, not so terrible. He's better looking than me. He's nicer, he'll get on all right. Less intelligent of course, and less honest – but that will be to his advantage. It was nice to meet you. You've been a very good host. But you look pale – you should get out more often.

The other head yawned, winked at me, then the fragile eyelids drooped and closed. He snuffled a little before his breathing slowed to a barely perceptible whisper in the air.

Douglas leaned back and the head swung behind his neck and subsided among the shadows of the armchair. His dominant head turned to look at me, as if he expected me to speak. Everyone was looking at me, waiting for me to speak. Jim had asked me a question and now he was repeating it:

– Are you all right?

I tried to pick up my glass, but my hand shook uncontrollably. Thankfully the glass was almost empty. Someone relieved me of it, there were other people's hands and faces everywhere, then Jim said something about there being too many for me.

– One too many, just one too many.

I looked at Douglas meaningfully as I said it and his eyes widened with baffled alarm. He stood up, and there was a sudden consensus in the room: everyone was standing up, draining glasses, putting coats and scarves on. The blurr of all that activity made me feel nauseous, dizzy. Voices kept offering me their apologetic thanks.

Jim, crouching down beside my chair, asked me again if I was all right. This really was the last straw. He brings enough people to my house to fill a small cinema – one of them a double-header into the bargain – then he asks me if I'm all right!

I stood up, pushing him aside and shouted:

– *I'm* all right. Ask your friend there how his other head is. Ask him if *he's* all right!

But Douglas was already shuffling hurriedly into the hallway, where a few of the others were already waiting to leave. Jim looked at me with puzzled concern.

– Take it easy now. We're going.

– About time too.

Jim turned and raised his eyebrows to the woman with red hair. It was evident to me that they had formed an unspoken pact. It would be back to his place, or hers, for sexual congress. But would it bring them closer to each other, or even to themselves? Somehow I did not think so. I suspected that their transaction between the sheets would leave both of them feeling lonelier than they had felt before, if either of them had ever felt truly lonely.

Jim said he'd call round in a day or two, thanked me for my hospitality and said they'd see themselves out. That was just as well, because I didn't feel particularly like standing around in my own doorway, exposed to the elements as I exchanged farewells with him and his army of film buffs. Let them go out into the street, under the empty sky. It was all right for them, they could do that with their eyes wide open and their heads held high, without the dread and the panic and the keeping near the wall and the scurrying for cover like a beetle when its stone is overturned.

When the front door eventually closed, I breathed more freely. The room seemed to settle into place around me, it became familiar again, but I felt exhausted by the evening's events. I wanted the warm cocoon of my bed. In reality it would be cold, unless I filled myself a hot water bottle, and I felt too tired to do that. It was hard work, being the host. It was all I could do to tidy up the glasses and bottles and ashtrays before going to the bathroom to clean my teeth.

As I pulled the switch-cord, the sudden bright light made my reflection jump out of the mirror at me. The roar of the Xpelair couldn't drown out my gasp of outrage at what I saw. It was there, no matter how often I wiped the condensation from the mirror with my sleeve, a mushroom-like swelling on my neck: the face was not fully formed, but already I could make out the mildly interested eyes and the constant, rather vacant smile.

Letters from a Well-Wisher

Helen Lamb

Dear B

You don't know me but I have been assigned to observe you – your habits, movements and so on.

And I'm not happy with what I see. The Bricksworth Building Society – Monday to Friday, your slow unwinding Saturday, sprawling Sunday – then like some jealous slob of a god, you survey Football Italia and see that it is good.

In the past few weeks, I've learned so much about you B, more than you will ever know. And yet CONTROL forbids me to pass my findings on, not even a hint as to where you might be going wrong. I'm sorry but I don't agree with this policy of non-interference. Somebody has to tell you. You need to be told.

It wouldn't be so bad if you actually built something. But where are the bricks? How are you supposed to start? Take my advice B, get some today. Also, may I suggest, a trowel and cement.

Yours constructively
A Well-Wisher

Dear B

Do you remember A, your fearless childhood friend? He was my first case-study.

A was some kid, wasn't he? Always tumbling out of trees and playing chicken in the traffic. His injuries were spectacular. Not just the usual collection of skint knees. He got concussion and compound fractures. And then there was the putting flag he speared through his left foot. The tooth embedded in his shin. Luckily, not yours. Though, at the time, you wished it was. Because you envied him, didn't you B?

You stole plasters from the First Aid Box and stuck them where they showed. But no one ever asked what you'd been up to. A always had a gorier story. He was just that kind of boy.

I say *was* – because A's not with us anymore, not since the poaching expedition. Remember? You were there as well. But A went over first and when the owner let the rottweilers loose, you hid behind the wall. You couldn't bear to watch. But you still heard him, his feet pounding faster and faster, and your heart raced with him, very nearly gave out too before the dogs caught up with him. You almost died yourself that day.

And A didn't call on you. Not anymore. Though, now and then, you thought you heard him. Times out riding your bike when he even got quite loud.

LOOK NO HANDS
LOOK NO HANDS

Of course, you were too sensible to listen to a ghost. You ignored him. You kept on ignoring him B. So he asked me to pass on this message for him.

Don't forget to have fun – he says. That's all.

A Well-Wisher.

Dear B

I was watching you at the check-out queue in Tesco's the other day and your trolley saddened me. The lack of taste, the poverty of imagination it displayed. You're not so hard up. You don't need to eat spaghetti hoops every day. Six cans – I counted. And one of ravioli. Anything for a change, I suppose. But that solitary can looked like a cry for help to me. Ravioli is desperate stuff.

And Cheddar cheese is for mice. Are you a mouse or a man? Try Parmesan and *real* spaghetti. Or something blue – a Stilton or a nice ripe Brie. It's not as dangerous as it looks. You'll survive. Think about it B, between now and next shopping day. Think about Parmesan.

A Well-Wisher

Dear B

Is your door locked and bolted? Are your windows secured? Is your little home fully insured against fire, theft, accident and sundry Acts of God? Lightning? Locusts? Earthquake? Flood? Have you saved up for that rainy day? I bet you have.

But do you sleep easier? I don't think you do. I've seen your light. At two and three o'clock in the morning, it flickers on and your flame curtains glow. Your bed is restless, your bed is on fire. Or that's how it looks from the outside. That's how it looks to me. I could be wrong.

Maybe a burglar broke into your dream. Or, sensing my presence, you woke with a start and decided to get up and check the small print on your policies. Are you covered for well-wishers? Do you have any protection against optimists like me?

Because I do have hopes for you, dear B. The insomnia, for example, that gives me hope. That is an excellent sign. And those lumps in your mattress, do you know what they are?

Possibilities.

Disturbing possibilities. Felicity from accounts is one. Office hours, you ignore her. But, at night, you can't avoid her. Her breasts hump the bed. You toss. You turn. Her knee digs into the small of your back.

Don't ask me how I know these things. Let's just say I'm the sensitive type. And I'm telling you B, Felicity is a distinct possibility.

A Well-Wisher

Dear B

You've been tearing up my letters. Don't think that I don't know. All my helpful hints reduced to useless scraps of paper.

I have written. I have written. I've put in for a transfer but until CONTROL gets back to me it looks like I am stuck.

My life is not my own. And yours is getting me down. If you were a half-decent host, it wouldn't be so bad. If you made some effort to entertain. But I don't even get to see your friends. You do still have some, don't you B? If not I thought we could invite Felicity round for dinner tonight. Don't worry, I can be discreet. She won't even know I'm here.

A Well-Wisher

Dear B

Just a quick note to let you know I'll be away for a few days. Orders from CONTROL.

I'm getting too close to the subject. That's you by the way. The subject. And what a boring one you are. You didn't ask her, did you? No. You didn't even say good morning.

AWW

Arbroath

Dear B – Hope you like the postcard of the Deil's Head (see over). You wouldn't wish to be here but it would do you good to stand on the edge of these windy cliffs. The erosion of sandstone is treacherous and quick. Where your toes curl today may be the void tomorrow. Or sooner. Who knows? Who can predict when the ground will give way?

AWW

Dear B

Got back lunch time yesterday and resumed my tail at once. Though I don't suppose you noticed. The extra shiver in the breeze? The slanted shadow that fell from nowhere? That was me. And twice we touched. We were that close.

So here I am. Again. I did enjoy the break but the comforts of the B&B had begun to pall and I confess I missed my vigil. Couldn't help worrying while I was away. And not without good reason it would seem.

I know I'm not supposed to write. CONTROL would not approve. And, I admit, I was the one who wanted more excitement. All the same, it's one thing to take a calculated risk, quite another to wreak havoc on the public highway. Yesterday evening on the way home from work, you jumped the lights five times. And all this doubling back on your tracks is downright anti-social in a one-way system.

Trust me. Nobody is following you. I would know. I keep a very close eye on you. So clunk-click for now and drive carefully.

A Well-Wisher

Dear B

I don't think you've met C. A fascinating character. Dangerously erratic on the road. And unreliable. I never know what he'll decide to do next. Will he/won't he grace the Bricksworth with his presence today?

We'll just have to wait and see. But first there's something you should know.

The thing is B – he looks a lot like you. And some of your less discerning colleagues have trouble telling you apart. Felicity sure notices the difference though, can't take her eyes off you. Sorry – I meant *him*. Just a slip of the pen but, now that I pause to consider it, fortuitous perhaps. For it suddenly occurs to me B, what with the resemblance and everything, if you were to impersonate him . . . ?

A Well-Wisher

Dear B

It is with deep regret that I write to inform you this will be my last letter. CONTROL says its got to stop and, as of 1400 hours today, I've been relieved of my responsibilities.

So B, you're on your own from now on. Wish the same could be said for me. At this very moment, as I force my pen across this final page, a hefty sour-breathed gentleman stands guard at my shoulder. Someone to watch over me. I think that's how CONTROL put it. And what is the charge? What did I do to deserve this foul fate?

Disruptive influence, apparently. They tell me you will never be the same again, B. Can't say I'm very sorry about that.

My jailer's shaking his head. He heaves another punishing smelly sigh. If I would just show some remorse – he says. This attitude will get me nowhere.

Of course, I fought the decision. You know me. Don't you B? You know me?

CONTROL tells me you don't want to. *You* are the one who got me locked away. You shopped me B. Is that true? Perhaps you're more devious than I thought. But no one can keep me inside forever. Not even you. One day, I'll be out of here. With good behaviour, my jailer says, who knows . . . ? When he speaks I'm obliged to hold my breath but the reek of his righteousness still gets up my nose. He says he might even be prepared to recommend me for parole. Not if I break out first he won't.

Expect me soon B – with a vengeance. I will be back.

A Well-Wisher

Like a Pendulum in Glue

Toni Davidson

I don't want to be here .

Louche screwed his eyes tight shut. He pressed his fingertips into his eyes and tried to chase the lingering orange blotches away from the darkness. For a few seconds he could still see the strip light until its glow slowly faded into nothing. He was lifted on to the kitchen units while the voice, his voice, kept repeating *I don't want to be here, I . . . don't . . . want . . . to . . . be . . . here.*

BRING IT ON, BABY, LET THE GOOD TIMES ROLL.

Louche heard his father singing, an off-key rendition, a vibrating sore that pulsed and throbbed, burrowing deep into his head. The tape was blasting in the empty kitchen and although he couldn't see him, Louche could hear his father's dance steps, tapping and scraping at the vinyl floor. His father was a good mover. Sometimes when Louche's eyes were half open, that frightening slit of light searing his world, halting for a moment his voice, he had seen the quick steps, the body swerves and hip sways. His father was in no doubt of his own abilities. In half vision Louche saw him linger in front of his image in the long mirror which hung on the wall. He swerved and veered in front of it, checking his step every so often to twirl then sweep a can from the floor, a swift drink that didn't break his tempo.

LET'S SHAKE, SHAKE, SHAKE.

Louche kept his eyes closed even when he heard his father tap his way closer to him, his hands keeping time with the rock ’n roll beat, drumming an insistent rhythm on the kitchen surface, a vibration that rippled his skin and made the hair on his arms stand up.

COME ON, BABY, WON’T YOU DANCE WITH ME?

The words were both in the air and in Louche’s face. His father took Louche’s bony arms and swung them from side to side but, still, he kept his eyes shut, not letting one ray of light into his head. The voice inside was still there; he didn’t have to check to make sure. It never seemed to go away.

I want to be somewhere else.

Suddenly the music stopped and he felt his father lean forward. His words were whispered, a long breath taken in and slowly released.

‘Son, you have to learn to enjoy yourself.’

‘C’mon, baby, come closer.’

Louche’s eyes were wide open in the pitch black. And he could see nothing. She wasn’t talking to him. Louche knew that. But for a strangely dark and sparkling moment he thought she was. Who she was talking to, who in fact she *was*, Louche had no way of telling in the blackened arch. He sensed her close to his body, not just her scent but that sense of movement that doesn’t require vision – like his own voice which didn’t need to be spoken. Of course, he could have reached out and touched but his heartbeat quickened and a voice in his head surged.

Take a step back, move away from this corner, get back into the open.

For a moment he hesitated, just enough to feel another presence close to him, brushing past his near-naked body. Scent, movement and, yes, expectation told him that it was a man. Louche pressed himself tightly against the wall he knew was behind him, and the woman’s insistent encouragement first faded then became muffled, her voice swallowed by a kiss, the sound of flesh against flesh, the sigh of release . . .

Inside, Louche could hear a voice again, its tone pulsing with threat, its persistent echo refusing to fade until he listened, obeyed and once again squeezed his eyes half shut and groped his way along the wall and into the next arch.

It was a little brighter, illuminated by the lash of candlelight. Here, the dozen or so figures moved as though exercising some kind of penitence. A slow walking monotony weighed down their steps, their bodies rigid and shackled by chains, but their heads and particularly their eyes were alert to their surroundings. Their clothing was elaborate but not particularly sophisticated. Stretches of rubber held by stretches of skin. Some men had rubber masks, some women thigh-length boots. It was uniform. In front of him an overweight, middle-aged man was led by an erstwhile dominatrix, chain in one hand, a whip dangling limply by her side. The entirely neutral look on the man's face terrified Louche, galvanised his own self-reproach into a frenzy, dragged him over burning coals, each with a spike that drove deep into his flesh, making his skin pop and sigh. Near one of the elaborate candlesticks that lit the poor brickwork of the arch a man leaned against the wall, his hands behind his head, his eyes tight shut, a grimace of something on his face. On her knees a woman dressed as in Victorian times was sucking his penis, her quickening, thrusting movements dislodging her emerald-green hat, the veil temporarily shifted to one side. There was a strange routine not only to their action but to the others in the room; single men mostly who watched with tight lips where lips were visible, with concentrated stares where eyes could be seen. But for the distant thud of music there was silence in the room broken only by metal links of the dominatrix's chain.

What is the point of this? I should be the point of this.

The other voice inside him, the one that rose above doubt's persistent echo, flashed like a torch in darkness. It reminded him why he was here. For a moment, just for one teasingly succinct moment. Until he felt overwhelmed by hope's bright glare, until he felt as though he was suffocating and unbearably hot, despite his near-naked state. Clothed only in rubber shorts and leather boots he felt restricted and, at the same time, both under- and overdressed. He shut his eyes completely, not wanting to be part of the silent stare, not feeling he had anything to share.

'Come on, let it fly, let it go . . .'

His father gave him the kite just as it gained some height. He was jogging backwards up the hill, struggling and fighting with the string, both laughing and cursing as it dipped then soared then dived towards the ground, its brightly coloured tail close to the grass. As it climbed again, Louche closed his eyes and hung on to its tail, feeling the lift and rise into the air, his own dangling legs becoming part of its tail. He was jogging half heartedly alongside his father, who was willing and wishing the kite into the air. For one moment his father unexpectedly lifted him up off the ground, desperately trying to give the kite a chance to fly in the light wind. When he lifted him up, Louche opened his eyes just the tiniest of fractions and saw the ground rush away from him. For that moment he too was airborne. But then the kite nosedived and he found himself back on the ground, his father huffing and puffing beside him, dragging the sadly grounded kite back up the slope. Some part of him was still soaring, yet another part was buried deep in the ground, lungs struggling for air, his eyes filled with earth. Louche sat beside him and watched through half-open eyes the sorry winding in of the tangled string. His father whispered into his ear, the words laboured, tense.

'You could maybe try a little harder, son.'

There was a peep show in another arch. Here there were more people than Louche had seen all night. They were two or three deep in front of the cage, which had been draped in black cloth. Around ten or so slits had been torn in the fabric, and the viewers, some with their hands on someone else, watched the participants of the peep show. There was both a sense of concentration and strange distraction as these bodies pressed against each other. Louche joined the viewers. Of course, inside his head a voice gushing with enthusiasm was veering from one suggestion to another – that he should be on the other side of the cage, that he should be running wild and feverish, that he could have been dipping and sucking and entwined, sublime among the assorted bodies splayed out in every stage of coitus. He worked his way to the front of the cage and shut his eyes, letting the thin wire of the cage press into his face, gently then forcefully. Then, another voice rose inside him.

What are you doing here?

Louche sank to his knees, and immediately people behind craned over him to view the orgy inside the cage. He felt a leg at his back, an elbow on his shoulder but these were accidental not intimate touches. When he opened his eyes there was only blackness and the relief that not being able to see brought to him. From open to shut there was no difference. That made sense to him, but again the hopeful voice in his head came back to him, forced open his eyes like rusty hinges and made his hands tear at the black material in front of him. A small gap opened, and his eyelashes brushed the hairs on a man's arms which were pressing against the cage. Contact. His wildest dreams had never been this abstract. His wildest dreams had him on the other side of the cage, his rubber shorts just another skin in a pile of limbs. His wildest dreams had brought him to this club of freedom, to set him free, to silence the undiminished voice in his head.

What are you waiting for, this is your chance . . .

The arm moved away from the cage, to be replaced by the smooth skin of a woman's thigh that suddenly buffeted the side of the cage, a rhythm growing ever more insistent. He tore more of the fabric away and more was revealed. He was so close he could smell something so personal that he scarcely believe it; he could see more than he had ever seen before. Louche put his hands down to his rubber shorts but his body felt numb, his nerves and senses blunted by the stimulation all around him until finally the persistent voice in his head reminded him what he already felt, already knew.

You are cold, cold, cold . . .

The conductor's eyes were closed. His head rocked forward then shook vigorously for a moment before jerking back, his wild hair falling around him. His shoulders were hunched but his arms raged around him, tentacles seemingly out of control then suddenly taut, suddenly loose. Louche turned to look at his father sitting beside him. His eyes too were closed, one hand brushing his eyelids while the other rested on the seat in front, his fingertips intermittently tapping the red velour. Through his own half-open eyes, Louche could see other people in the audience in a similar state to his father, all of them reacting to the music as it raged towards a crescendo, the drums thundering through his seat.

At a quiet moment, his father whispered into his ear.

'Marvellous, isn't it?'

He took his hand away from his face momentarily to squeeze Louche's hand.

And it was marvellous; Louche believed what he was told. His first concert, his first experience of live music, it was an evening of firsts. He should be proud. He was the only child in an audience of adults. There was something special about his presence there and yet his eyes remained only half open, his vision squeezed into a loose line of blurred colour and unfocused bodies. He wanted to rock his head like the conductor, he wanted to run his hands along the harp, back and forward, laughing as the notes slid upwards. He wanted to run on to the stage and leap on to the cymbals, crashing his way through the music. But a voice in his head offered no encouragement, teasing him only with the possibility of public humiliation.

How terrible it would be to be suddenly on that stage and expected to play . . .

He drew his body closer in, hugging his arms and legs, gathering his limbs tight against his chest. He needed to go to the toilet, he needed to clench his fists and stretch his legs so taut they would break and then there would be relief, a wash of wonderful warmth spreading over him and he could shut his eyes without thinking they should be open, he could let his voice out without fear of it being heard. He would not have to try anymore.

The Street of Shame, a central corridor of the club, was littered with couples in various states of sex. The light from the candles placed at even intervals along the narrow arch was surprisingly still, with little flicker to move or animate the bodies stretched out on the cobbled, uneven floors. Louche walked through these bodies with stealth, there still remaining a sense of expectation, a desire for invitation. Ahead of him, he saw another man, similar age, similar synthetic look, stop at one couple engaged in the early stages of arousal and kneel by them, outstretching a hand to the man's head and reaching down with his head to the woman's bare chest. Their arms welcomed him and drew him into their embrace. Louche smiled. This was what the evening was about. Encounters with strangers, exchanges of brief passion without guilt or long-term attachment, a sense of revolution and sexual freedom He'd been told it was an ideal way to explore yourself and lose inhibition about sex and intimacy. His optimistic voice, that hopeful half of him, reminded Louche to retain the smile, to shore it up, fix it and anchor it in the face of doubt, but even in the shadowy light of candles it was clear to see there was little humour creasing his thin lips.

Don't you wish that was you? Why can't it be you?

The warring voices in his head were the only thing Louche could hear at that moment. Yes, there was music, the sound of boots on cobbles, the grunts and groans of sex all around him, but he was both deafened and muted by his own rage, clamouring for him to join in. Or not. He found another dark corner and pressed his bare back and legs against the cold brick. Now he was invisible, a white stain on the wall. He tried to stop all sound within him, to tighten it, strangle the words which kept coming back, on and on until his own breath stopped. Silence, somehow.

All they could hear was rain. The tent had begun to be weighed down by the torrential pour which had lasted more than three hours, just after the sun had set hurriedly at the end of the field. Louche could understand why. The enjoyment of the day had gone with the sun, the light drops of rain coming on as dusk shrouded them. It seemed to Louche that, with the sun gone, the clouds had rolled down from the hills surrounding them, rushing to coral them in their tents, one for the children, one for the adults. His cousins were enjoying themselves. They shed their given skins and let their naked limbs loose, a burst of energy, a smell of earth, sweat and something else. While in the adults' tent maybe ten metres away he could hear the clink of glasses, the low murmur of conversation; inside the children's tent there was a worm out of control, tunnelling its way in and out of the sleeping bags as the other cousin tried to kill it with one of the plastic picnic forks. Out of his squinting eyes, he could see the worm get closer to him, but rather than watch the small figure burrowing towards him he watched the fork in the other boys hand, raised and poised to strike.

I need to be somewhere else.

Soon the torchlight began to dim and he felt able to open his eyes. His cousins smothered the light under the material of the sleeping bag and the bright-red glow became eyes in the gloom of the tent, their still playful bodies the tentacles of a serpent, the rain outside was the hiss and spit of its hunger. Louche was so lost to the sensations around him he could barely talk, though when they spoke to him he replied. He told them his favourite games, his best sport, he reeled off the expected litany of likes and dislikes, but whether they knew it or not he was simply going through his paces. An expected recitation. The inevitable rituals. With raucous pageantry they showed him theirs while he hid from his, the palms of his hands pressed together, glued between his thighs.

He waited for the torches to die, their batteries to deaden, until they were unable to ignite the darkness with their penetrating beams. When at last they were plunged into darkness, Louche began to emit low noises, part animal, part machine that came from the back of his throat, maybe from somewhere deeper. They hung in the air with menace. His cousins stopped talking and giggled at first and called him names, half surprised, half impressed. But when Louche continued to vocalise these sounds they asked him to stop, they wanted to sleep, they didn't know why he was making the sounds anymore. It wasn't funny. But he thought it was. Simply, naively funny.

After ten minutes Louche's father poked his head into the tent and told them to be quiet. He addressed himself to the cousins and not to Louche and this case of mistaken identity quietened him more than his father's gentle chastisement. While his cousins went to sleep he lay on his back, unable to curl up as they did, unable to get foetal as they did, unable to soften his grip on consciousness as they did. He lay awake all night, the sounds in his throat thwarted and held.

Near the end of the night, Louche made it to the last arch, a narrow corridor hung with black drapes. Instead of candles, there were lanterns held on metal poles, which splashed tight, yellow spots on to the ground. The sound of his footsteps, the throb of music faded until all he could hear was the snarl of a whip.

He had expected to find more people in the arch. Everywhere he had gone that night there had been a throng of people, their desire and urgency, their lust and lingering desperation, being the brightest of lights, a beam that penetrated his half-closed eyes.

A sign read 'The Dungeon', and an attempt had been made to re-create some medieval sense of torture. Whips of differing lengths and widths were racked on to the wall, as were restraints and other devices, their function uncertain to his inexperienced glance. The lash of the whip had not been a performance to a large crowd but the action of one solitary, hooded man. A strangely angular man who stood in front of one of the walls, raising the whip and then bringing it down, sending the dust from the loose bricks flying in clouds around him.

Turn back, turn back; this isn't for you.

Now or never, Louche, now or never.

The voices in his head were dominating everything, their ceaseless tussle reverberating as much as the sound of the whip in the empty arch, but he swallowed hard and tried to take the voices with it, tried to take the voices and bury them somewhere deep and inaccessible. He didn't want to listen to them anymore, and left alone he would have inevitably heard their insistence; left with no other distraction he might have surrendered and walked back along the gravel trail. The hooded man stopped mid-strike and through the black cloth Louche could see him squinting in the light of the lanterns, his eyes meeting his. He quickly looked away, but just as his gaze suddenly found a missing brick in the wall his hand was taken and led towards it. The same hand was raised into one of the shackles, attached to the wall, joined quickly by the other.

One, just one voice, like a deep and unwelcome sigh, surfaced quickly.

Is this what you want?

For once the question was left unanswered in the air, swirling incoherently with the clouds of brick dust. Without a word the hooded man stepped back, and Louche heard the whip trail along the floor. He was close to the wall, close enough for him to lick the dust from between the bricks, close enough for him to smell the dampness. He opened his eyes, fully, taking in all the available light, taking in everything within the limited scope. It seemed the richest of views. He waited for the persistent voice to say something, to make him balk and doubt his actions, but he heard nothing. The silence brought forward a surge of emotion, of tears and anger and laughter, rolling and gathering pace with each passing second.

Somewhere he heard his father sing BRING IT ON BRING IT ON BRING IT ON.

Somewhere he saw a young Louche hanging on to the kite that disappeared into the clouds.

•

Meat

Laura Hird

Dad and I never talk. We just ask each other the same questions and give each other the same answers, day after day after day. Since I was about twelve, it's just seemed simpler that way. Prior to that, when he used to take me for walks in the Pentland Hills, or out in his brother's boat, he was always too busy showing and teaching me things to talk about everyday stuff. Days out with Dad always seemed more like geography field trips.

We've not been fishing for as many years as he's been pestering me to go fishing with him again, and it just seems like the best place to tell him. Somewhere neutral, that we spent time together when I was young. So however he reacts, it'll remind him I'm still his son.

Our wordless drive to Cramond is starting to stress me out, though. One part of me's trying to convince the other not to tell him, and is being very persuasive. I don't know. Maybe I just want to spend time with him and get a few hours' shelter from the storm that's been going on in my head since last Wednesday.

The tide's already coming in, by the time we get to Cramond.

'Let's get our gubbins together, then.'

Dad's full of stupid wee expressions like that. We get the fork and bucket from the boot, and walk down the heavily littered, sandy grass on to the soft, blackened beach. Aeroplanes roar past, swooning over the Bridges into Turnhouse, tin cans of holidaymakers, bringing back God-knows what, from God-knows where.

'Alright for some, eh?' Dad sighs, looking up.

What does he expect me to say? He's the one who's insisted we couldn't afford a holiday for the past ten years.

'I suppose.'

Stopping in front of me, he draws a circle in the sand with his garden fork and begins digging.

'Here, get they twa big soosters in that bucket,' he orders, in the teuchter voice he speaks in when he's excited, pointing at two of the biggest worm-like creatures I've ever seen outside a fifties B-movie. I don't want to touch them. As soon as I do though, their sliminess reminds me of a wee boy who was once me, cutting them into pieces, watching them slither like maggots, then putting them down the wee girl next door's dress. Someone once told me if you cut them in two, each half grows into a new worm. But really, you just end up with a disorientated beast, trying in vain to reconnect itself before it dies.

I watch the poor sod dig out about fifteen circles before offering to take a turn. His face is completely purple, sweat's pouring off him and he's gasping for breath, but he seems like it's making him happy. He even tells me several times what a great team we make, as he watches me dig. Really though, I'm bloody useless – peching and sore before I've finished my first circle. It depresses me how weak I feel. With every forkful of wormless sand I shift, my resolve that this was a dreadful idea deepens. Luckily, Dad seems to notice I'm suffering, dips the bucket into a pool of water and chucks in some sand.

It takes about forty minutes to reach the picture postcard wee harbour at Dysart. On the way there, Dad manages to point out a hawk, a buzzard, a squashed badger, numerous fields of rabbits, the sun, the moon and various unpronounceable cloud formations. When we arrive, he struggles into his waders as I transfer the equipment from the car into Uncle Duncan's boat. It's only a seventeen footer but there are a couple of bunks and, thankfully, a small engine. Dad manoeuvres it down the slipway, into the sea, as I stand with my hands in my pockets, doing nothing apart from worry about how I'm going to tell him. It's ridiculous. I'm getting more worked up about what I'm going to say than I am about the bloody illness.

Then we're sailing into the unexpectedly ocean-like Forth. We stop near a buoy and let the boat drift. Dad stands behind me to demonstrate how to drop the line, then reel it in. I enjoy the unusual sensation of having his arms around me. He squeezes my hand round the line, trying to show me how to tell when you've hit the seabed. My smooth, waxy fingers look girlish cradled in his rough, powerful hands. I don't care about fishing; I just want him to hold me and be close to me. A strong sense that this is my dad and I am his son makes me feel momentarily safe and untouchable. The sudden sight of worm's blood rolling along the groove at the side of the boat, though, reminds me why we're really here.

Dad makes our lines irresistible by over-loading his home-made mackerel flies with the creatures from the black lagoon he dug earlier. Apparently, they don't feel pain, but as we impale them round our hooks, they do a great impression of agonised writhing. My rod is soon jerking in appreciation, not with mackerel but cod. Kamikaze cod. It's too easy! It's like they're tired of the sea and want to get caught. I just reel in; Dad unhooks and chucks them into the crate inside the boat. The first one is still slapping about in shock when we throw in the second and third. You'd think they'd just give up after a while, but they seem to take hours to die.

We catch so many in the initial flurry; I suspect Jesus has walked past on the water while my mind was elsewhere. Any smaller than a pound we use as bait, or slit open and lob into the air, to be gulped down whole by seagulls in flight.

'Bet if we threw them chunks of ourselves, they'd eat that too,' says Dad, the sea air making him momentarily profound. He's right, though. We're all just part of the same, huge food chain.

I lose all sense of time. Hours fly by unnoticed. Dad's glowing, delighted to be fishing with his 'boy' again. He looks like he does in old photos. His face is relaxed, not screwed up in frustration like usual, and his wrinkles seem to have vanished. I can't shatter all that. Then again, while he's oozing with paternal goodwill like this, it's probably the perfect time.

Taking my rod, he trawls our lines behind the boat and brings the lunch bag from the cabin. How come tomato and chopped-pork rolls taste so good in the outdoors? I wouldn't touch them in any other circumstances. As we share the flask top of coffee, Dad puts his arm round me, and points at a seal. It takes me a while to make it out amidst the grey choppy sea and fog that's starting to steam off the waves. By the time I've manage to focus, Dad's attention has moved to a family of puffins bobbing past on the other side.

He notices things nobody else does – birdcalls, the names of different types of mushrooms, which animals do which droppings, birds sleeping in bushes. Even if it's just a way of avoiding talking about real things, it must make him more likely to understand. I don't mean for him to tell Mum. I just want to give him the chance to know me like he knows his animals and plants.

'Looking awfie deep in thought there. Bit of a dreamer, like me, eh?'

I have to say something.

'Know Shirley, Dad?' Shirley's my best pal. She likes it on the scene because guys don't hassle her. She chummed me for the test. Dad likes her.

'Aye, super lassie. You couldn't have done better.'

Shit. What does he think I'm about to tell him? I've always assumed he knew we were just friends, but I suppose it could look like more. We see so much of each other and I've never bothered to explain otherwise.

'Naw, Dad, this isn't exactly about Shirley. Well, she sort of knows and that, but I just mentioned her so you'd know she knows, y'know, and she's okay about it . . .'

My tongue is tripping me. The part of my brain that forms coherent sentences has packed in.

'Get engaged. Why not? You don't need to play the minefield.' He laughs at his attempted joke. 'Look at me and your mum. That was my first real relationship and we're okay.'

Now he is joking? Him and Mum okay? Does he really enjoy his every utterance being shouted down or snapped at? Is that why Mum's so bored she knocks herself out with Diazepam and goes to bed at half seven every night. He's right. They truly are a wonderful advert for getting hitched.

'. . . or get a flat together, when you get your degree. Mum and me have a bit money stashed for when you get married. You dinnae need some bit paper if you're happy anyway though.'

'Naw, Dad. It's not like that. We're not going out together. She's just a pal. Seriously.'

He grins.

'Don't be embarrassed. Mum doesnae mind. She's hardly a prude, y'know?'

'Dad, please, listen. Shirley's my friend. Just my friend.'

'Rubbish. Stunner like that? You'd have to be bent not to fancy that.'

The very idea makes him guffaw.

'I am, Dad.'

It comes out so quiet I'm not sure he's heard me. His smile remains fixed, but his eyes say it all. I think I see the wrinkles breaking out again. I wait for him to cry, or scream, or belt me one, but he turns around as if nothing has happened, and reels in his line.

'It's getting dark. Better get our gubbins together.'

He starts clearing up – dismantling rods, putting the flask in the bag, not looking at or acknowledging me. I try to help but he pushes me away, emptying and rinsing the bait bucket, he throws it, clattering, into the cabin. The harsh, loud noise makes me jump.

'Did you hear what I said, Dad?'

'Loud and clear.'

Tugging on the engine cord until chugging drowns out any other attempt at conversation, he glares straight ahead and guides us back towards the harbour. I sit in shock.

By the time we get the boat back up the slipway and transfer our stuff to the car, the fog is heavy and it's starting to get dark. Aside from a few shouted orders on the boat, nothing further has been said. Getting in the car, we pull out of Dysart on to country roads. As we came here on the motorway, though, I'm not sure where we're heading.

'Is this a different way back?'

'Aye,' he barks.

I've not seen him this close to losing it since the time he found out one of his pals from school had drowned while she was on holiday. It's the only time I've ever seen him cry, and he seemed to cry for days. It was years ago, but I still remember feeling really scared, because Dad suddenly wasn't in control. Like now.

'Why are we going this way?'

'I don't bloody know.'

The fog gets worse as we manoeuvre our way round winding roads, barely wider than the car itself. It's impossible to see further than a few feet ahead. Dad's doing forty miles an hour though, cursing each time we mount the grassy verge on corners. Are we even going in the right direction? Why won't he say something? I have so much more to tell him! We're going to end up wrapped round a tree at this rate.

'Dad, please. Go back on the motorway; it's dangerous here. You can't see where you're going.'

'I've driven in fog before.'

Suddenly, out of nowhere, the headlights pick out something on the road.

I let out an embarrassingly effeminate shriek as the car veers off to the left and slams against a fence. I lurch against my seatbelt. When I come to, Dad's hyperventilating, glowering at the dashboard as if it's somehow to blame. I lean over to check he's alright but he yanks himself away and lunges out the car.

By the time I catch up with him he's kneeling in the middle of the road, hugging a shapeless bundle. In the little light left, it looks like a bag of shopping. Reaching down to touch sticky, matted wool, though, I realise it's a lamb. My fingers slip into some slimy, unseen gash. It makes me squeal. Dad responds with a look of disgust as I wipe its syrupy blood on to my trousers. It smells like a butcher shop on a hot day. Jesus, don't let me be sick.

'Is it dead? What'll we do with it?'

Dad looks down at it and smiles.

'Know how much these things are worth? Know how much meat you get off a wee thing like this? There better be plenty room in the freezer.'

Staggering back to the car, the animal weighing his body into a slouch, he puts the still warm body in the boot. Hopefully, it died before it had time to register the pain. I wonder if its parents are looking for it.

Thankfully, Dad decides to go back on the motorway. He's persisting with the strong, silent crap, though, so I just watch Fife scooting past, through the window. 'Dad, about what I said. Can't we ta–'

'You've told me, alright?'

North Queensferry is reached in silence. Just as we get back on to the Bridge, though, the car starts shuddering and banging, as if the engine's about to explode. The shock makes Dad swerve slightly, into the path of a massive, speeding juggernaut, which only just misses us, horn blaring. I want us to stop, but the traffic heading into Edinburgh is so heavy, it's impossible. It sounds like someone's shooting at us. Jesus. The car's going to blow up, if one of us doesn't beat it to it.

'What is it? Is it the engine? Has it happened before?' I ramble, as the clattering seems to get louder. Then I realise he's sitting there laughing. Laughing at me.

'It's our friend.'

'How d'you mean?'

'That bugger. Rumours of his death have been greatly exaggerated.'

I think he's getting some dig at me, then realise he means the lamb. He's right. It's coming from the boot! At least they don't have tollbooths any more. God knows what they'd make of it. There are brief lulls then it starts up again, demented drumming and the most awful wailing, more like a whale mourning a dead partner on a beach, than a half-dead lamb. Dad still finds it hilarious though.

'What'll we do with it? Mum won't let us keep a sheep in the back garden.'

He sneers at me.

'I wasn't planning on making friends with it. I'll kill it! Great stuff. Lamb chops till Christmas.'

'Kill it? But it's survived and everything. You can't do that.'

'Oh, dinnae be so bloody wet. If we'd knocked it down and killed it, that would have been fine, like?'

'Aye, but that was an accident. What are you going to do, poison it?'

Dad's laughing again, not in the warm way he usually laughs but in a malevolent, unhinged sort of way that makes me shudder.

'Clunk it on the head, what d'you think? It'll probably bleed to death by the time we get home, anyway.'

I feel sick. The mewling sound is going right through me. I keep imagining the poor wee thing, spending its dying minutes scared, in agony, confused and alone in the petrol-smelling boot of a strange car. Dad's less concerned.

'Shut up back there. We'll get you some mint sauce and a nice Chianti soon, ipff ipff ipff ipff ipff.'

Is this sudden macho shit for my benefit; I'm gay because he's too sensitive? If he acts like a hard hetero for five minutes after seventeen years, I'll be cured? He doesn't even know what's wrong with me. What's really wrong.

As we drive past a bus stop on Calder Road, I'm sure a few people hear the commotion. Someone's going to phone the police with our registration number. How can a half-dead creature make so much noise? We'll never get it out of the boot if it's having convulsions like this.

When we finally pull into our street, it's been raining and the neighbour's two boys are kicking a muddy cushion about. Dad makes me get out to open the garage. The kids follow me.

'That's some fucking old banger, Mr Frazer. Can you no afford a real engine?'

I try to ignore them as I wait for Dad, but they're still going on when he slams the garage door shut.

'What's in the boot, Mr Frazer? You kidnapped someone's wean? They let Mrs Frazer out for the day wi'out her strait-jacket?'

Dad blanks them and goes to the kitchen to tell Mum about the invalid, while I stand and wait for him in the living room. Ages seem to pass. What if he's telling her about me? Surely not. Mum's hated poofs since a teacher interfered with her friend's wee boy. She thinks gay equals paedophile. He won't have the nerve to tell her. Besides, they never talk about important things. Just National Geographic monologues from him and snidey comments from her.

I can hear the lamb bleating, faintly, as I stare at a photo of Eddie, Mum's brother. If they only knew the half of it.

Dad comes back through and makes me follow him to the garage. I try to sense if mum seems different towards me as I pass her in the kitchen, but she's only interested in the imminent free meat. Naturally, that's much more important than me, than my life.

'Shouldn't you take it to a butcher's to chop up? You don't know what bits are edible, Ewan. It's maybe full of disease.'

When Dad eventually opens the boot, the combined stench of blood, piss, fish and dung is overwhelming. It makes my eyes sting. It squeezes my windpipe and I have to puke on the concrete. The lamb, still mewing pathetically, has rolled on to its back and become wedged between our debris and the fishing bag. One of its front legs is bent up the wrong way. I don't know if this happened when we knocked it down, or if we shut the boot on it. Splintered bone juts out at the back of the knee. Its matted fur is caked, purple and black. One whiff is enough to send Mum back into the house with a tea towel over her face, though whether this is to block out the smell or the carnage, I'm not sure (it's way past her bedtime, anyway).

Dad picks an oily sheet from the ground and wraps it round the lamb, but it starts squawking like a car alarm, painful to listen to. I realise it has an ear missing (the car must have wrenched it off). Part of the skull is gone and there's pinkish, grey blubber, oozing from the wound. How is it still alive?

Its crying gets louder as Dad tries to take it out the car. Its three good legs wriggle frantically, like a cartoon character running, as it tries to find the ground, and then it's bad leg is up in front of it, as if it's pleading with us to stop.

Dad makes me hold it as he searches for something to carry out the execution with: the axe, some cheese-wire, a saw, the Stanley knife? He settles for a hammer and starts swinging it about at his side, grunting and pulling weird faces like a Maori warrior preparing for battle. It's so not Dad, it's scary.

The lamb takes fright as well, losing control of its bladder and soaking my jeans with hot, bloody piss. But I can't let go of it, even though it's skittery, and the more it struggles, the more it slobbers and bleeds on me. Several times, I have to swallow my own sickness.

Dad tells me to grab it and keep its head steady, and though I'm hating it, I try to think of it as putting an end to its suffering. I have to.

'There, yeah, right there,' he growls, pornographically.

The animal, sensing it's about to die, starts wriggling more than ever, refusing to stop fighting. Then suddenly the hammer is down, and the lamb roars as the edge of the metal ball splits its eyeball apart. Fresh blood sprays my face and open mouth. But the struggling has stopped. We both look down at the wet pool that was once an eye. I loosen my grip to let it fall to the ground, but the remaining eyelid flickers and it wheezes out another agonised *mehehehebeh.*

'Again! Again! Do it again!' I shout, grabbing it back and offering its head for another whacking. I'm hardening to the awfulness of it, bracing myself for the next impact.

But Dad just stands there, trembling.

'Come on, do it now . . . now! Christ c'mon!'

It lets out another tragic bleat and I look up at dad, who's started sobbing. 'I've hurt it. I've fucking hurt it.'

Dropping the hammer on to the concrete, he runs out the garage, leaving me with the stunned creature burring and haemorrhaging on my lap. I stroke the sticky, wheezing bundle, as I wait for him to reappear.

But he doesn't come back. It was his fault, but he's left me to sort it out. I went out today, hoping for support, but instead I'm the one that has to be strong. It suddenly feels like the lamb and me are the only living things left on the planet. We've been left alone to die together.

Wrapping the oily sheet round it, I put it back in the boot, removing the fishing bag and tackle to give it more room. Its eye is still bleeding but the gash on its head has scabbed up. It's too weak to bleat any more. There's only a wheezing kind of death rattle coming from it now. If I close the boot it'll probably die anyway, but it just seems so helpless and desperate, I can't bring myself to.

This time last week, everything was fine. The lamb was probably scampering round a field, chewing grass and doing whatever it is lambs do. I was doing whatever it was I used to do, thinking I would live forever. Now look at the pair of us. It manages another mehehehe, its hollow eye socket fixed on me, begging for an end to its pain.

Picking the hammer off the concrete, I apologise and take aim.

Gothic

Ali Smith

This actually happened to me.

It was an afternoon in spring not long ago, in the mid 1990s. A man came into the bookshop where I was working. He looked like a bank clerk or an accountant or some kind of businessman; he had distinguished-looking hair and was wearing a suit and tie. I straightened my shoulders. I was already in trouble at work and didn't want to get into any more trouble; he looked like he might be important.

I worked in a more old-fashioned bookshop at that time; what I was in trouble for was not wearing the right kinds of clothes. Shortly before the day I'm talking about I had gone to work wearing a sweatshirt with a designer slogan on it. It said across my back, IN A DREAM YOU SAW A WAY TO SURVIVE AND YOU WERE FILLED WITH JOY. The sweatshirt had caused a major staff commotion and I had been called to the boss's office and given a dressing-down (as it were), a row about always wearing trousers instead of a skirt, and thirty pounds' unprecedented allowance to go and buy some proper blouses. There was a lot of anger in the staffroom about me getting money for clothes. The old members of staff, who smoked a lot, thought it was outrageous, though they already thought I was outrageous anyway for not wearing the right kinds of clothes, and the young members of staff, sitting resentful in the veil of thick cigarette smoke, thought that it was unfair and that they should get a blouse allowance too.

I was wearing one of the proper blouses the day I'm talking about. They both itched and I disliked the cowed, dulled person I felt I'd been made to become by wearing them. But I smiled at the man who'd come in. He was nothing like the man standing over there, behind him, at the shelf where *The Chronicle of the Twentieth Century* was kept.

The Chronicle of the Twentieth Century, until a couple of weeks before, had always been out with its pages open somewhere in the middle of the century on the lectern specially supplied to the shop by its publisher. Three of us worked on the ground floor and we had decided to remove the lectern because every day this man came in, took out his wet handkerchief and hung it over the back of the lectern while he read the *Chronicle*. Every day the same; he would come in, he would hang it up, read for hours then finger it to see how dry it was, fold it up, put it in his coat pocket and leave the shop.

We were always getting people acting weird in that shop. It had been a bookshop for hundreds of years in the same old building full of of hidden corners, sudden staircases, unexpected rooms. People had died in that bookshop. Old members of staff were always talking, huskily through the breathed-out smoke in the staffroom, about the day one of them found the lady lying dead among her shopping bags, her legs sticking straight out, her coat askew and a look of surprise on her face, or the day another of them found the man sitting on one of the windowsills on the third-floor stairwell staring straight ahead, dead.

We had a man who used to steal books, bring them back again after reading them, slide them on to the shelves and choose new ones to take away with him. We called him the Maniokleptic. We had a man who would fall asleep as he stood leaning against the shelves. We called him the Narcoleptic. We had a woman who would come in and pick up whatever was on the New Books table, turning the pages very fast like she was taking photographs with her eyes. We called her the Critic. We called the two old ladies who always came to any readings at the shop so they could drink the free wine Raincoat and Mrs Stick (Mrs Stick used a stick to walk with). I much preferred working down on the ground floor; where I'd worked first, up in a room off a staircase at the back of the second floor, we were always having to clear up after the people who urinated in True Crime, the spines of *Dead by Sunset*, *The Yorkshire Ripper*, *Massacre*, *Crimes Against Humanity*, *Perfect Victim*, *The Faber Book of Murder* dripping again under the fluorescent light. We called the urinators the Gothics.

Our name for the man with the handkerchief was Toxic. The day we took the lectern away all three of us gathered at the front desk nudging and shushing each other to see what would happen. He came in as usual. He stood where the lectern usually was. Then he came over to the counter. Barbara stared at the floor. I stared at the light fitting. He asked Andrea if she could point him in the direction of *The Chronicle of the Twentieth Century*.

Andrea blushed. She was the ground-floor sub-manager. She raised her arm and pointed it out to him in Non Fiction. Then she said, wait. I'll show you. She took him over and found it for him. We all watched him spread the book open on the shelf at reading level, shake his wet handkerchief open and hang it off the edge of the bookshelf; it draped over the books on the shelf below. When it was dry he closed the book, put it back where it came from and left.

He was there again the day I'm talking about. He was always there. I could almost see its contents evaporating into the air, circulating throughout the shop in the ancient rattling heating system (although it was April, that morning there had been a white frost up the sides of all the church spires when I was on my way to work, frost across the endless tenement roofs). Earlier while I'd been watching him I'd been wondering again about leaving bookselling. I had turned away so as not to have to see him standing in his coat with the grey belt hanging; I looked out of the window instead at the busy Old Town streets and the blackened church and shops, the taxis passing and the wind whipping the people about as they stood by the pelican crossing or hunched themselves against the weather up and down the street where the museum was. My blouse was too tight under my arms. I stretched my shoulders and wondered if the material would rip. I wondered what it would be like to be working at the museum with its glassy-eyed stoats and stuffed hawks and foxes cordoned off behind the Do Not Touch signs, the dinosaur bones wired together the height of the grand hallway, the sound of genteel heels tapping on marble, the scholarly, weighty, methodical air. But they probably had a dress code at the museum too. Probably people like this man would stand about there all afternoon as well, hanging their handkerchieves to dry off the toe-bones of extinct creatures, urinating on the predators. I stood and wondered if there was anywhere in this city I could work where I wouldn't feel that while I was doing it life, real life, was happening more crucially, less sordidly, somewhere else.

Then the smartly-dressed man came in and stood at the counter. I smiled at him.

Can I help you? I said.

He put his briefcase on the counter. It was large, old leather, bulging. A businessman wouldn't own such a briefcase; maybe he wasn't a businessman after all. Maybe he was an academic, I thought, since the bookshop is only yards away from the city's medieval university campus, and now that I had thought of him as an academic I could see how his hair was slightly overgrown, how his suit was a little worn and how there was something defensive and clever about his eyes when he looked at me, which he did while he opened his briefcase. It was full of the shining spines of brand new hardback books. Maybe he was a Christian or some kind of religious book-rep. I frowned.

I am an author and historian, he said. You have probably heard of me. You have almost definitely sold some of my books here already.

He told me his name, which I didn't recognise, though I

nodded and smiled a suitably respectful smile. It was still mildly exciting when an author came into the shop in those days, the days just before authors were always appearing in bookshops like they are now. Now it is rather mindnumbing, always having to associate a face or a voice with a book so that the face and the voice and the name, the body of the writer, are all sold as part of the £9.99 package, tiny peeled slivers of him or her inserted for readers between the pages like erratum slips or bookmarks.

He took one of the books out of the briefcase and put it down on the counter. It had a picture of Hitler on the front. I read its title upside down. It said something about true history.

This is my latest work, he said.

I opened my mouth to redirect him to History. He held up a finger to stop me.

It is the English translation, he said. Because this book is only available in this edition in English, I am having to sell it personally to booksellers and institutions like yours, which is why I am here today in person selling it to you. It will be available, in time, in a more mainstream edition than this one, which, as you can see (he turned the spine so I caught a flash of an imprint insignia), has been produced by a small American press. But I would like this book to be available now, sooner rather than later, to all my readers, even though it is only at the moment available in this difficult-to-find, difficult-to-order edition. You understand?

I nodded.

I know that a bookseller such as yourself, he said, would like to have all available editions on your shelves as a matter of principle.

He seemed to be waiting for me to nod so I nodded again.

We – I said.

You see, he said. Much of what reaches us, much of our everyday knowledge, from our knowledge of current affairs to our knowledge of history itself, is heavily censored, you know.

The man leaned forward.

This book, he said, is in its own way a kind of rebellion against exactly what we've been talking about.

He looked boyish, coy. He smiled charmingly. Censorship, he said smiling close to my face, is the death of true history. You could say it's the death of truth. We are all censored, every day of our lives. You know what I mean.

Yes, I said.

It is vital that we fight back against this vile censoring of our identities. For example, he said. I have been conspired against, in all sorts of ways. In fact there is a conspiracy against me right now. In everything I do I have to work against others who are working against me.

He nodded at me now, so I would nod back along with him, which I did, though I had no idea what he was talking about.

And this means, he said, standing his book on its end in front of me, that my work is often censored, because I am writing the true history that no one wants to hear. I write the truth that a paid conspiracy of Jewish publishers, bankrolled by a Jewish majority in whose sole interest the truth is daily denied, will not be courageous or pure enough to publish.

The man drew breath. His face was slightly flushed. I was still nodding though I had stepped well back by now and was scratching my head. I was wondering where the rest of the ground-floor staff was. There seemed to be nobody else in the shop, just me, the man in the suit and the man whose handkerchief was drying over the books as he read his way chronologically through *The Chronicle of the Twentieth Century.*

You see how it is, the man in the suit said. He smiled at me, a winning smile.

I had slid my hand under the counter and had my finger resting on the button we called the Panic Button, which was for people who tried to hold up the till or for whenever staff felt threatened by anything. But if I pressed it and Security came, what would I say? *This man is a bigot. Please remove him.* Or *I do not agree with what this man is saying. He is a dangerous liar. Please have him ejected from the shop.*

I fingered the button. Um, I said.

He was unloading books out of his briefcase; there were ten or more on the counter.

No, – I said.

He stopped. He looked straight at me, a book in his hand.

Are you Jewish? he said.

No, I -, I said. It's not – . It's just that I'm not a book buyer. I'm not a manager. You need to be a manager to buy the books in. I can't, I'm just, a, a.

The man looked angry. For a moment he looked vicious. Then his face settled.

I wonder if you might call the manager, he said.

I can call the sub-manager, I said.

Can the sub-manager buy in books? the man asked.

I nodded. I pressed the numbers on the phone. The man and I stood in silence while we waited for Andrea to come down. He looked at his fingernail, rubbed at it impatiently with his thumb. I stood by the till looking hard at the old peeling sticker on its side giving everyone information about how to process barcodes. Andrea came down. She came under the divide and stood beside me behind the counter.

I'm sorry, she said. We don't stock books like yours in our shop.

The man almost looked pleased. Vaguely smiling, he put the books back into his briefcase, closed the clasp and left the shop.

The door swung shut.

Jesus, I said. Christ.

He'll be back in a minute, Andrea said. He always does this. He'll come in the side-door and go up and try History. Bet you a fiver. What did you say to him?

Nothing, I said. I didn't say anything to him.

Then this is what happened next. The man we called Toxic folded his handkerchief up and shut the *Chronicle*. But instead of going straight out of the shop as usual, he came over to the counter. He stood in front of us and he looked directly at me. He shook his head. Then he looked at Andrea and he tapped the side of his head lightly with a finger, twice. Mad, he said. She's mad, man. Then he left the shop.

When the door had closed behind him Andrea said to me, you know, every time I see that man I'm filled with shame at what we did. Some nights I actually can't sleep because of it.

Then she said, okay, you can go and take your break now.

On my break I was in a terrible mood. The staffroom really smelt of stale smoke. It was a deeply anti-social place. That was the day I decided to make the No Smoking signs and stick them round the yellow walls. It almost caused all-out war.

But soon after the fuss about whether people could smoke in the staffrooms or not, I moved to the new chain down in the New Town. First I helped install the new computers that automatically reorder books which sell more than three copies. Then I was made ground-floor manager. I can wear what I like now (though I am always smart) and I let my staff wear what they like too, within reason.

I have kept an eye out for that Toxic man since I moved. I have never seen him again. We don't get the same kind of person in this shop, I don't know why, other than that it is a clean shop, with wide-open wooden floors and a clean line of books and shelves; and nobody urinates here either, it wouldn't be easy to without being seen. People rarely enough even sit in the armchairs, because, as company policy suggests, we leave them in open positions so people won't be comfortable in them for too long. We do have prostitutes; I don't remember there being prostitutes in the old shop. Maybe it was too difficult to negotiate, too obviously nooked and crannied, not open enough to make browsing an innocent-seeming-enough activity. Maybe it was because there was no café at the old shop.

But I tell you. I'm ready. I stand at the counter behind the computers and I'm waiting. If that man comes in here, if that man ever dares to come in here, I will have him removed. Believe me. I have the power to do it now and I won't think twice about it.

A Hole with Two Ends

Michel Faber

'It was nice of us to come, wasn't it?' said Sandra to Neil, as they were walking back to their car. She kept her voice low, so as not to be overheard by the woman whose horrid little cottage they'd just left.

'Of course it was,' sighed Neil. 'It's this little anti-English game they play – making you feel like a complete bastard even when you're bending over backwards for them.'

'Can one refer to a woman as a "bastard", I wonder?' mused Sandra as they stepped up to the Daewo. 'I mean, in the pejorative sense?'

'Don't see why not.'

Neither of them needed to voice what had been obvious to them as soon as they'd arrived for the interview: that this latest candidate was yet another Highlands loser, a waste of their valuable time.

Neil pointed his electronic key at the car and its doors obediently unlocked themselves. As he and Sandra swung into their seats, they got a clear view of the vehicle parked in front of the cottage a junkheap of uncertain pedigree, speckled with rust. When Sandra, right at the beginning of the interview, had reminded the woman that anyone working at Loch Eye Pottery would need their own transport, the woman had waved her cigarette at her 'motor'. In fact, she'd pushed for a petrol allowance on top of the wage. Then later she'd admitted that the car 'needed serviced' (ugh! illiterate expression!) and in any case it belonged to 'Hughie' and Hughie was 'down the road' just now and it would surely be easier all round if Neil and Sandra could just bring the pottery here and then pick it up again when it was painted?

That was the problem with making anything entrepreneurial happen up here. Your workforce had to be drawn from people who were stuck in the stagnant shallows of self-deception: the long-term unemployed, the nervous-breakdown survivors, counterculture failures, alcoholics, benefit scroungers, small-time dope dealers . . . a whole countryside full of perpetual losers stranded in decrepit cottages that stank of cigarette smoke and baby shit and booze.

Neil noticed, as he was revving the engine, that the folio of (really quite good) watercolours the woman had originally sent them was still lying on the dashboard.

'Damn,' he said. 'Shall we . . .?'

'No, I *couldn't*,' groaned Sandra. 'We'll post them back.'

There wasn't an SAE, of course, but then, equipping the back rooms of Loch Eye Pottery with a few halfway reliable workers had cost them so much hassle already, another fifty-two pence wouldn't make much difference.

They pulled out of the farm road, wincing in unison as the potholes rattled the Daewo's suspension. Between the two strips of crumbling concrete, a furrow of grass had been allowed to grow so thick that it bashed and scraped against the underbelly of the chassis. In their quest for a couple more people to copy Sandra's elegant Loch Eye designs on to bowls and jugs in a serene and beautiful workplace for a very reasonable £3.75 an hour, they might be rewarded with a puncture.

Thankfully, they cruised on to the bitumen road unscathed. The drive between here and their home in Loandhu would be a smooth and pleasant one now, through drowsy farmlands and forests turning gold and emerald in the late afternoon sun.

'We shouldn't have let that blonde girl go – that Alison,' said

Neil, slipping his Ray-Bans on. 'She was the most reliable we had.'

'Yes,' murmured Sandra coolly, tidying her fringe in the sunvisor mirror. 'I know you liked her.' She frowned as she flicked a stray lock of hair back and forth: perspiration had got to it. Her big brown eyes were, she noted, a little bloodshot, and the flesh around them was finely wrinkled. For forty-eight, though, she was in pretty good shape – better than *him*, if honest truth were told – and her determination never to go to a hairdresser north of Edinburgh was paying off.

'It has nothing to do with *liking* her,' said Neil, accelerating. 'She didn't have the usual disadvantages.'

'Oh, I'd love to know what those are,' she volleyed back. 'Perhaps something to do with – ? *Look out!*'

Her shrill cry sharpened his focus on the road ahead, but it was too late. A flash of grey had passed in front of the car, and was swept under the wheels with a sickening jolt, a muffled soft collision of steel and rubber with flesh and bone. Sandra spun round in her seat and saw the creature leaping through the scrub at the side of the road, then wriggling frantically through the barbed-wire fence of the field beyond.

Neil slowed the car and brought it to a stop as close to the road's edge as he could manage.

'It's dead for sure,' he cautioned her, as she wrenched her door open and sprang out.

'It was still running,' she called over her shoulder.

He hurried to catch up to her, squinting in the fierce sunlight, following her silhouette with its windblown halo of honey-and-grey hair. 'It's a nervous-system reflex,' he said. 'They're dead, but they keep going for a few seconds. Like chickens with their heads cut off.'

'We ran over its back legs,' she said. 'I saw it dragging them. It's injured, that's all.'

Farther back than they thought possible, they found the accident site. An unspectacular smear of blood, lightly garnished with fur, glistened on the grey tar. Sandra was already leaning against the barbed wire, peering into the empty field. It was an unkempt expanse, stubble in parts, churned-up mud in others, engraved with the dried footprints of cows long moved elsewhere. The farmhouse appeared to be half a mile away, barricaded with a phalanx of hay-bales sheathed in black plastic. In the desolate middle distance, nothing moved.

'We can't leave it to die,' she said.

Neil was about to argue, but realised he didn't know what they would be arguing about. 'What do you think it was?'

'A wildcat. Scottish wildcat. Rare. Only three thousand left in all of Britain.' She began to climb over the barbed wire. 'Hold this down for me.'

He lowered the tense cable of steel as far as he could push it while she swung her legs over. The flesh of her buttocks bulged against the delicate beige cotton of her trousers as she strained to keep a safe channel of vacancy between her crotch and the snarly metal spikes. Coming down on the other side, she yelped, not because she'd been snagged by the barbed wire – she hadn't – but because there was an unexpected drop through insubstantial scrub.

'You'll have to be careful,' she called up at him, annoying him with her presumption that he'd follow. She was already stretching her arms high, grabbing hold of the barbed wire so she could hang on it with all her weight. Her breasts looked good that way, pressing out through the yellow cashmere of her pullover; her sharply upturned face smoothed the wrinkles out of her bare neck, stripping years off her age. He hesitated, then climbed over the wire himself, landing rather gracelessly beside her.

'Come on,' she said. 'It must be hiding in this verge somewhere. It would hide in the closest available spot.' Already she was visualising the magic moment of discovery: a shivering, cowering creature yanked rudely out of legend, blinking up at her from a nest of grass. A tabby the size of an ocelot, golden-eyed and panting with fright.

She stumped off, peering intently into the tangled embankment as she moved along the field's perimeter. There was precious little grass underfoot; most of it was bristling out of the earthy barricade, lushest near the top as if nourished by the fence-stakes. Beneath this furzy mane of vegetation, the bulwark of clay was crumbly and embedded with stones and lumps of concrete. It was also riddled with rabbit holes.

'It'll have crawled into one of these,' decided Sandra. Spot judgements were her *forte*; in matters of instinct she was rarely wrong.

'If so,' said Neil, 'it's probably dead by now. Or vicious as hell. What are we supposed to do, call "Here, pussy"?'

'We ran it down,' she reminded him. 'It's our responsibility.'

Neil breathed deep and counted to three. If any single factor had inhibited the growth of their business, it was Sandra's occasional attacks of sentimental scruple, which could flare up, like hormonal flushes, at the strangest times.

'Jesus,' he said, visualising the wildcat from memories of infra-red pictures he'd seen in newspapers. 'This isn't some old lady's beloved moggie, you know.'

Sandra didn't reply. She was already making her way along the line of the barricade, no longer expecting the cat to be revealed entire, but straining for a fugitive glimpse of gleaming eyes, striped flank, twitching tail. Inside the snug-fitting lid of an earthenware sugar-pot she could imagine a tiny painting of a cat's face, staring out as if from a hole, hidden there to surprise the Loch Eye Pottery customer. Did any of her staff have the skill to paint such an image? Alison might have, if she hadn't minxed herself out of a job.

Sandra snatched up a lone birch twig from the ground, denuded it briskly by tearing off its sprigs and leaves, and poked it into the nearest rabbit hole. Then, a few steps farther on, she poked it into the next, and the next, each time testing how far the stick would go. Most of the passages were narrow, too narrow to fit a large feline; some of them had been collapsed by erosion or were clogged, like dead arteries, with ossified debris.

'Hey, I didn't lock the car,' said Neil, when they'd moved fifty yards or so from where they'd begun.

'Forget the car for a minute, can't you?' she said. 'This thing's still alive, I know it.'

He squared his shoulders, preparing to argue the point, but there was a hint of pleading in her eyes, a flustered lick of her lips, letting him know she didn't want to fight. He smiled, let his shoulders fall.

'I hope you don't have your heart set on having it stuffed,' he sighed. 'If it's badly injured . . .'

'It's going to be fine,' she insisted, pressing onwards, stick in hand, Neil following on.

Only a few moments later, her hunch was proved right. A rabbit hole she'd poked her stick into emitted a dull scrabbling noise, and Neil, six feet behind her, was startled to see the furry tip of a big striped tail trembling out of the nearest hole to him. He uttered an inarticulate shout, causing the creature to jerk back inside, but he hadn't imagined it: a flurry of loose soil puffed out of the opening. He and Sandra, a man's span apart, were clearly standing at opposite ends of a horizontal tunnel through the curved embankment, a simple sinus in the soil.

Without a word, Sandra lowered herself to the ground, and squatted in front of her aperture. Neil did the same at his.

It was late afternoon by now, almost dusk. Somewhere beyond the road they could no longer see, the sun was disappearing behind trees, casting a flickering glow over the fields. All around Neil and Sandra, the picture quality of the world was being adjusted as if by contrast and brightness buttons on God's remote control: the sharper contours of grass and scarred earth were sharpened further, almost luminescing, while the duller stretches were retreating into darkness.

'The car . . .' said Neil.

'Forget the car,' hissed Sandra through clenched teeth. She

leaned closer to the hole in the embankment, squinting into its horribly pregnant shaft.

'Your trousers . . .' he warned her softly, as she shuffled forwards on her knees across the dirt.

'I can see its eyes,' she said. 'It's frightened.' Neil watched her settle onto all fours, her palms balancing gingerly on the ground. Her bosom was pressed between her arms, bulging forward, a soft glow of cashmere in the twilight. He suddenly wanted her more intensely than he'd wanted her for years; he felt like mounting her here and now in the field.

'I – I can well imagine,' he said. 'But what can we do?'

'I'll poke the stick in,' she said. 'That'll make it back up, towards your end. Once its tail pokes out, you grab it and pull.'

He snorted in disbelief. Trust her to leave that part to him . . . Fire the difficult employees, grab the wildcat by the tail: Neil'll fix it!

'What if it tears me to shreds?'

She groaned at his dullness.

'We ran over its legs! It's just dragging its hindquarters back and forth.'

'So you say.' But he kneeled forward, bracing himself. The sound of the animal's anxious breathing was having a weird effect on him, as if it were a drug he'd sniffed into his bloodstream. Imagining himself a broken animal trapped in a claustrophobic shaft, he was almost intoxicated with pity.

Sandra inserted the stick carefully, almost tenderly, into the hole. On her face was an expression of intent curiosity, an ardent childlike wish for the desired outcome. Her lips were parted, her eyes half-closed.

From inside the tunnel came a fierce hiss and the sound of scrabbling. But no sign of the animal at Neil's end. Sandra leaned further into the hole, her arm disappearing inside it, her cheek brushing against the earth, her hair mingling with the rough grass.

'I need a longer stick,' she breathed.

'Well, find one,' he urged her, his voice shaking with anticipation. 'You're liable to get your fingers bitten off.'

She withdrew her arm. Her sleeve was covered in soil, dark brown against the dry-clean-only yellow. She glanced all around, but didn't get up off her knees.

'I can't see anything better than what I've got,' she said, studiously examining the end of her stick as if for blood or saliva. 'And I'm not leaving this hole.'

For another few minutes they squatted there, while the world grew darker all around them. Their eyes were well adjusted to the fading light, and they could still see each other and, of course, the holes in the embankment, perfectly well. But the rest of the environs – the empty field behind them, the long lampless road, the treetops of the hidden forest – were inexorably merging with the deepening mauve of the sky.

'The car's parking lights aren't on,' said Neil.

Sandra turned her face to him, stared directly into his eyes through the gathering chill of dusk. Her left cheek was smeared with dirt, her white teeth were bare.

'Forget the fucking car,' she warned him, each word enunciated with crystal diction.

After a moment's hesitation, she leaned forward again, and started to claw at the edges of the hole with her fingers.

'Dig,' she said.

He watched her, mesmerised. Her red fingernails disappeared, to be replaced by grimy black ones. Earth showered over her trousers.

'Dig, you bastard,' she hissed.

He dug at his own hole. There were skiing gloves in the boot of the car, which would have made the task more comfortable, not to mention more efficient, but he knew better than to suggest this. Instead, he jabbed at the soil with his fingers, fumbling for purchase on larger clumps and stones, grunting with effort. It was penance, he knew: a more potent offering than denials and red roses.

They worked doggedly as the light was extinguished all around them. They burrowed in rhythm, panting in unison, swaying on their knees. Their flushed faces looked bone-pale under the rise of a colossal moon. From inside the earth before them, an anxious, inhuman moan made itself heard, growing steadily louder and more despairing.

At last, when they had excavated so much soil that there was only about a metre of tunnel left undisclosed, the moment came. The wildcat's striped tail, bristling electrically, convulsed into view, and Neil grabbed it in his filthy hands and yanked. There was a grotesquely loud shriek of terror, then his fist was being savagely bitten – as if a mallet had slammed several iron nails right through his flesh. The creature was a squirming chaos of fur and muscle on the end of his arm, its claws ripping at his thighs and elbows as it flailed through the air.

Unthinkingly, he ran towards Sandra and, even as he released his hold, she lunged at the creature herself, arms thrust forward in a fearless, angry embrace. For a split-second she had it clutched tight to her – it might, in that instant, have been an ordinary cat after all – but then its huge yellow eyes blazed with fury, and in an eruption of brute force it clawed its way up her breast, on to her face. Its crushed hind limbs swung crazily as it clung to her head for an instant, then tumbled down her back and hit the ground. With a slithering of skewed bone, it heaved itself away, hyperventilating, into the darkness.

'Don't stop! Don't *stop*!' shrieked Sandra, as Neil fell back in horror at the damage to his hands, the blood running down her face. 'Useless fucking coward!'

A deep claw-gouge from forehead to brow to cheek – missing her eye by a miracle – was bubbling and spattering blood all over her chest and shoulders. Yet she ignored it, and instead whirled around and stumbled off into the gloom, hunching down like some sort of primate, her arms swinging low through the air, brushing the inky vegetation.

Suddenly there was a screech, not of a living being this time, but of tyres on a road surface – a short, surreally musical screech, and then a loud crash of metal on metal.

'Jesus Christ, the car . . .!' barked Neil.

'Come *on*!' yelled Sandra, still pursuing her prey.

'But don't you understand – ?'

'I understand everything!' she raged, fetching up a stick – a much larger and heavier stick than before. 'Whatever's happened has happened. Who gives a fuck? It's over! It's over!'

Cudgel dangling from her fist, she pushed on into the gloom, her hunched form a piebald pelt of yellow and black. He wanted to follow her, to restrain her, to enfold her in his arms, to carry her home, but he was half-blinded by the pain in his hand, a nauseous mixture of numbness and agony, a greasy mess of bloody fingers. He heard his own voice grunting and whimpering as he strained to get his legs to move, but he just stood there shivering on the churned earth.

He knew that this was all madness now, that they couldn't hope to save this creature, this half-crushed, fear-crazed demon of pure instinct. But it seemed his wife understood this too. She was swinging the stick into the undergrowth, not in a tentative, exploratory way, but with all her might. Earth and grass exploded into the air, gobs of raw clay flying around like flesh, as she flailed, viciously, over and over, her weapon now clutched in both black fists.

'I see its eyes!' she kept screaming, hoarse with feral longing as the whole countryside was falling into blackness around her and all the tiny stars came out of Heaven to bear witness. 'I see its eyes!'

You are Here

Maggie O'Farrell

The landscape flattens as she nears the border, stretching out like a cat in sleep. Then the jagged, red rocks of the coast appear, just as she knew they would, on the equator line of her windscreen, the sea invisible but roaring somewhere below the road.

She arrives early, too early for what she's come for – delivering an art prize to a primary school – and so she sits in a café, waiting. The town is hot, the sky drooping over the building tops, low and heavy. Through the salt-speckled window, she watches men in black bodysuits, with masks that throw back opaque fragments of the sky, emerge from the oil-slicked water of the curving harbour.

She enjoys the drive back, the sense of a job done and the road unspooling before her and the miles back to Edinburgh narrowing down on each signpost. The dashboard softens in the heat and the steering wheel burns like a rope in her hands. She overtakes more recklessly than usual, winds down all the windows, finds a distant radio station airing old, scratched songs and, while the breeze whips her hair over her forehead and eyes, sings fragments of lyrics she didn't know she knew: 'There may be trouble ahead . . .'

The traffic in the city is slow, locked, cars inching over tarmac that is melting and bubbling, lights turning and turning back with no movement. Music from other radios drifts in through her windows. She cranes sideways, trying to see up ahead to Princes Street, then, wrenching the wheel around, she takes a right up Calton Hill.

But when she rises to the summit, the cars are moving in a slow and sonorous line. She becomes aware of her wheels crunching over shattered glass and a slight anxiety begins pulsing in her neck. Police in yellow jackets that hurt her eyes are waving her away, blue cones of light circling above them, hazard tape hanging limp in the still, heavy air. As she passes the wrung-out, twisted mess of metal and glass she tries not to look. But of course she does. Twin mud scars in the grass verge, wheels spinning in mid air, slow as a waltz, and the shank of one of the cars folded like a paper fan, a deep-blue colour that gleams in the sun. And as she moves by all she can think is that the colour reminds her of something, something someone used to wear, a shirt was it, who was it now, she almost has it, a deep blue shirt that exact same colour . . . Jamie. Jamie's blue shirt.

Gilmore says that she ignored him when they first met. It was at a private opening in the Gallery of Modern Art, where she works. She had been pouring the champagne, meandering about the room with two cool, condensing thick green glass bottles in her hands, grateful not to have to make conversation with all these people dressed in clothes cut from expensive, smooth-feeling cloth. She doesn't remember seeing him there at all. 'I drank so much champagne off you that night,' Gilmore says, 'I was sick on my porch.'

Two, maybe three days later, she is going down some steps into a basement café with a few people from the gallery on their lunchbreak, and Jamie slips into her mind again. She came here once with him and the recollection makes her smile. Because she so rarely thinks of Jamie. Because it was so long ago. Because she's been here so many times since and it seems funny that she should suddenly think of him now.

They sit at a table by the door. The window is a swirl of stained glass and the light bleeds red, blue, yellow and green into their skins, the menu, the table top, the salt cellar. A child on the next table, washed blue in this light, is squeezing mashed potato through narrow slits in his clenched fist. He stares unblinkingly back at her.

She and Jamie had sat over by the counter with white towers of napkins for people to help themselves. Jamie had taken too many, a thick pillowy wedge of them that he dented with one of his elbows. He'd learnt a magic trick. She smiles again, amazed at the sudden clarity of her recall. Something with trying to separate interlinked hoops that hadn't worked and made him swear and frown, glowering for the rest of the meal.

'. . . Faith?'

At the sound of her name she is jerked back down into the present. Her colleagues are all gazing at her.

'Sorry?' she says, gripping the menu between both hands. 'What did you say?'

Gilmore is thirteen years older than her. She told her mother it was ten. The first night they spent together, he stayed awake for hours debating which age-match would have been the most indecent: 'Nine and twenty-two,' he said. 'No, wait, how about four and seventeen?'

She has one foot braced against the wall, bones spread flat against the plaster, and she is balancing on the back two legs of her chair. A newspaper is spread over her lap. One hand winds hair around its index finger. Behind her, Gilmore watches TV. She can hear him shift position every now and again, clothes rub and resettle on his body, the sofa springs sigh, the scratch of fingers against hair. She is half-reading an article about the manufacture of ice-cream in the Lothian Region.

Suddenly, even before she is aware of hearing it, her head snaps round to the TV. 'Oh my God,' she says.

'What?' says Gilmore.

She gets up, newspaper pages sliding to the floor, and walks closer to the set. It's an advert for a mobile phone. A tiny computerised figure is using a small, sleek, silver handset as a surfboard. 'This way, you'll always be connected,' says a voice coming from inside the black, depthless speakers either side of the screen.

'I don't believe it,' she says, and laughs. 'It's Jamie. That's so weird because–'

'Who's Jamie?' Gilmore says from the sofa. 'What is Jamie?'

'It's Jamie,' she repeats. 'The voiceover. It's Jamie doing the voiceover. He's . . . I used to go out with him . . . oh, ages ago. He was trying to make it as an actor.'

'Hmm,' says Gilmore, scratching at the raised, red parabola of an insect bite on his shin. He takes a dim view of actors.

'He wasn't very good, though, so I never thought he'd make it.'

'Maybe it wasn't him.'

'No.' She stares at the screen, which is now filled with an image of a woman flipping her curtain of golden hair over a suntanned shoulder. 'It was definitely him.'

The next day she wakes early, but not early enough for Gilmore, who leaves the house before seven. She finds his coffee cup in the sink, a slurry of unreadable grains swirled around its curved china hollow. It's another hot day, but there's a cooling, restless movement in the air, so she decides to walk to work.

Leaving the house, there is a smarting behind her eyelids. With every breath, she imagines the invisible, malevolent molecules of pollen penetrating her, latching on to her tongue, her throat, the thin, delicate membranes of her nose. By the time she reaches the Meadows, a swelling rash is spreading over the soft part of her mouth, and hot, griefless tears are streaking down her cheeks.

She skirts the grass, keeping to the pavement, a tissue

clutched in her fingers. In hot weather the city haemorrhages people; they emerge from buildings and cars and offices into the heat bowls of the street. All around her people are walking the pavements, like she is, the sun pressing down on their hair, the hot air moving inside their clothes. She passes a man with a tiny baby strapped to his chest, a boy with a red streak through his fringe, a woman turning to her companion and saying, 'She's going to get it. I tell you, she is.'

Passing through Tollcross, she sees a man coming towards her – same height as her, that thrown-back set of the shoulders, soft, yellow hair, the bouncy walk. Jamie. A slight confusion buzzes through her brain like a faulty electrical current, and she is raising her hand to wave when a oppressive, suffocating feeling rises without warning to the front of her face. She clamps the tissue over her nose and her body folds into itself as she sneezes. Once, twice, three times.

When she lifts her eyes again, Jamie is close by her, close enough to touch him. And all of a sudden it isn't Jamie at all, but someone who looks nothing like him – face too wide, eyes too set back. She sniffs itchily into her tissue and glances away at a wooden stand at the edge of the pavement with a map of the city trapped beneath a sheet of plastic. 'You are here' it tells in squared black letters. But the arrow that should show her where has been scraped off, peeled away. It disturbs her, unbalances her, that arrowless assertion, the idea that she is somewhere but no one can tell where. She rubs a hand across her forehead and the woman in the surface of the plastic does the same. She turns away.

He's coming out of Haymarket Station when she sees him for the second time, and her heart leaps and knocks against her ribs. This time he's too tall, too thin. And when she is across the road from St Mary's Cathedral and he is coming towards her again, she doesn't smile, she doesn't want to raise her hand. She wrenches at the teeth-like clasp of her bag, pretends to be looking in it, and when the not-Jamie has passed her by, she looks after him, watching him until he's turned a corner and is lost to sight.

In her office, the fan turns towards her, blasting her hair away from her face, then turns away, as if offended. She has to weight down her papers with bottles of water, staplers, her silver bracelets. At lunch time she walks through the white rooms of the galleries, dehumidifiers humming, people milling, arms folded, among the exhibits. She passes a small sculpture of a woman bent over backwards, walnut wood stomach arched into the air, a painting of black and beige circles, a square of fake grass implanted with tiny speakers that whisper and mutter unfathomable sounds. She stands for a while next to the entire body of a car crushed and compacted into a narrow oblong, metal folded into glass, leather into chrome.

Gilmore phones in the late afternoon when the sun has elongated into rhombuses across the floor.

'So,' he says, 'how the devil are you?'

Gilmore won't tell anyone his first name. When, just after they met, she begged him to tell her, and he said, 'I could tell you, but then I'd have to kill you.' One afternoon, him out of the house, she slid a bureau drawer along its runners with stiff anxious fingers, and found letters and documents and certificates. The name, that word of six letters, stuck there in front seemed odd and indigestible. She never mentioned it again.

'The devil I'm fine,' she replies. 'How are you?'

'Eh . . . Frankfurt,' he says.

'Oh, Gilmore,' the words leave her mouth in a long, thin sigh. 'No.'

'Five o'clock tonight.'

'Bollocks.'

He laughs. She can hear the office behind him, the droning buzz of money-making. 'Bollocks to you,' she continues. 'And your employers. And to everyone in Frankfurt.'

'I'll pass that on.'

'Good.'

'I'm back on Wednesday,' he says after a pause. 'It's only four days.' He starts to tell her about where he's staying and the extraordinary ugliness of the man he is going to see. She pushes her finger into the resistant coils of the telephone wire, moves her feet inside the hot leather of her shoes, her mind slipping its moorings and drifting off.

'. . . hello?' she hears his voice saying, and she jumps, the muscles in her neck tensing. 'Are you still there?'

'Yes,' she says, 'sorry.'

'What were you thinking about?' he asks.

She's so appalled to realise she's been thinking about Jamie that for a moment she cannot answer.

She finds herself lying diagonally across the bed, splayed like a starfish. Her teeth are clamped shut, set together like a trap, and her mind is still running on the dream she'd been having: she was in Jamie's flat, on Jamie's sofa, with the stink of the woodworm-treated cupboard filling her nose and the sound of Leith traffic booming outside the windows. She hadn't been able to see Jamie, but she knew he was there, somewhere out of sight, in the next room, or the kitchen; she could hear the sound of his voice running like a tap.

Jamie was one of those people who was never silent. When they were going out together she couldn't imagine him alone, as if he might cease to exist when he wasn't with anyone. Once, after they'd been on the phone to each other, she'd picked up the receiver to make another call, and discovered that she was still connected, that he hadn't replaced his receiver properly. She tried pressing her connection button, shouting, screeching, trying to make him hear her. Then she realised, with a kind of cool sinking sensation in her chest, that through the muffled silence of his flat, she could make out his voice – and hers. 'Hello Faith,' he was saying, 'hello Faith.' And then in a different tone, 'Hi Jamie, howreyou doing?' It was said at a higher pitch, with a north-east coast lilt. Hers, exactly, unmistakably, echoing back at her. 'Howreyou doing,' she heard him trill again, 'howreyou doing.' She'd had to look down at herself, standing in her own flat, on her own carpet, one foot angled slightly away from the other, to reassure herself that she was in fact here, that she was herself. Her hand had reached out from her body and pressed the receiver down into its cradle, careful and deliberate as a mime, as if he might hear.

She curls into herself in Gilmore's bed. The sheet crackles against her limbs. She is seized with an urge to look round the room, to check he isn't there, to check that Jamie isn't standing by the mirror, staring at her. But then she realises she's afraid to – just in case he is. She billows the sheet up over her head. Her heart is beating so hard that her head feels fragile, boneless, as if it might burst.

She sees two not-Jamies on the bus, and another queuing outside the gallery for the new modernism exhibition. At lunch time she can't swallow her salmon sandwich after her mind plays her a memory of watching him slit the grey-green shimmer-skin of a fish on his draining board, the guts and gullet sliding across the stainless steel. She reads a report on government arts funding, but has to stop because she is hearing each word inside her head in his voice. Every time she looks down and sees herself – her hands, her lap, her ankles, her arms – she is recalling his hands on that part of her body, the touch of his hair against her face, the weight of him on her.

'Are you OK?' the education officer enquires, knuckles curled white against the surface of her desk. 'You look awful peely wally.'

She says she's fine, it's just the heat, she's a bit tired actually, she didn't sleep well last night.

She looks out of the window when the education officer has gone, and sees a Jamie flit past, his hair bright gold in the sun. She presses her fists into her eyes, and when she looks again the window seems still and strange, like an empty stage, filled only with the trees and the rhododendron bushes, weighty with red-black blossoms.

* * *

She doesn't like being on her own in Gilmore's house. It's old and large, with reverberating dark rooms, corridors, and too many openings into the garden and street. The things that she likes about it in Gilmore's presence turn into things she hates in his absence: the trees that press the undersides of their leaves to the windows, the empty spaces of the ceilings that catch sharp light darts from the pond, the rumble and creak of the underfloor copper water pipes, the loudness of her feet against the tiles. The weather has strained and split open: wind tosses, restless and melancholy, in the trees, and rain falls sharp as needles against the panes.

Before she goes upstairs she walks twice around the ground floor, making sure all the doors and windows are locked. She isn't allowing herself to think about what it is she's scared might come in, but the long cracks under the doors are making her nervous, edgy, and she has to resist the temptation to run adhesive tape along them. She presses her fingers to the narrow sliver-gap around a sash window and feels the cool, thread-like breath of the outside. She snatches her hand away as if it's burnt her. She has her foot on the bottom tread of the stairs when she turns, drags the thick weight of the leather armchair to the front door and pushes it up against the lock. For good measure.

Undressing she thinks of how she had this skirt when she was with Jamie, and immediately envisions his hands unzipping it. Going to the window and seeing the wet stretch of the road makes her remember his bike and how he fell off it one day, the grain of the tarmacadam flensing his arm. Reading a book, she hears him talking. Running a bath, she sees his body, pale as marble beneath the water. She feels cursed like Midas, that everything she touches turns to Jamie. She can't stop him invading her mind, as if there is a mistuned radio signal from a pirate station interfering with her mental processes.

She lies on her back, the carpet rough through her nightdress, and tries to remember the procedure for clearing your mind from a meditation class she went to once. This is ridiculous, she scolds. You just have to get a grip on yourself. Then she remembers that she went to the class with Jamie and she sits up, tears stinging her eyes. Across the room in the darkening mirror, her reflection is staring back at her, wide-eyed, shocked. What is going on, she asks it, tears spilling on to the thin cotton of her nightdress. This airwave is taken, she wants to shout, get off.

Gilmore is describing a store in Frankfurt where you have to have a numbered ticket to enter each department. She is putting one foot in front of the other, her fingers curled into his arms, feeling her breath filling and leaving her body, concentrating very hard on not calling him Jamie. It has almost happened three times since he got back early this morning, once during sex. She had to press her teeth into his shoulder to swallow the word, to stop it escaping and filling the room like gas.

Gilmore stops, blocking her way. They are on Arthur's Seat, Salisbury Crags bisecting their view, Calton Hill looking hunched, diminutive in the distance. He puts his hands on her shoulders and looks straight into her face. She smiles at him, pulling up her mouth in the way she knows she should, at the same time disturbed by how distant he suddenly seems, as if he's just someone she's met a couple of times.

'Where is Faith?' he asks. 'What have you done with her?'

She laughs, then stops, jarred by how close to tears she is. He regards her, a slight frown on his face, his head on one side.

'What is it?' he says, his voice low and serious now.

She coughs and rubs her nose. 'This weird thing's been happening,' she says.

When she and Jamie walked together, he held her hand unnaturally high, against his chest. He used the word 'avatar' a lot. He wore his shoes without socks. He liked to hold her head between his hands, as if memorising its dimensions: 'I'm reading your cranium,' he said once when he was standing behind her, just out of sight. 'I want to know what it's like to *be you.*' He would without warning cup her breast in his palm when they were in public. When he didn't have an acting job, he would spend whole days walking around the city, or out to Corstorphine or the sands at Cramond. 'I like the feel of concrete under my soles,' he said in his stage-actor voice. He lost his temper with his car, with an electric blender, with his agent, with her. When she left him for the last time, he held on to her wrist, bracing himself against the doorjamb, so that her hand was the only part of her left in his flat. 'You will never get away from me,' he whispered at her as she struggled, his voice strangely tender, 'never. Do you understand?' All she could feel was the terrible grind and stretch of her tendons as she strained away from him.

'How long were you seeing this guy for?' Gilmore is looking the other way, as if transfixed by a dog nosing its way through the scrubby grass. His hand feels inert in hers, a loose collection of skin and bones at the end of his arm.

'Hardly anytime at all.' She is already worried she's said too much, that she should never have mentioned it. She feels that if she took a step, just one, she might very easily tip over and fall. 'Four months. Five maybe. I don't know. I can barely remember. It was ages ago. Ages and ages.'

'And you can't stop thinking about him?'

'Yes, but–'

'And it's a recent thing?'

'Gilmore–'

'I see.'

'Please–'

'Have you seen him? Are you in touch with him?'

'No. No. Please. Listen to me. Please.' He looks at her. Now that she has his full attention, she isn't quite sure what she wants to say. 'I don't want to think about him,' she begins, uncertain, stretching out her arm ahead of her for balance. 'I mean, it's not good thoughts or, or . . . it's not that I'm pining for him or anything like that. I'm not. I'm really not. I just . . . I just can't stop him . . . getting into my head all the time.'

There is a pause. Gilmore is staring at the dog who is now looking at them, two people having an argument on a path up a hill, its yellow eyes expressionless.

'Do you know what I mean?' she asks.

'No,' he says, walking on, his hand sliding out of her fingers, 'I don't.'

Above her, the trees fill like lungs, and the river to her right hisses and boils through the wet earth. Her shoes are heavy with mud and she leans, one hand on a tree trunk, waiting for her pulse to stop catching in her throat.

You are walking, she tells herself carefully, you are going for a walk. The row with Gilmore has left her empty, wrung out, bleached like cloth left too long in the sun. She has come here, to the Hermitage of Braid, to walk, to take some air, to see things. She straightens up, her palm still pressed to the grooves of bark, her muscles contracting and stiffening. You are walking. A point in her head, to the left of her eye, jitters and throbs with the beginnings of a headache. She looks at what's in front of her: 'river' she hears Jamie's voice inform her, 'stone', 'path', 'moss'.

She crushes her eyes shut, her hands clenched into each other. Then she looks left, into the centre of the pain. Her retinas flash a red ache to her brain and there, through the trees, she sees him, arms folded across his blue shirt, his hair gleaming in the sun-shot leaf canopy. His head is tilted, looking at her, his lips curved in a smile. Above him, the trees fill like lungs, and the river to his left hisses and boils through the wet earth. A low sound, half scream, half growl, bounces away from her mouth and back. She starts up on the path, her sodden shoes slipping in the mud, her hands reaching out for the trees. The city forest slides past her, giddy and unsteady, then the streets and gardens and lights. She doesn't look back.

In the hall on her way back in she meets Gilmore, newspaper in hand. Her chest is heaving, trying to draw oxygen into her bloodstream. He stops, smoothes her hair back from her face, and cold sweat glides between her scalp and his palm. His lips are moving and she has to focus hard to see what he is saying.

'Maybe you need some time out,' he is saying, sadly. 'Your own place.'

She tries to shake her head, but his hand is holding it too firmly. 'No,' she says, 'I don't–'

'Maybe this,' he shrugs, looking round the hall, the house, 'all happened too fast for you.'

She twists away from him, pushes herself up the stairs, wrenching at the banister, treading dark clots of mud into Gilmore's red carpet. In the upstairs room she seizes her address book and sits at the desk.

There are two numbers for him, one scrawled in fading pencil, the other in rather neat blue ink. She tries the blue one, punching in the numbers with such force that her fingernail splinters. She has the receiver clamped to her ear, hard, and it pulses a hot, flat pain into her skull. Then there is a distant ring on the line, and a woman:

'Hello?' Hesitant. Middle-aged. Well-spoken. His mum.

'Hi,' she says, 'Sorry. I wonder if you could help me. I'm trying to reach Jamie. Do you–'

There is a sound like a gasp, or a sudden expellation of air, and the woman saying 'Oh God,' but not to her, to someone else, someone in the room with her. Then a silence stretches, long and fine as a thread of silk, between Faith and the room. And a man comes on the line, his voice cracked like ice: 'He's . . . he's not here. He was killed in a car accident, a couple of weeks ago. On Calton Hill.'

The Woman with Fork and Knife Disorder

Jackie Kay

Her name was still Irene Elliot. Irene Elliot had been drying her dishes and putting them away for years. She was quick and methodical and she didn't even notice what she was doing. It was second nature where things went: the cups and saucers, the pans, here, the dinner plates, there, the tea plates up there. She'd lived through, oh, at least two hundred tea towels. She'd experimented with all sorts of rails and holders for tea towels; the ones that bit into the towel like shark's teeth; the ones that stuck on to the edge of a cupboard. It was a thing she never seemed to get right. She'd burnt a lot of tea towels really because there had never been the perfect place for them and also because she didn't believe in oven gloves.

The daughter, Mary Ann, was out at high school the day it first happened. The fork and knife drawer was open and Irene Elliot was just drying the cutlery and putting it away. *Woman's Hour* was on, the comforting, safe voice of Jenni Murray. The clouds had broken up and gone off their separate ways. The sun was filtering in through the kitchen windows, sliced through the blinds. She was humming to herself in a way that was not unlike conversation or odd thoughts. She went to put a knife in the knife bit and it slipped out of her hand and joined the spoons. She said *Silly Irene* to herself. She had always had this habit of naming herself aloud as if she were outside herself, a character.

(How could you make yourself real?) You could have knocked Irene over with a feather when I heard, she'd say to Sandra over the fence. Or, Irene will just have a wee cup of tea to herself. Silly Irene, she said and took the knife out and placed it in the knives bit. A moment later the same happened with a dessert spoon. Somehow, it upset the forks. For a split second, Irene felt uneasy. Her attention must be slipping. (What makes attention slip?) She was one of those women who got angry easily. If she forgot something she should have remembered, the name of the place where she'd been staying on holiday. If she forgot to pack something to take; if she dithered at a crossroads. If she struggled to find a word, she would get into a tight-lipped fury, a white, sharp anger. She sighed and kept her eyes peeled on the cutlery drawer. Still a fistful of knives and forks and spoons to put away. Dizzy *Dozy Irene.*

Irene Elliot kept on putting the cutlery away, humming to herself, *I gave my love a cherry it had no stone. I gave my love a chicken it had no bone.* She used to sing that to Mary Ann when she was a wee lassie. Mary Ann hated her singing now. She told Irene her voice 'trembled too much'. When Mary Ann was out, she sang. Who would have believed her girl, her lovely girl, who used to worship her, follow her around and look at her with such devotion, such love in her big wide childhood eyes, could find so much of her revolting, as if Mary Ann hated her. But the worst thing was that part of Irene could not resist seeing herself through Mary Ann's teenage eyes. It was a strange close thing living alone with her adolescent daughter. The smallest of movements could annoy daughter dear. A simple thing like drying her hands on her apron infuriated Mary Ann. Even the sight of the apron incensed her. 'Nobody wears aprons anymore, Mum,' Mary Ann would say. 'I do. I like my pinnie,' Irene would say back, knowing in the small, sick, glad bit of her heart that this reply would make Mary Ann seethe. Or when she kissed her lips together after putting lipstick on and made a tiny phut-phut noise. And Mary Ann thought Irene was overweight, she could tell. Too much on her hips, her thighs. A bit under the chin. Fat arms. Whenever they were going out somewhere, rare these days, Mary Ann would look Irene up and down in such a way that made Irene uncomfortable. Her daughter's criticisms could be heard even if they were unspoken.

When Iain left (though *left* was hardly adequate – when Iain split up their home, when Iain took an axe to their house, a machete to their marriage, when Iain abandoned them, when Iain cut loose, cut adrift, cut the knot, severed the tie, when Iain broke up their family), Irene could tell Mary Ann thought it was all Irene's fault for being fat and deeply unsexy. Somewhere in the depths of her, Irene knew, there was a wild sexuality that no man had ever the finesse to bring out. Iain was hopeless really. He made the whole business seem really silly and over the top, a huffing and a puffing till they all fell down.

Irene knew better now than to kiss Mary Ann or to hug her. The last time she did it, Mary Ann's body went so rigid and hard, fighting against her. Her daughter's muscles – tensed up and hateful. It was odd to consider that Irene had actually given birth to a girl that would turn on her like this. In her darkest moments, Irene was upset with her own body; it had clearly betrayed her; it obviously had a hand in the matter. 'It'll pass, Irene,' she told herself. Irene didn't remember ever being like this to her own mother when she was a teenager. She remembered having the odd bubble and greet when she got her period, but that was the hormones definitely. With Mary Ann, Irene couldn't put her hand on her heart and say that it was the hormones. Part of her it seemed had just been waiting, ever since she turned, what, nine? Was that fair? Were families fair?

* * *

When she looked down, everything was in a terrible state. Four of the knives were splayed across the forks. Two of the forks were lying with the spoons. Five of the spoons had joined the knife section. Some teaspoons were on the edge of the forks. Exasperated, irritated, a little edgy. *Bother,* she said, and when she saw that the sharp knife was lying, serrated edge staring into her face, she said, *Bugger*. She assumed her head was wandering and that was that. (Where did it go, did it wander back, lost, over the years?) She took the wrong cutlery out and put it back where it was supposed to go. All the spoons lay gleaming inside one another. The knives lay on their sides, flat and passive. Everything was neat, properly sorted. In the right place.

Maybe she wouldn't have thought anything of it if the same thing hadn't happened a week later. She went to put a knife away in the knife section. When she next looked down that same knife had somehow cut loose and joined the teaspoons, lying blatantly across them, almost smiling, a wide silver smile. That was when, looking back, that was the moment, the turning moment, when she felt as if someone had stuck a carving knife into the side of her ribs. She was frightened. She dropped the whole lot of cutlery on the floor. It made a terrible racket like screeching music in a horror movie. Clattering and crashing on to her kitchen tiles. It seemed to go on and on and on as if she had a whole canteen in her hands. She rushed upstairs, pulling herself up, her two hands clutching the banister, closed her bedroom curtains, yanked back her covers and she went to bed and she cried.

Of course the daughter came home and wanted to know what was going on. A pile of cutlery on the floor, no dinner, her mother in bed. Irene knew better than to tell her that the forks and knives were acting up and had a mind of their own and that she couldn't get them to lie in their right place. She told her that she had a pain in her left side and had had to lie down. Mary

Ann scowled, a look that was the double of her father's scowl, so close, the same craggy, jagged face, the cheeks hollow and sharp with anger, the chin jutting out righteously, that it was as if he was standing just behind her. It made her gasp. Mary Ann's eyebrows worked themselves into a hateful state. She didn't like her mother having mysterious pains. She didn't believe in her pains. Whenever Irene said any simple thing to Mary Ann like 'My head's tight screws fastening into me,' or 'My stomach has got a small man inside chewing' or 'My chest has a snake wrapped round and round stopping me from breathing properly,' anything like that, the daughter froze. Mary Ann nodded slowly, chewing, with her skirt too high and her knees like scrubbed round potatoes.

That evening, Irene sent Mary Ann out for fish and chips from the fish shop. They looked so reassuring when they came back wrapped in their hot paper, the smell so comfortingly fishy, so reliable. Nice light batter. Vinegar. Plenty salt. Big mug of tea. Nothing like a fish supper, Irene said. Mary Ann ate hers straight from the paper, *that's the whole point.* Irene put hers on a warm white plate she'd preheated in the oven. Irene ate hers with a knife and fork. Mary Ann tore at hers with her bare fingers. 'Fingers were made before forks,' she said in her deadpan teenage voice which hardly ever went up or down. 'So they were!' said Irene as if this was a revelation to her.

Irene took a deep breath, then said airily to Mary Ann–

– It's you for the drying, me for the washing,

– What? I hate drying. It's stupid. Let them drip.

– I'm wanting the place tidy. I want everything put away.

– Tidy for what? Nobody's coming.

– Does everything have to be an argument with you?

– You make me argue.

– Just dry the bloody dishes!

– I hate putting cutlery away.

– Do you? Do you?

Irene moved closer towards her. Why?

Mary Ann shrugged. Don't get all excited. I just hate it. It's boring.

Irene watched from the corner of her brown eye, Mary Ann putting all the knives and forks in their right place, no bother. They watched a bit of telly together, *The Royle Family.* They didn't speak much. Mary Ann didn't like talking when the telly was on.

Irene woke up at seven thirty to wake Mary Ann, who was big enough to wake herself but never did. The daughter was even worse first thing in the morning. Never looked pleased to see her mother, or the day. What time is it? she growled. Why didn't you get me up sooner? I'm going to be late now. She pushed past Irene into the shower, slamming the door. Irene shrugged. Why couldn't she yawn pleasantly and say good morning, mum, and maybe give her a bit of a kind look, a smile? It was awful this. To feel this constant hatred fuming away, already up and steaming first thing in the morning. You would think animosity might need a roll or a coffee or something to get going.

Down the stairs she went to put the kettle on, holding on to the banister again. Already rattled, uneasy, she felt she was living on a knife-edge. She was wearing her Chinese caftan dressing gown that Mary Ann thought was hippyish and embarrassed her in front of her friends. She had on her oriental slippers. She liked occasionally buying things that bit different. Not the same as the rest of the flock. A splash of colour and country. She picked up her *Glasgow Herald* and brought in her pint of milk and padded towards the kitchen. As soon as she opened the door, she knew something had happened. Slowly, she walked to the blinds and pulled them open. The daylight peered anxiously through the spaces. She filled the kettle, put it on. She put some toast in the toaster and went to get out a knife to butter it. That was when she gasped. The knives were all missing. There were no knives in the drawer at all. The forks were there like a bunch of strange people missing their spouses. The spoons were there, still sleeping. The teaspoons were there at the top where they should be. Irene picked up a spoon and stared into it. Her distorted reflection loomed in a spoon, upside down. She stared at herself in the spoon for a terrible moment, transfixed.

She rushed up the stairs and barged into the bathroom. The lock didn't work properly and could easily be forced. Mary Ann was still steaming in the shower and the room was thick with mist. Irene Elliot coughed as Mary Ann's steam fingered her throat. She waved her arms around dramatically in the fug. Mary Ann covered her breasts with her arms. 'You can't barge in here like this. What's going on?' Mary Ann wrapped herself in a white towel and swept out of the steam into her bedroom, banging the door shut. What was this thing with banging doors? What did it mean? It meant she wasn't supposed to go in, but what else? It meant that Mary Ann was shutting herself in, tightly, furiously. Mary Ann did it so much she almost became the closed door. Her face looked like it, shut and silent and wooden. There was no give in her face anymore. When she was a wee girl she used to look up and there was so much give, so much enthusiasm there spread all over her wee cheeks. Gone now. Who was she, this girl that swept out of the bathroom and banged her door on her? Irene breathed slowly to herself. Mary Ann did not come out, that was certain. She couldn't have come out or else Irene would have seen her. Irene went back downstairs, holding on to the banister as she did do. Her back felt wobbly as if the centre of herself was losing gravity. When she opened the drawer, the knives were all there again as plain as day. Oh Jesus, Irene, she said to herself. Irene's going to have to see somebody.

* * *

Mary Ann came clattering into the kitchen with her big gangly teenage self. 'Why did you barge in on me like that?' 'I don't know. I forget.' Irene said hesitantly, laughing a silly, breathy laugh. 'You forget!' Irene could hear Iain's coldness. She had borne a daughter that had turned out to be her husband. She knew it in her bones. The way her daughter talked to her cut deep. Now that she loathed him, she partly loathed her for being him, for being so like him, so snide and superior. It was a terrible feeling – to suspect her own daughter of being her husband.

Irene Elliot made an appointment to see her GP, Doctor Aspinall. Two days' time – Thursday morning. Mary Ann had left for school banging out of the house. The minute she went, Irene sighed with relief. She felt lonelier when Mary Ann was at home, more strange to herself. There were too many things Irene didn't know and Mary Ann liked to point them out. Clever and arrogant like her father was the daughter. Irene had never been clever. Clever people frightened her and bored her almost to death. If she happened to get stuck in a conversation with one of them, caught unawares, she felt herself seize up and all language leave her. She didn't like people who asked her what she thought of such and such. The new Labour government, what was going on with the white farmers of Zimbabwe, the situation in Sierra Leone, what to do with paedophiles. It all alarmed her. Nor did she like to be asked which painters or writers or singers she liked. Mary Ann had a clever friend home with her one day who asked her if she'd read *The Catcher in the Rye* or if she'd read *Catch 22*. 'No,' Irene replied, 'but I've heard the expressions.' Mary Ann's friend looked blankly through her it seemed, as if beyond Irene, there was another world. Mary Ann burned. Her cheeks took on a glow not of embarrassment, but of anger. Clever people made Irene Elliot feel trapped and claustrophobic. She couldn't wait to escape their talk in her ears. It was exhausting for her trying to concentrate, trying to take in what was being said and remember things. Clever people liked to show off their knowledge; they were never content just acquiring it, they had to bang on and on about it. Irene was never a show off.

She went into the kitchen to make herself a coffee. She steeled herself. Mary Ann was out so it wouldn't happen. She was sure it was something to do with Mary Ann. She opened the cupboard and pulled out the jar of Maxwell House coffee. The lid was open and a spoon was sticking out of it. She opened the fridge for the milk and it all fell out of the fridge, slashing, stabbing, smashing onto the floor. The knives, the forks, the spoons, the carving knife, the bread knife, the fish knives, the steak knives, the meat cleaver, the soup spoons, the dessert spoons, the serving spoons, the ladle, the potato peeler, the potato masher, the knives, the forks, the spoons. 'Knife, fork, spoon. Knife, fork, spoon,' she said as she picked them all up. 'Knife, fork, spoon, soup spoon, tea spoon, that's a fish knife!' she cried out triumphantly. 'That's a steak knife!' she screamed. She moved it around, flick-flick, as if it was a sword. 'This is a fork!' said in a low, slow voice. She was sweating. There was sweat between her cleavage, under her arms, between her legs, in the join of her arms, under her double chin. She ran a basin of hot water and put some fairy liquid in. She threw all the cutlery in there and let it sink like her heart. 'She's not going to get me this way. There's nothing to be done except carry on, Irene,' she said to herself out loud. 'Get this washed, dear, and put it away.' She took the sponge with the green crust on it and scrubbed. A small sharp knife sliced open the tip of her thumb. She stood quite detached watching her blood swim among the knives and forks and spoons. She felt dizzy as if part of herself was falling away, as if her womb was loose or some organ had floated free of everything else inside her. Her mouth filled with saliva and she swallowed fast trying to keep the sea in. Her eyes were watering furiously and it was as if somebody was inside her stomach pulling the ropes, letting the boat out. She heaved and rocked and threw up into the basin with the blood and the forks and the spoons and the knives.

She had to go upstairs; she had to lie down. This short journey upstairs clutching the banister was becoming so desperately familiar. If she could just get horizontal, she might be safe. She washed her face in her bathroom with a cold flannel. Her hair was sticking to her scalp. She was hot. She took off her blouse and her skirt and her stockings and she lay down on her bed in her pants and her bra.

Sleep opened its jaws and let her in. Her dreams when Mary Ann came barging into her bedroom were still there and if Mary Ann hadn't been so urgent, she might have been able to grip them. There was a deaf girl who didn't want her to write a note in capital letters; there was a boat, the bottom slashed, leaking water; there was a man who ejaculated into the choppy sea with Irene Elliot watching. There was so much of it, creamy, frothy; she was quite enthralled. It mixed with the froth of the sea, the high, wailing tip of the waves. It was windy, salty. The man's hair flew about his face. She was just trying to snatch more of him, to remember who he was, when Mary Ann came in.

The daughter surprised Irene then. She sat down on the edge of her bed; she put her hand on her forehead. 'Mum,' she said in a really kind tone, such a lovely kind tone that Irene could have fallen happily asleep to it, 'Mum. You're not well. You need to go to the doctor. I'll clean it up. Don't worry. Shall I call the doctor out?' Mary Ann asked. 'No, I've got an appointment for tomorrow.' Irene felt the tears in her come from a long way off: across a mountain, sliding down a hurrying waterfall, along by a babbling brook. Finally they caught up with her and she heaved and rocked, sobbed and sighed – Mary Ann beside her saying,

'Don't, don't get in such a state. Don't. It's probably a virus or something.' Irene laughed in the middle of her sobs, happy that Mary Ann seemed to care. She sniffed and smiled. The snot ran down Irene's face and Mary Ann rushed up to get some toilet paper. Mary Ann hurried back into the room with a big wad of it wrapped round her wrist like a bandage.

Doctor Aspinall always stood up as a patient entered his room. He sat back down when they were seated. 'So, Mrs Elliot, what's the problem?' (The problem? Where to find the containers for problems.) The doctor smiled with a pained expression on his face. Not a genuine smile, Irene thought. It looked as if it was hurting his face, false and stretchy. 'How can I help?' he looked up again, trying to swallow his irritation. He had a lot of patients outside still waiting to see him.

'I've been having trouble with my cutlery,' Mrs Elliot said tentatively.

'Oh yes?' He tried to keep his head down looking at the prescription his hand was obviously itching to write. A bloody lethal dose of morphine. 'This is a new one on me. Go on. I'm intrigued.' Doctor Aspinall smiled a small smile. 'When I go to put the forks and knives in the right place, my hand just can't,' Mrs Elliot stabbed around for the right word, 'how can I put it? Well it just won't organise itself to do it right.' Organise was not the right word. 'I can't co-ordinate myself,' she said, seizing on this word *co-ordinate*. It's as if I've got two different sides and they won't work together. Then yesterday I went to get a spoon for my coffee and all the cutlery fell out of the fridge and I didn't put it there. I know I didn't put it there. My daughter denies it as well. It's just too much. It's all too much. And a lot of it is very sharp and dangerous. My husband liked sharp cutlery, so that it would cut his steak properly. A lot of our knives have those jaggedy edges.'

Doctor Aspinall stared at something on the wall just beyond Mrs Elliot. Irene actually turned uneasily and looked at the spot behind her. 'I'm going to be frank with you, Mrs Elliot. This knives and forks business is beyond my ken. I'll have to recommend for you to see another doctor.'

'I hope you don't mean a psychiatrist?' Mrs Elliot said anxiously. 'I think I'm just tired. Maybe my mind is playing tricks on me.'

'Well let me prescribe some Prozac and see how we go with that. If it happens again, you come back and see me. It could be a problem with your brain. A left-side, right-side thing.'

'A problem with my brain?' Mrs Elliot echoed, impressed. As far as she was concerned there had always been problems with her brain. Her brain wouldn't do what she wanted it to do. She could feel the limitations of her own mind. She'd always been able to feel them. Like shutters coming down. Like blinds blocking out the light. But sometimes she wanted to know things like who first thought of putting a buttercup under somebody's chin to see if they liked butter. 'Yes, a brain scan would maybe not be a bad idea.' Doctor Aspinall repeated looking back down at his prescription.

It made Irene Elliot wonder at herself. What was it like inside her brain? What activities were taking place? How busy was her brain? Was her brain like her mother's brain – her mother was always called harebrained like Irene – or was it like her father's brain? Her father was tall and bald and supposedly brainy. He had the bold walk of the very bright, quite a surprising, long stride.

The very next week Irene was back, sitting in front of Doctor Aspinall who was sitting behind his desk. Could you just give me a check up? It's been happening again. Could you just listen to my heart? Somehow, it seemed if the doctor listened to her heart, he would know it was broken. This time, Doctor Aspinall insisted on recommending her to a psychiatrist, who, for all he knew, he added ruefully, might be a specialist on people with knives and forks disorder. Irene suddenly felt excited. You mean other people have it?

I was being ironic, Doctor Aspinall said, privately thinking to himself that irony was lost on the mentally ill. When people went bonkers in Doctor Aspinall's experience, they shed their wit, lost their sense of humour.

Doctor Aspinall gave Irene a number to ring – a very sympathetic woman called Jenny Spence. He himself would be ringing her to pass on the details of her case. He also increased the strength of her Prozac prescription. Irene returned home. The light was strange in her street; Kenmuir Drive looked different to her now. Her whole street was full of sadness, hidden behind the curtains. She knew it for certain now. Her own unhappiness allowed her to see everybody else's. She counted the pavement slabs till she got to her own number like a child. Everybody lived behind a hedge or a fence or a gate or a post. Each neighbour was neatly divided from the next. The hedges were too neatly trimmed; completely flat on top. Most of the houses were well painted. A dowdy dirty house stood out. Most of the houses had blinds. A house with just curtains looked poor. The borders of the small suburban gardens were full of sad little flowers, pansies and geraniums, people making their best effort, but no flair or imagination. It seemed outrageous that she should possess a key to a door to a house that meant nothing to her. She stared at her own key dumbly before opening the stranger's door. She nearly passed out.

All along her narrow hall corridor, cutlery was laid out as if many people were expected to a banquet on her dark, red carpet. All places set, but wrongly. Even Irene could see that. Some places were all spoons. Some all forks. Some with knives across the top and tea spoons down the sides. A lot of cutlery was in the middle laid out at intervals. Irene had forgotten that she owned half of it. A silver ladle. A huge serving spoon with a marble handle. Some African salad servers, wooden, that Iain had brought back from somewhere, whose name she can't remember. Proper napkins, white and rolled in their holders, which she never used these days, were at each place in various positions, some on the top, some at the left, some at the right. Irene thought she saw one of the napkins float for a minute and then drop. Her first impulse was to straighten things out. Lay things out properly. The whole hall was as big a challenge as any she had had in recent weeks. It was a matter of putting the right bit in the right place. There was faint music playing in the background. A fine, airy, elegant waltz.

Irene stood up and waltzed down her hall. One two three. One two three. Pas de bas. Pas de bas. She had to be careful not to stand on any of the cutlery. Her feet had to be as dainty as someone born with a silver spoon in her mouth. Iain was a dauntingly good waltzer. Irene was adequate. When Irene watched Iain with women who really could waltz, graceful and nimble, straight backs, long legs, noses turned up in the air to the music, waltzing women that looked as if they had been specially made for the sole purpose of waltzing, she knew that Iain felt as if he had a wife that didn't work properly. Like a clock that didn't keep time, Irene would lose the beat in her head after just a few turns. Concentrate! Iain would whisper into her ear, viciously, steering her body with his overly masculine arms. One two three. Listen. Can you not hear the beat, woman? But that would only make matters worse. Irene felt her steps disintegrate into a slow, shoe shuffle, a scramble, one foot desperately chasing the other to the same silly spot. Until she had to put her hand across her head and wipe the sweat from her brow – no one else seemed to sweat – and say I'm deadbeat, dear. Have a dance with Iris Murray. Iain would settle her down somewhere and go off and that would be that. He wouldn't ask her to dance again until it was all over. One two three. One two three. The music got louder. Knife fork spoon.

* * *

Suddenly Irene was seized by an overwhelming desire to take a sharp knife and stab it into her heart. The desire was so strong she could almost see herself doing it. A stab, a slash, a sharp slit; a cut, a chop, a slice. All of them so tasty. If she could just mark herself, one creative cleave with the carving knife. Rip her own useless, pathetic skin till it split, till she was wounded, till everything burst forth from the gash. If she could rock her own foundations, rupture herself. It was so exhilarating, the picture, the temptation to do herself this final harm. Her mouth was dry, her eyes steady on her own flesh. One part of her was crying out to shred herself, to make mincemeat. She could visualise the dynamic and dramatic red of her own blood, sputtering, stuttering, saying see, see see, I told you so. Out of the pit of her black handbag, she pulled the number of the Spence woman. It felt like calling 999, her fingers trembling and hovering above the numbers until they punched them out, one by one. She felt as if she might explode by her own telephone into a mass of tiny wires and veins and bones. Out of breath. She could not still herself. A voice came on, a recorded voice, friendly, asking for a name and a time and a number. Irene forgot her own number; she could never remember anything under pressure. The phone went into its handset on its own, it seemed. Irene let out a huge, windy sigh. Outside the wind was slicing the trees, clipping the grass, snipping the hedges.

The cutlery in the hall was set for the banquet. Mary Ann would deal with the guests. That one could be sociable with other people if it suited her. Quite the charmer like the father. For a moment, she couldn't think who could be coming. Most of the joint friends had plumped for Iain after the separation. All the folk she had cooked for, dinner after bloody dinner. They had all branched off. They'd followed his swallowtail. Puff! and away that life went, just like that. Lives are silly. Friendships that seem detailed and trusty enough, that seem to have accumulated enough intimacies, knowledge about each other's likes and dislikes, that evaporate into nothing. What was she to make of them? What was she to have thought about her life? Was it real at all? Or was it all fake, sham, pretence? Oh all the hugs in the hall when leaving. Oh all the 'That was lovely, Irene. You excelled yourself.' All a load of hooey. Baloney. Shimmy shammy. Pointless, empty talk. Nobody meant a single word of what they said. Flannellers. Lying, cheating, false teeth. None of those joint friends that had shared the Sunday joint of lamb or beef, or that had gone on joint holidays, none of them so much as phone her now or drop by to see how she is. There was the fork in the road and off they went in her husband's direction. It was beyond belief. The people she had never been all that close to moved forward. They surprised her with their kindness and support. They were a revelation. The ones that she expected nothing from.

Into the kitchen she went and pulled from the fridge a free-range, corn-fed, yellowing chicken. She put rosemary on it. Some lemon juice, some olive oil, and she shoved it straight into the oven to roast. She went to peel some potatoes, but there was no peeler. She found it in the hall, posing as a soup spoon. It would have to be plain fare. She was never much of a cook anyway, not even when she tried cooking lamb cous cous or chicken karachi. All of her efforts tasted the same – spicy stews that made pleasant guests' eyes water. Plain fare was best. Her grandmother from Kirkcudbright liked nothing but plain fare. Plain fare for rosy cheeks, she used to say. Carrots. Parsnips. Onions. Irene hadn't known she was giving a dinner. She went upstairs to lie down while the cowardly chicken cooked. This was the parting of ways. Bed, bed, bed. She could lay a wreath on her bed. She could plait her auburn hair and lie down next to her wreath. All she felt like these days was sleep. Sleep the great I am. Sleep the great pretender.

* * *

It was as if Mary Ann belonged to a different life now. The day was so long it seemed like a journey. Mary Ann's malice, temper, sulleness, slyness was far away. Hazy. A scowl over the hills. Irene wanted to die. Let Mary Ann go and live with her father. She had been asking why she couldn't. Well let her fuck off and go and live with him, Irene shrieked to herself, enjoying the shock of swearing inside her own head. Fuck off, she said again. Just fuck the fuck off. Irene had been tempted to tell Mary Ann that Iain didn't want her either, but she had managed to stop herself. She got up. At least Mary Ann could have a nice dinner when she came in. She had her own key. The wind whispered and hooted like an owl. All along Kenmuir Drive the bushes and the plants and the flowers shook and trembled. The sky was aghast and drained and serious as if it had just been through a long illness.

What would Jenny Spence want her to tell her? Irene walked quickly in the wind with no hat, no scarf, with her thin cream raincoat, no brolly. She remembers digging in her bit of back garden as a child, which was all earth then, no grass yet, digging with a spoon in a pair of tartan trousers and red wellingtons. Digging for fat juicy worms, translucent and other-worldly. The dirt under her small nails, the earth of her tiny, trusting fingers. She walked to the end of her own street and down to Calder Street. She would go to the park. She would go to the park and have a coffee and feed the ducks. She would make herself sane doing a sane thing. She could feel herself split. It wasn't like people said this feeling of madness. She was not out of her head. She was in her head too much. She was beside herself, that was true. Beside her selves. Married and separated. Mother and daughter. Part of her knew what she was doing and knew it was bad; but the other part couldn't stop her. She just couldn't stop her. She didn't want to stop her. She wanted to go all the way. To cut herself in two. Knife and fork.

* * *

The photograph that was still on their mantelpiece why didn't she take it down, did she think he'd come back, did she think she'd have him back? – of Iain and Irene on their wedding day, cutting the cake. Both hands holding the knife. Irene had spoiled their tenth wedding anniversary when Iain took her to a posh restaurant in Callander and they had a four-course meal and Irene started eating from the inside out. From the minute she had sat down that time, she knew things were going to go wrong. Just the sight of all the cutlery made her anxious. She didn't like fancy places really, all the hush and seriousness about the food. She was more comfortable in a canteen. She never knew what to say or do. Iain coloured and then hissed, The other way for Christ sake. For some reason, Iain always thought himself superior to Irene even when it came to sitting down and eating a dinner. Irene's napkin always slid off her knee and on to the floor. Iain's napkin would never do that. Well perhaps Iain had more practice since his job involved more and more fancy dinners. He was a long way from the Gorbals boy she had fallen in love with. This Iain had acquired all these particulars.

She got to the park. The café was quite busy despite the bad weather. Irene hoped she didn't look strange. She was sure it must show on her face. Her top lip hesitated on the bottom. She ran her tongue along the top row of her teeth. Why hadn't she put a little lipstick on to brighten herself up? She was as pale as a ghost; her reflection shocked her in the café's mirror. She ordered a coffee and a Danish pastry. The woman said *Here you are, dear* and seemed to relate to Irene as if Irene was normal, so that was something. That was surely something. There hadn't been a word of warning. They had not been getting on as well as in the early days, but all marriages descended into squabbles and squawks and shrieks and silences. In the early days, Irene could no wrong and in the late days Irene could do no right. That was the journey of their marriage: from right to wrong.

Iain criticised just about everything. He even said *Stupid Woman* fairly regularly. Irene disliked Iain doing his crossword puzzles. When they were first married, she was proud of his smartness. Working-class, scholarship boy, went to Allan Glens. But as time went on his cleverness seemed so self-contained, almost exclusive. Irene couldn't get in. It was all double Dutch to her: crossword puzzles. It seemed as if Iain was often cross doing them or correcting them the next day. Christ. That was staring me in the face, he'd shout at the obvious answer.

But it had come from nowhere. One evening at dinner when Mary Ann was out, Iain had said simply and coldly, I just can't do it anymore. Do what, dear? Irene said. This. This bloody marriage. It's a farce. We don't even love each other. The sex is practically non-existent and not very good. I'm packing my things.

It was typical of Iain that even as he was leaving he had to blame Irene. All her fault like everything else. She was the inadequate. No sorry. No *I'm in love with someone else.* No tears. Just a tight cold stranger's face.

She took a knife, a fork and a spoon and a napkin from the café when the kind woman wasn't looking. She put them in her raincoat pocket. She went to the pond where the Canadian geese and the More hens and the white geese and the male and the female mandarins lived out their theatre on the water, remembering and forgetting their lines. She took the bread from her pocket and fed the birds. They knew her. She knew them.

She peered in and saw her reflection wobble and distort. The wind forked her hair. Kneeling, almost crawling, she set an empty place for herself at the side of the water. She put the knife very carefully on the right. The fork on the left. The spoon at the top. Then she sat back spread-eagled on the grass, both legs sticking out in opposite directions, like a child. At her place, Irene methodically cut her way through bits of grass and turf. Her mouth was full of the taste of earth, iron. She wiped the side of her mouth with her napkin and continued chipping and chiselling and chewing. There was nothing like it. A picnic to herself at the park with the Canadian geese watching Irene and Irene watching the Canadian geese.

Serving the Regent

Andrew Murray Scott

During the endless night, on the seventh floor of Joe's Hostel behind the Port Authority Terminal in midtown, I had been acting out my desperation, drowning in my own sweat, winding myself ever tighter in the greasy sheet. On a clapped-out mattress on an old iron cot, without air-conditioning, with only the coughs and creaks of other destitutes nearby, sleep was impossible. The sun glared in at some early hour and set fire to the room. The concrete chasms were already discordant with sirens, horns tooting somewhere by the bridge, the rumble of traffic heading for the Lincoln Tunnel.

On the sidewalk it was worse. It was coming at you. Everyone was on a short fuse and liable to explode. In the heat and decay, in the death-bringing muggy water-clogged air, it was too hot to do anything at all, except what was expected. And the thermometer behind the desk was already clawing its way up to the eighties. Chattery orange faces on TV screens pointed to an absence of isobars. The handsome kid at Slattery's had the right idea. He was sitting spread-eagled in his shorts inside the front of the icebox, crooning in its cold breath.

'Mornin, Mr Gray, gonna be a hot one.'

'You're right,' I mumbled, adding 'my usual.'

Without moving his face from the blue ice-light, he shouted down the hatch to Slattery's man. 'Usual for Mr Gray.'

'Comin right up,' the voice in the basement yelled.

The air-conditioner being defective, propeller blades slowly pushed already warm moist air around the low-ceilinged diner. There were a few other solitary breakfasters, like ghosts, sipping coffee, trying to keep awake, their silhouettes blurred against the glass. And even in here, the stink of the drains, the pervasive odour of Manhattan overheated milk, mingled with despair and human sweat could be smelled over the black steam of coffee. That was all as usual.

Lee, the desk clerk, had a message for me when I got back across the street. From the Regent Agency: work of a sort, in a hostel off Central Park West, which I knew. A Mr Malkouf, 2pm, cash in hand. The regular tutor couldn't make it.

I took the stairs rather than risk the elevator. The carpets, a crimson colour originally, had a central track worn greasy by feet. The faded, washed-up wraiths who were Joe's main clientele, sidling from locked cell-like rooms, mostly windowless, to grim white bathrooms at the ends of corridors. Some doors slightly ajar; mad eyes peering out. A rat ambled along the corridor towards me and passed by, then came back along the other side.

In my room, I slumped on the sagging mattress. The open window might as well have been a furnace. Fetching up to close it and draw the curtains, I saw something in the block opposite. A statuesque nude black woman on the sixth floor, fanning herself at the window in the cool shadow of the neighbouring blocks. She caught sight of me, began to scratch her crotch aggressively and finally gave me the finger.

The Regent Agency supplies its tutors with a basic textbook and two sampler exercise books. They expect you to improvise. It's not the kind of agency that widely advertises its services. Its clientele tend to be the kind who wouldn't want to be seen abroad in daylight. Mr Malkouf sounded typical; the import-export business and connections with Third World countries. Probably no genuine visa, but then, neither had I; mine had expired four months ago. Since then I'd been a non-person, most active at night. Forty dollars for four hours' work would help to supplement income from my evening regulars.

Instinctively, I gravitated to the shady side of the street. As I passed coin boxes and coffee booths, catching a hazy reflection of myself as a creepy mister with no sure outline, I slid cards inside the glass or stuck them to walls with a tiny lump of stickit. That's another little sideline of mine, for Jorge and Mario. I reckon I've displayed thousands of their little cards around midtown. Everywhere: 'hot black pussy', 'teen virgins'. It's thirty blocks north, a nightmare in those canvas sandshoes. Worst are the intersections. Steam explodes from the manhole covers like volcanic ash and the tyres of cabs melt into the tarmac. The sun blasts into these narrow fissures and has you scuttling for the shade of the next block.

I was grateful to get to the place and rode the elevator to the eleventh floor. It was indistinguishable from my place, even the shiny, rutted carpet looked identical. A tall foreign man opened the door to a shabby little darkened room. He looked vile, but few of my clients were nice people, even if they appeared to be. They all had different needs. Malkouf drew me inside and swiftly checked the outline of my jacket and pants.

'Mr Malkouf?' I mumbled. 'Regent Agency sent me.'

He nodded, and pointed to the bed. I sat down and unwrapped my books: *Good English for Business and Pleasure* and handed him the complimentary Regent Agency exercise book. He looked at it, but continued to examine his fingernails.

'Mr Malkouf?' I queried. 'The book is free. Yours–'

He smiled thinly. 'No want,' he said. He was odd-looking, gaunt; there was a bloodless intensity about him. He had long yellowish teeth. Most of all, he was ominously silent. I couldn't see how I was going to teach him. A rapport has to be established. I felt that he didn't trust me. The cheap brown curtains billowed slightly in the acrid breeze, but the room was stifling. I heard arguing voices in the room next door, Spanish probably. It was the typical room, a cube roughly ten by eight, with an iron bed, a ricketty chair, writing table, a mirror screwed to the back of the door and a peeling poster about fire regulations.

'I need to know what you want me to teach you,' I said, 'what level you're at.'

Malkouf grinned and put a skinny finger to his emaciated lips. He was listening for sounds in the corridor. I didn't like it and stood up, ready to leave. Fuck the Regent Agency, this was a drag.

'You wait,' he said, holding up his hand. As his off-white jacket fell open, I realised he had a stiletto inside.

'I have no money,' I said.

Malkouf grinned in that sidelong way. 'No money,' he repeated with a heavy accent. 'No, no, you make . . . money. You wait.'

After a few more moments, he heard the sounds he was waiting for, eased back the door and swiftly opened it fully. The draught of cooler air was a welcome relief and with it came in another man whom I faintly recognised. He stood beside Malkouf and they grinned loosely at each other, revealing yellow teeth and thin gums. He was short and sweaty, damp stains spreading under the armpits of his linen suit, and around the bulge of his belly. I'd seen him in the brothel on West 27th when I went to pick up my boxes of cards from Jorge.

'You know me?' the stranger enquired. 'I am Hernandez. Real good friend for Mario and Jorge.' His accent was if anything heavier and more outlandish than Malkouf's but the 'real good' was phoney yank. 'You want work? Real good money . . .' he gestured at the books in my hands. 'Much money. No trouble.'

'Okay,' I said, after a moment or two, 'what is it?'

'You inarest?'

'Yeah. Depends.'

'Good. Real good friend Mr Malkouf . . .' he half-turned to grin at the thin man, 'Malkouf in import-export business. Big,

big business . . . lots of place. But busy man. Busy, busy man. You go airport for him. To meet hees . . .' he paused, 'girl-friend. He busy. Much busy. You go? Bring her back for him?'

I thought about it. Took a deep breath. 'Okay, sounds fine. When?'

'You go?'

'Said I would. When?'

'You go . . . tonight.' He held up three fingers. 'In morning. La Guardia. We got car. You get, come back, everything alright you get money.' He held up two fingers. 'Two hundred dollar.'

'Okay, what's her name?' I asked.

Malkouf grinned intensely. His eyes seemed to glitter. A bloated fly had somehow gotten itself into the room and distressed itself in the curtains. The other man held up the forefingers of his left hand.

'We got picture,' he said. He took out a shabby small photograph. Its edges were ragged as if it had been torn out of a page and its surface seemed greasy, or else the focus was slightly out. The girl was smiling, a pretty blonde. She was wearing a white bikini.

'Okay. And her name is?'

'Name?' the fat man frowned. 'Name . . . is Elena.'

'Okay. 3am, La Guardia, Elena. And where do I take her?'

'No understand,' the fat man said wearily. He pointed for me to sit down. 'You get girl. Malkouf he going drive you.'

'And she's his girlfriend?'

Malkouf grinned. 'Yes. Girlfriends. Yes.'

Hernandez held up both hands. 'Girlfriends. Much girl-friends. He too many girlfriends. Wife also. You meet. Take her to him.'

'Well, you tell me where to meet . . .'

'No!' Hernandez shook his head emphatically. 'You stay.' He indicated with his fingertips the rest of the room. 'Stay here.'

Hernandez left the room, leaving me with the vacuously

grinning Malkouf. He came forward and switched on the TV. A wave of a sour, foreign-smelling sweat emanated from his open shirtfront. I looked at the picture again. Seaside, cool sea-breezes, like a mirage. She was a pretty girl alright, but a teenager maybe, too young for Malkouf. I knew a white slave racket when I saw one. There was nothing I could do. It was going to be a long night.

The TV bilged out pictures and noise entirely alien, loathsome jovial commercial junk. Buy this! Buy this! What I wanted was a top-quality air-conditioner that worked, or an icebox I could get inside. Malkouf didn't seem to feel the heat. He paced about, brushing past me. He had locked the door. Occasionally he pulled apart the curtains to stare down ten floors, and then I caught a glimpse of the massed greenery of Central Park. Down below the sheer blocks of the upper east-side. The argument in the next room became louder and erupted into violence. There were several loud thumps on the wall, then silence of a sort, except for the prattling brightness of the ball game from some Florida playpark. I began thinking of women in the abstract. The lights of the sex shops would be flaring in hot neon, advertising new depths of isolation for the human soul. Getting close to a live nude girl – only a pane of glass between – where you could see yourself like a sordid ghost, jacking off. One-way windows. Two bucks for two minutes. The smell of cheap scent and lysol. A male voice complaining and the girl chewing gum in the peep show, snarling 'Fuck off, asshole!' and starting to smoke a cigarette while the shutters click all the way round. All those nights, unable to sleep, desperate for a cool breath, flittering in the muggy heat and sour light around Times Square, stepping over broken-down bums sacked out at the intersections. Municipal garbage trucks grinding slowly round the trashcans. Manhole lids clanking every time a tyre hits them. The black man with the shopping cart full of plastic bags making endless circuits of the sidewalks. A busker's electric guitar thrashes the discords of the night. Two cops, a male and female, wide-hipped in blue uniforms, hands hovering at their belts, ambling by like zombies. That same pervasive smell of burnt chocolate or wet rubber. Always. Always.

Often we sat in the Burger Rack feeling rumblingly hungry, but the food was stale, cardboard, cloying, unsatisfying, had no taste. Cigarettes made no impact on our numbness, our isolation. A gaggle of late-night tourists and young blacks in alpaca caps reflected in neon in the windows and an anorexic whore in black cadged money at the junction. We never discovered if she worked for Jorge. Two cops on horses entered the square, created difficulties for the yellow cabs. A black man in rags lay flat on his back in the doorway of a block of apartments and passersby stepped over him incuriously. Some Puerto Rican youths gave him a desultory kick or two as they passed. He rolled into a ball like a hedgehog, and later uncoiled himself and sat up. The youths came into the Burger Rack and loudly ordered milk shakes and jostled each other. The air-conditioning is the best in New York, the reason why we went there. After a few minutes it made us sneeze. The sex shops busy, sidewalk hustlers accosted passersby: 'drugs', 'young virgin', 'best clean pussy'. A siren clawed at the usual tumult, distinctive in its nameless terror.

In the room, Malkouf's colourless eyes were at me. I realised I'd been drowsing. It was only 1am. I didn't know how I was going to get out of it and I didn't care. Probably I was going to do exactly what they suggested. Two hundred bucks. Some chat show, laugh, laugh, every five seconds, but nothing I could see was funny. A siren in the street, probably on Columbus for the Roosevelt Hospital.

At 2.30am precisely, Hernandez was back, waking me up, and they shuffled me between them into the elevator. It was cooler on the street and the black stretch limo had good air-conditioning. After the jolting lights and miles of blocks and lights, and empty sidewalks, up over the Triborough Bridge on to Wards Island and then the Hell Gate bridge into Queens. Over the glistening open sewer of the East River, along Shore Boulevard to 20th Avenue. We pulled to a halt at the cab rank of the airport's Delta Shuttle Terminal.

'You understand?' Hernandez said, hand on my sleeve. 'Wait for girlfriend, she come long way from Romania to Boston, arrive Gate 1. You bring her here. No trouble. Understand?'

'Okay. When do I get my money?'

Hernandez's teeth seemed pearly under the fluorescent light. 'He pay.' He nodded at Malkouf who sat beside the driver. 'Two hundred.'

I stepped out of the car and inside Gates 1–9 Arrivals. It was busier than I had expected. I saw on the monitor that a Boston shuttle had landed at 3.15. I made my way over to the escalators. In the cool shade of the airport fresh breezes ruffled my soured shirt and pants. I had the photograph in my hand. There's a particular spot just beside the entrance where you can see into Baggage Reclaim, and I waited there. My eyes were sore and tired and I rubbed them. They watered and I stared through the mucus at the queues building up inside around the carousels. I realised why Malkouf and Hernandez needed someone to meet Elena. They didn't want to be captured on security cameras. But in the ebb and flow of arrivals and departures, I noticed one particular man out of the corner of my eye. He was leaning against a pillar watching me. I'd suspected there would be someone else. In this racket, you expect it. I had several false alarms. Blonde girls were flooding into the country by the dozen, even at that early hour.

Right up to the point where I first caught sight of her, I had intended to hand her over. It wouldn't be the worst thing I had ever done. But when I saw her there, in her pretty pink dress, with her pathetic little cheap suitcase . . . something in the timid way she was standing, something about the bright enthusiasm of her eyes . . . I knew I couldn't do it. She was about a dozen back from the gate, ticket in hand. I sauntered round the Arrivals Hall, aware of the other man watching me closely. When a gaggle of nuns with suitcases piled high on trolleys interceded, I glanced into an alcove where the cleaners' trolleys are kept. A girl in faded, open-kneed jeans hunkered down against the wall between the trashcans. Her eyes, glazed over with a mucus film, stared vaguely at me in a myopic stupor. She was a blonde but only just – her roots were showing. She'd pissed herself.

Back at the gate, Elena was straggling out with her suitcase, looking around. Out of the corner of my eye, I was watching the man by the pillar. As soon as I saw him look away, I waved wildly at her.

I leaned over the crack-head and dangled a five-dollar bill. Her eyes focused on it hypnotically between the dangling wisps of her straggly hair. She managed to struggle to her feet, seeing five dollars' worth of rock on offer. She shuffled after me into the concourse.

Elena came up to me. I turned to smile at her. 'Wait,' I whispered. 'Two minutes.' She let me take hold of her suitcase – let go of it. She watched me carry her suitcase in my left hand and with my right propel this other girl towards the front entrance. Elena half-heartedly followed us. As I had expected, the thickset, dark-haired thug by the pillar quickly emerged, neatly removing the suitcase from my hand, and firmly grasping the crack-addict's shoulder. At the car, he expertly bundled the skinny deadbeat inside like a ragdoll. Malkouf was handing me four fifty dollar bills through the open window. The car sped off with a flicker of tail-lights.

Elena looked like a lost child in the middle of the huge concourse, her eyes wet at the inexplicable loss of her suitcase. She was a natural blonde, prettier in real life than in her picture. Meekly, she let me take her arm. She wouldn't quite realise, until I had taught her enough English, just how grateful she was going to be to me, and all my new friends – at Joe's.

Lana

Alison Armstrong

The woman wore a red-sequinned dress that was so long, it covered her toes. It was slit so that she could walk, and when she moved she glittered like the mirrorball overhead. Her gestures were a little stiff, and when she spread her hands for the high notes, her fingers tensed like talons. MacFarlane watched her closely, although he was not a musical man. He was not really a club man either, especially when the club was a small room in the back of a poor hotel. The decor was dirty-red plush, with chipped refectory tables and ricketty Windsor-style chairs. It suited the woman, he thought. Cheap.

He sipped a whisky and water. He rarely drank, but he would have drawn attention to himself if he'd ordered a coke. He looked like a whisky-drinker; he was a raw-boned tweedy man with blue eyes and pale-auburn hair receding from his temples. A true Scot. Whenever he visited Edinburgh, tourists asked for his photograph.

It was good to fit your surroundings, the country of your birth. But MacFarlane was a nomad, forced to drive, and seek out the small, dead towns. Now he was at the east coast, and if he stepped outside the club he would smell salt and be beaten down by the wind. It was no incentive to leave, and take his eyes off that woman in her sequinned, scaly dress.

MacFarlane had an erection, which at that stage of the evening he regarded as a waste of energy. His own father had had no children after the age of thirty-two, and there were younger men in the club who were showing no interest in the woman. She was unnatural, a stage creature got up to simulate desire. Her hair was too blonde, too curly. And no woman walked around with those nails, that make-up, that dress.

'Thank you,' she said into the microphone. 'This next song is called "Fantasy"'. As the taped accompaniment began, MacFarlane reflected that there were certain words that popular music had cheapened. Fantasy was one word, and love was another. They couldn't express real feeling anymore, yet people still tried. People used words casually, as if they were paper tissues.

MacFarlane was a words man. As a student, he had loved the roll of them, the grape-like feel of sound on his tongue. He had thought that losing his virginity would ground his words in matter – give them a subject, make them real in some way, and end his dry separation from the rest of the world. But when it happened, the girl – a student, like himself – went to the lavatory to piss him out.

He moistened his lips with his whisky. His fingerprints were all over the glass, but it would be odd behaviour if he got out his handkerchief. There had been no ice at the bar; they'd laughed and said it was cold enough. Maybe this was true outside, but here in the club it was much too hot. And the smoke made the heat worse. Everybody was smoking, except him.

He considered the other people in the club. Maybe they were fishermen who no longer had work. Fishermen with their wives, their girlfriends, their mothers, even – women who had no smell to scrub away because of the downturn in the economy. The woman on stage was not a fisherman's wife. She was a siren, responsible for many deaths – yet here she was tolerated. Strange.

MacFarlane sold words. He once sold Bibles, then encyclopedias, and now he visited schools for an educational book firm. His job made him travel, but it was the weekends that brought him to the small dead towns. He came because the women were not students, or doctors, or any type of clever, clever person. They never pissed him out – he made sure of that – but it didn't solve the real problem. When he finished with them, he was still dry and separate. Occasionally he sensed ghosts, with dead, sad eyes and fingers that tried to clutch him. Sometimes, when the wind blew, they laughed at him . . . but this all was nonsense. Superstition.

'I want to dedicate this song to all the lonely people out there.' The woman was bending forward, talking to him, and her breasts made dangling U-shapes. The song had roses in the title, and the chorus. Roow-ses. It was bad pronunciation, but he made himself smile at her. The red dress was a mermaid's tail, curved by her belly and her hips. Undulations, he thought, allowing the word to ripple silently over his tongue.

She was smiling back at him, so he raised his glass to her discreetly. Her voice was gruff, a little smoky, and he placed her as forty-something, perhaps as old as himself.

This would be her last song. He had cast, and she was biting. Even so, she was not yet in the bag. There might be a boyfriend or a husband waiting to take her home.

'Thanks. You've been a great audience. Good night.'

Her platitude was too big for the room. A few people clapped her, and in the silence after she'd left, MacFarlane's ears started to ring. The small stage went black, apart from the mirrorball that scattered silver pieces.

People started to leave. MacFarlane glanced at his watch and saw it was late. He still had most of his whisky and water, but he did not drink it. He rotated the glass meditatively as he had seen drinkers do, and began to sense that the barman was watching him.

He waited for about half an hour. Then he heard a clattering sound, and she came into the sphere of the barlights from the back of the stage. She had changed into tight jeans and a red leather jacket, and she was wearing very high stiletto heels. A gold zip ran from her crotch to her belly, straining because of the flesh packed underneath. 'Would you care to join me?' asked MacFarlane, indicating a chair at his table.

'Thanks.' She flashed a showgirl smile, full of teeth. As she sat down, she pushed a shapeless nylon bag under the table, and he withdrew his feet. Perhaps she was staying in the hotel overnight. Perhaps she lived in cheap hotels – a nomad through her work, like himself. Then he shrank from similarities. All they had in common was the table top.

She crossed her legs, swinging right over left, and called to the barman, 'Get us a large rum and diet coke. I'm gasping.' As an afterthought, she pointed a fingernail at MacFarlane's glass. 'And whatever–'

'No – no,' said MacFarlane quickly.

'You sure?'

'Quite sure,' he said, and gave her a tight smile. The barman brought her drink with the coke still in its can, and she ripped back the ringpull with the sides of her fingers and her thumb. She poured some of the coke in her glass, and gulped more in one mouthful than MacFarlane had drunk that evening. Then she fidgeted in her jacket, and laid cigarettes and a lighter on the table. She offered the pack to MacFarlane, and when he declined, she lit one for herself and turned away from him to blow a plume of smoke at the stage.

'So what brings you here?' she demanded.

'Nothing. I'm just passing through.'

She gave a smoky cackle. 'Passing through! Where're you going to, mystery man? Down to the bottom of the sea?'

MacFarlane kept his smile, and said nothing. He watched the woman's hands as she toyed with her cigarette. They were smoke-knotted, twig-like hands – old, in spite of her red lozenge nails. After a while, she laid her cigarette in the ashtray, and twisted around to face him. Her eyes were pale blue, and if they hadn't been tired and bloodshot they might have been beautiful. 'I've seen you before,' she said. 'Are you famous?'

'Oh no,' he protested, and told her about his job with the book company. As he talked, she rocked back in her chair and began to hum a song. Her smoke ascended like a Mackintosh flower, and MacFarlane felt a love for her melody that made his heart glow and swell. As the tune lapped against his ears, he realised his outline was dissolving. 'What's your name?' he asked, quite sharply.

'Lana. After Lana Turner.'

It would happen tonight, he decided. Lana would crack his dry shell. 'Would you like a lift home?' he asked.

She considered, pouting a little. 'No thanks,' she said, 'I always get a taxi.' She emptied her glass, then looked at her watch. 'It's normally here by now.'

She went to look, rising awkwardly because of her tight jeans. MacFarlane's foot slipped and he kicked her bag – then he kicked it again and again and each time his foot went in, a voice in his mind whispered *fuck*. It was a word that he never spoke aloud.

The barman was sending odd looks. MacFarlane stopped kicking, and groped for the handles of the bag. It was a large grey stomach, sloppily packed with soft things and a few hard objects. MacFarlane thought of make-up, curling-tongs, and that red dress . . . He carried the bag past the barman, who commented, 'The age of chivalry's not dead."

'No indeed,' said MacFarlane. 'Goodnight.'

He stepped into the lobby. It was freezing cold and the stark light forced him to blink. There were two high-backed green armchairs and Lana was sitting in one of them. He could only see the back of her head, with its false blonde curls that snaked across the upholstery.

He approached her. His tread was quiet, but she turned. 'It's not here yet,' she complained, gazing up at him with her bloodshot blue eyes.

'I've brought your bag,' he replied.

She smiled at him. 'Oh – thanks. Put it down.'

He placed it on the vacant armchair because he didn't intend to sit. She was sitting with her legs parted, and he could see the X of her jeans-seams at her crotch. He had an impulse to retreat with her bag, and squeeze inside her dress. He was not a burly man, although he was strong. When he was at College he did a little boxing.

'It's cold,' she remarked. She hugged her waistline and jigged her legs so her shoes clattered like a typewriter. When they'd quietened down he agreed with her – then he repeated the question he'd asked earlier: 'Would you like a lift?'

'Och – I don't know –' She pushed back her sleeve and looked at a gilt watch. It had a square face and a little chain that hung down in a loop.

'It's very late,' he pursued. 'And taxis can be unreliable –'

'Okay,' she interrupted. He waited patiently while she lit a cigarette, before rising. When she stood, he noticed that they were the same height, but without her heels, she'd be five or six inches shorter. As they walked to the exit, he carried her bag once more, and she called him a real gentleman. 'I've seen you on television,' she said. 'I know I have.' This was untrue because he had never been on television, and as he listened to the noise of her heels, he found them neurotic.

Outside, the sky was bluish-black, and the moon wore a slouch hat made of cloud. There was salt in the air that made MacFarlane lick his lips, and wonder if the process of corrosion had started on his car. It was the only vehicle left in the carpark, apart from a rusty van that possibly belonged to the barman. 'That your car?' Lana asked. She sounded impressed.

'Yes,' he said. There was still time to leave her and drive off with her bag, but he asked 'Shall we go?' and steered her ahead by touching the small of her back. As soon as they left the doorway, the wind blasted them with wet salt. Lana squealed girlishly, but he kept his lips shut. She threw away her cigarette, then took his free hand. Because of her long nails, she held it in a flat, peculiar way, then she started to hang back, as though pulling him to drown in the air. 'Sorry,' she called above the wind. 'It's these shoes.'

They reached his car, and Lana dropped his hand and went to wait by the passenger door. The car had central locking but Lana hadn't realised, for she was still shivering outside. He reached over and unlatched the passenger door, allowing her to pull it wider and get in. She slammed the door, as people did who were used to old cars. Then she reached for the radio dial, and, despite her nails, managed to twiddle the dial to a pop-music station. The song playing was a bedtime smooch, sung by a girl with a high, syrupy voice. 'Someone to comfort and hold me,' she sang, 'In the long lonely nights –' Lana joined in, singing the words almost under her breath. This time, her voice didn't affect him.

Then the song faded, and a DJ cut in. 'Hi,' he drawled. 'That's for all you lovers out there.' Lana tutted, and yanked MacFarlane's rear-view mirror in her direction. Then she found his reading light and switched it on, in order to inspect her face. 'Christ,' she muttered in her smoky voice. 'What a hag.'

'Tempus fugit,' said MacFarlane. He didn't expect her to know what it meant.

'It's not the tempus,' she told him. 'It's the sodding weather.'

She repaired the damage. First, she produced a lipstick from her pocket, and, squinting into the mirror, she applied some, stretching her mouth. As she worked on her face, the smell of her wet hair mingled with the wet, wool smell of his jacket, and the windows began to steam up.

Finally, she turned to MacFarlane. 'Do I look okay?' she asked.

'Fine,' he said. 'Just fine.' He switched the ignition full on, and drove away from the hotel. The road's course held him firm: it was a ribbon that stretched behind sand dunes, with no deviations apart from the turning. He'd noticed the turning on the way to the hotel. It wasn't on the map.

He asked Lana where she wanted to go. 'Just carry on,' she said. She was lulled by the wiper blades, and the music that she'd turned low. He thought she'd fallen asleep, then she exclaimed, 'I've got you!'

'What do you mean?' he enquired. His heart froze, and his knuckles gripped the wheel tightly, but his voice was its usual quiet self.

'I know who you are. You're Gordon Jackson!'

'No I'm not,' he said, and sealed the fact with his tight smile.

'But you are,' she persisted. 'I watched you every week in *The Professionals*.'

'Gordon Jackson's dead,' he interrupted. He added, rather brutally, 'So is Lana Turner.'

Lana took a breath, sharply, then she giggled. 'Isn't it funny that we're both dead people?'

'No,' he said. 'I don't think it's funny at all.'

The road continued monotonously, and the wind from the sea whipped his aerial. The dunes didn't blow away because they were tussocked with gorse. He couldn't see the gorse, but he could picture it, tough like pubic hair. Coarse gorse.

He nearly missed the turning because it wasn't marked. As he turned, his car lurched into a pothole and gave Lana a shock. 'Where are we going?' she demanded. 'You're meant to be taking me home.'

'Just a short diversion,' he said.

He drove down a slope to a jetty, whose limit was marked by a rusty post. When he turned off the headlamps the post vanished, leaving them hanging in sea and sky. 'Shall we go for a walk?' he asked, as a squall blurred the windscreen.

'In that stuff?' she retorted. 'You must be mental.' She reached to turn up the music. In the light from the radio, he saw that one of her nails had broken, the one on her middle finger.

'Leave it,' he said. 'The music's loud enough.'

'For what?" she asked huskily, and rested her hand on his knee. Her knotty old hand was repulsive, but he touched it, and stroked back towards the wrist. She gave a little sigh, as though she was happy, but he didn't visit dead towns to stroke hands. He took her middle finger – the one with the broken nail – and started to bend it back. 'Ow!' she went. 'What d'you think you're doing?' He kept pulling and pulling, and only let go when he reached breaking point. She didn't try to escape because of her ridiculous shoes.

He reached for her throat, and she made horrible noises as she fought for breath. After he'd strangled her, he wiped the saliva that she'd dribbled on to his hands. The radio was still on, and a black voice was singing falsetto. It annoyed him, so he switched the radio off.

The moon was showing faintly, through a cloak. MacFarlane unclipped Lana's seatbelt, then clambered out of the driver's seat and scurried round to the passenger door. He opened it and extended Lana's seat to make her lie back. He unzipped her jeans, and pulled them to her ankles along with her pants, then unzipped his own trousers. He was limp, although it was now the right time to have an erection. He tried to lose himself in dumb repetition as he crashed his pelvis against her.

The handbrake of his car was too close to his leg. It dug into his knee, and before he could lose himself, he was forced to abandon Lana and crawl painfully out of the car. He rubbed his knee, and the wind shrieked. It seemed to be laughing at him.

Another car streaked past on the road. It was probably Lana's taxi. All his pain, his discomfort was her fault; he'd never had problems with the handbrake before. She was laughing at him, and so were all the women, right back to the student years ago who'd pissed him out. He tried to quieten them by pulling Lana's body out of his car and shoving her repeatedly with his good leg until she rolled off the jetty. The splash she made quietened everything – then the laughter resumed, crazily, in the wind and the roar of the sea. MacFarlane realised that he was still unzipped. He felt ridiculous.

He returned to his car. It was warm inside, even humid, after all his exertions. His wet clothes began to feel uncomfortable and he worried about catching cold. He didn't have a change of clothes. Normally he packed a valise, but this time, for some reason, he'd forgotten. Then, in his rear-view mirror, he caught sight of Lana's bag, sprawled on the back seat.

He reached over and unzipped it. The red-sequinned dress glittered and winked at him. It was a dead queen, surrounded by trinkets: a hairdryer, bangles, a pouch full of stage make-up and some chiffon scarves. MacFarlane caught his breath. There was something about those objects, and the way they breathed Lana's perfume . . . he didn't feel ridiculous anymore.

He turned up the heating and wriggled out of his wet clothes. He extracted the pouch of make-up and applied sparkly blue powder to his lids. To do this, he squinted in the rear-view mirror, just as Lana had done when she fixed her face. Then he found a pan-stick foundation, and smoothed it over his face. It had a thick, sweet smell that he remembered from his mother, and if he hadn't applied the eyeshadow he might have shed a tear. His eyebrows were now covered, so he redefined them with mascara, then he gave himself cherry-coloured lips. Halting for a moment, he surveyed himself and saw no trace of MacFarlane, apart from the receding red hair. This he covered with a chiffon scarf, then smiled at himself coyly. His transformation felt so complete that he was surprised to glimpse his own teeth.

His heart raced as he lifted the dress from the bag. It was heavy and externally cold, like the pelt of some sea-creature. The lining still felt warm, and he could see Lana's sweat-stains under the arms. He got out of his car again, and stepped into the dress as though he was entering a volcano. Once it reached his thighs he had to pull and wriggle, and despite the satin lining the sequins flayed his skin. He didn't mind; it was only his shell that was hurting. He raked the dress over his buttocks and his belly and his chest, then faced the sea and raised his arms to heaven. 'A star is born!' he screamed, and the wind became hysterical.

The dress gaped at the back. He couldn't fasten it. Then invisible fingers came, and began to inch the zip up his spine. At first he didn't notice, then he loved the feeling of a tighter, tighter waist. The fingers edged the zip further, and the dress started crushing his ribs.

He tried to get rid of the fingers. He tried to shake them off, and brush them away, but his own hands touched nothing. He tried to scream, but couldn't move his chest. Besides, there was no one to hear.

The fingers took their time. They were good at waiting. They closed the zip tooth by tooth and when they finally reached the top, they fastened the hook and eye.

The dress reached the ground. It took root, in spite of the weather, and held MacFarlane up to face the morning.

Mouse

James Robertson

Gilchrist sat on the edge o the bed, his haun rubbin at the reuchness o his unshavit jaw. His unblinkin gaze wis fixed on the gap at the side o the electric fire whaur the moose had disappeared.

I ken fine whit ye cry me. Dinna think I care a haet. Ye daft wee stupit lassies.

He'd waukened wi a jerk frae a dream aboot the shop an sat straucht up in bed. Somethin wis scartin awa at the back o his mind. Syne the scartin sclid frae his mind doun the waa an unner the bed whaur it jyned tae somethin squeakin. There wis a moose ablow him, a bluidy moose.

The clock said ten tae five. He'd be risin onywey at five. He raxed oot an turnt the alarm switch aff. Syne he flung back the covers an swung his pyjama'd legs ower the edge. A moose. His bare feet landit on the linoleum like lumps o leid. Auld, calloused, hard as bluidy buits they were. The soun o them on the flair wis like buits stampin an the moose shot oot atween them an ower the flair an in ahint the electric fire.

Gilchrist sat rubbin his face, an his mind turnt ower the arrival o the moose, the ovens heatin even nou at the shop, an the stupit wee lassies that wud be at the shop later. The ovens wis permanent an unyieldin an Gilchrist himsel wis permanent but the lave wis like stour ye flicked awa wi a clout. They cud cry him whit names they likit but it wudna shift him, he'd be there lang efter they were gane.

It wis a guid while sin he'd had a moose here at hame. In the shop ye expeckit them, a bakery wudna be muckle o a bakery athout the odd moose. But it wud be a year or mair sin he'd seen yin here. Sin afore mither had dee'd. Ay, an she'd hae haen plenty tae say aboot a moose kythin. He cud juist hear her at it.

It wis the season richt eneuch. October, an the hairst wis in. In the shop it wis different. But here at the hoose, backin ontae aw these fields, it wisna surprisin that the mice cam in at this time o the year, herriet oot o their simmer nests an preparin for the winter. Ay. Sae there it wis, the first moose. The first cuckoo merkit the stert o simmer an the first moose pit an end tae it. No that Gilchrist had time tae listen oot for cuckoos. Gowks, his mither aye cried them. There wis naethin couthy or sentimental aboot the wey she said it either. Ye had tae say that for the auld bitch.

There wis naethin sentimental aboot Gilchrist. He dealt wi life day by day an he'd deal wi mice juist the same wey. He had traps at the shop an he'd bring some back an catch the brutes afore they got oot o haun. He believed in preventative medicine in awthin, includin capital punishment, an onybody that telt ye hingin didna prevent onythin, weill, it wis juist bluidy haivers. It preventit the buggers daein it again, for a stert. It wis cried deterrence an it worked for humans an mice juist the same. Ye punished yin an the ithers sat up an tuik tent. The same at the schuil. Either ye got the belt an ye felt that, or ye saw some ither wean gettin it an ye felt that tae. That wis the auld days, o coorse, when schuil wis for lairnin, no like nou. The mice cud dae whit they likit in the pairks, but yince they set fuit ower his lintel they were as guid as deid.

He stude up an pou'd aff his pyjamas an pit on his breeks, leavin the galluses hingin doun at his knees. He pit on his socks an shuin an aw, an gaed throu tae the bathroom tae synd his face an shave it. His heid wis a wee thing dozent wi the drink frae last nicht, but that wis aw. He didna get sair heids frae drink, he didna hae the sentiment, the waikness. It wisna sae muckle that he didna *suffer* sair heids, mair that he wudna *thole* them. Na, na, he wis hard as nails, Gilchrist, an tuik the effecks o drink as ye micht duntin yer knee on the door-jamb – a curse an it wis by wi. He drawed the razor ower his stibble wi the same lack o respeck for the pyne – the water wis only hauf-warm. The pyne'd be better respeckin him!

He'd uised tae work maist o the nicht wi the breid, but no these days. Nou he redd up awthin in the forenicht an preset the ovens tae heat at five, an he cud still hae het breid on the shelves by hauf seiven. The big orders for the schuil an the auld fowk's hame werena required afore nine o'clock sae there wis plenty time. Gettin in at hauf five gied him three oors forby afore the lassies an Mrs McGibbon cam in – three oors o guid hard-workin peace his lane.

An in spite o the automation the work hadna got that muckle lichter doun the years – guid work wis hard as buggery, aye had been, aye wud be, it wudna be work if it wisna. But he'd lairnt hou tae manage his time better, an tae delegate some o the basic tasks tae the lassies. No the important yins, mind, like the buyin o flouer an yeast an the bakin itsel. Christ no, a wummon dae thae! An the coontin o siller, the bankin an the wages, he'd niver let ony ither grabbie haun in at thae bits o darg! Mrs McGibbon, that'd been wi him twal year, cud organise wha wis servin at the coonter an wha wis scoorin trays an pans, the tea-breaks an siclike, but that wis as faur as her or onybody's rule wud rax as lang as he wis the gaffer. An whit wey wud he iver no be? He'd niver had a day's illness in his life the whisky see'd aff ony o thae dreepin nebs an hoasts the weemin aye seemed tae cairry aboot an as for holidays, weill, whit need had Gilchrist o a holiday? He had his Wednesday efternunes an his Saubbaths, had he no?

He gaed back throu tae the bedroom an pit on his semmit an a clean sark. Nae tie – it wis a bakery, no a restaurant. He made a mental note aboot gettin the traps an gaed oot, lockin the door ahint him.

It wis only a mile frae the hoose tae the High Street whaur the shop wis, but in the time it tuik tae stert the motor an drive doun Gilchrist thocht again aboot whit they cried him. Psycho. That wis it. It wis short for somethin, an he kent it wis a term o abuse; it meant he wis a bad bastart that planned tae murther them aw ae nicht, but mair nor that he didna ken aboot it. Ay weill, as weill for them he wis juist a baker. If he wis a flesher he wud dae them in for shair wi a cleaver.

It wis juist sair gripes on their pairt. He wis a fair employer. Whit did they expeck, a tea-pairty insteid o hard work? He'd be daein them nae favours if he didna cam doun on them for puir standarts. An he peyed no bad wages – no bad for the toun an for retail, onywey – an aw they did wis serve the customers an tak the siller affae them an clean the place – it didna exackly require a degree. Nou. See if there wis ae kinna person he wud niver employ but, it wis yin wi a degree. A bluidy student. Naethin but bother, thocht the warld awed them a livin when the warld – ay, Gilchrist an his like – had peyed their taxes tae let them slounge aboot readin Shakespeare an that for three–fower year, syne they were haunless for ony job that needit yer back pittin intae it. Na, na, for aw that they were stupit he kent he wis better aff wi the yins he had, but he wudna be saft on them. Ae thing he'd say for that English bitch Thatcher, she kent aboot the worth o siller an the worth o labour. Ye meisured the yin agin the tither an naethin else entered intae the calculation. Nae sentiment wi that yin either. He cud respeck that.

When his mither wis alive she tuik in bed an breakfast in the simmer, juist tae mak uise o the spare chaumer an get a puckle extra bawbees. They'd fell oot wi the wummon in the tiny wee Information Office because she niver recommendit them tae ony visitors – the only trade they were gettin wis frae fowk that got their nummer oot the guide-buik. They cud hae dune wi some o thae rich Yank tourists that whiles cam out frae Embro, but fient a Yank did they see. Mither gaed doun there yince tae fin oot whit the problem wis: the wummon shairly wudna hae the impidence tae tell her the room – the haill house – wisna spotless, wud she? (That wis hou mither wis sae ill-pleased if a moose iver shawed itsel, she tuik it as a personal affront.) The Information wummon hemmed an hawed an wudna come oot wi't at aw. They had tae conclude it wis juist plain malice; she'd taen a scunner at them for some reason. She worked for the Cooncil, but there was nae uise in ludgin a compleent wi them, they ayewis jyned thegither tae defend theirsels.

Efter mither dee'd he'd meant tae tak the hoose aff the list o accommodation but he'd forgot, syne ae nicht a young wummon turnt up at the door an asked if he'd a vacancy. It wis that lang sin the last yin he didna ken whit she wis on aboot. Syne he realised an juist cam oot wi: 'Weill, I suppose ye cud come in if ye've nae place else tae bide, but I dinna really tak fowk nou that ma mither's deid.' Mebbe it soundit queer but it wis the truith, wis it no? The stuck-up feartie bitch backed awa an said it wis aw richt, it wis juist a general enquiry, but did she no tak the tale back tae the Information Office the neist day, sae when he phoned up tae hae the hoose tuik aff the buiks the wummon said, 'Oh, yes, Mr Gilchrist, I heard that was the case now that you're on your own out there.' Oot whaur, for God's sake? Ye cud walk tae the toun frae the hoose! She made it soun like they were oot on the bluidy muirs. It wisna lang efter aw this that the lassies stertit cryin him Psycho ahint his back tho – he fun oot quick eneuch, catchin snatches o their daft claik – he'd bet that interferin besom in the Tourist Office had a haun tae it.

The smell o new breid aboot ready tae come oot o the ovens hit him as sune as he'd pit aff the alarm. But he wis early, it wantit anither five minutes. There wis a press for aw the buckets an brooms an siclike, an he fun three moosetraps in ahint a pokefu o mop-heids, a wee thing rousty and yin o them wi whit luiked like spleiters o auld bluid on the plate. He tuik them oot tae his motor so's he wudna forget them later, syne gaed back tae tak oot the breid.

Aboot eleiven that mornin, he tuik a dauner doun the street for a paper an stepped intae Lawrie's for a bit cheese. He didna eat muckle cheese himsel, in fact he hardly iver had ony food in the hoose, preferrin tae eat a big meal at denner-time in the pub. 'Juist a quarter o cheddar,' he said tae Lawrie.

'Now, is it the mild, or the mature white you're wanting?' said Lawrie, in that mim-mou'd wey he had that got Gilchrist's birse up, as if he cud fool onybody that his apology for a shop was some kinna delicatessen.

'Yer cheapest,' Gilchrist growled. 'It'll be juist as appreciate whaur it's gaun.'

'That'll be the mild, then,' said Lawrie, poutin. Syne he said, 'Do you have a wee problem, Mr Gilchrist?'

'Whit?'

'A wee problem? A wee visitor, perhaps?'

Whit bluidy business wis it o his? He refused tae cam doun tae the man's level. 'A moose,' he said, 'if that's whit ye mean.'

'Oh, well,' said Lawrie, as he cut the cheese an wappit it, 'see if this disna work, you mark my words, a wee bit of chocolate does the trick. Nothing they like better than a wee bit of chocolate. Sixty-seven, please.'

Gilchrist haundit ower the siller. 'Chocolate?' he said. 'Chocolate? It's a hoose, man, no a bluidy hotel.'

'Ay, of course,' said Lawrie, wi whit luiked like a smirk playin aboot his gab. Gilchrist resistit the urge tae tak his nieve tae it. Mair fother for their jokes, nae dout. Ach! They cud think whit they likit.

Whiles it wis hard keepin yer heid up amang aw the cuifs an eejits that surroondit ye. But Gilchrist got a kinna pleisure oot o rubbin shouthers wi them. It wis as if he needit tae sperk aff their imbecilities, as if he wud turn intae a big sumph, a daud o dough, if he juist sat hame at nicht watchin the television. That wis hou he steyed on at the shop efter the lassies' lowsin-time, fed himsel on a couple o pies or whitiver wis left, redd up for the morn's morn, syne tuik himsel back tae the pub for a few drams. Better that nor cuttin yersel aff frae the common herd. Whiles fowk wud speak tae him in the pub, whiles they wudna. It juist dependit.

'Ay, Mister Gilchrist,' said Sandy, the barman, settin the gless in front o him. 'Hou's things?' Sandy wis a young lad but he wis aw richt, kent his place, aye cried him Mister.

'No sae bad, Sandy. Gie's a hauf tae gang wi this, will ye?'

Doun the bar sat auld John Douglas, that uised tae drive the buses afore takkin early retirement. Ye wunnert why fowk did it, Gilchrist thocht. There wis John, he'd had somethin tae occupy himsel wi aw day lang, kept him awa frae the wife forby bringin hame a wage, an he'd gane saft on himsel. Naethin wrang wi his health either, as faur as Gilchrist kent. He juist wantit the easy life, sittin up at the bar aw nicht readin his Westerns or his paper like nou, an wantin a crack wi onybody daft eneuch tae listen. The easy life: there wis nae sic thing.

Ivery twa–three minutes Douglas wud gie a snicher or a gasp, as if he wis actin in a play, an wag Sandy ower. 'Wud ye credit it? That's the Japanese for ye, eh?' Syne, 'See this, Sandy? It wisna like that when I wis your age.' Wud ye no juist bluidy shut up, Gilchrist thocht. Let a body hae his drink in peace.

Syne John stertit tae read oot a haill story. Gilchrist fun himsel takkin it in, tho he made damn shair his face didna shaw it.

'More Indian victims of mouse virus,' read John. 'Three more Navaho Indians have died of a rare disease associated with desert mice in New Mexico. The mouse population in an area of Southwestern USA which includes the Indians' reservation is believed to be widely infected with the virus. If transmitted to humans it causes extreme pain and eventual asphyxiation when the lungs fill with blood and froth blocks the respiratory channels.' By Christ, ye wudna want tae be a Navaho, wud ye? First ye get the hell beaten oot o ye by the US Cavalry, syne when ye've fun yer feet a hunnert years later alang comes a wee moose an chokes ye wi yer ain bluid. Did ye hear that, Gilchrist?' he cawed doun the bar. 'I wis juist readin aboot thae Rid Indians.'

'Ay, I heard ye,' said Gilchrist.

'The best laid plans o mice an men, eh?' said John. 'I bet the Navahos arena gaun aboot addressin the wee sleekit cowerin timrous beasties. Nae fear!'

Of coorse they're no, ye're talkin shite as usual. Whit wud a wheen savages ken aboot Rabbie Burns? Gilchrist had forgotten aboot the moose, his ain yin. He cowped his dram an his hauf an had the same again. Twicet. Syne he gaithert himsel tae his feet an drave hame.

At three in the mornin he woke wi a stert. There had been a snappin soun frae ower by the fire. 'That'll bluidy lairn ye,' he said oot lood, an rowed ower an back tae sleep again.

The neist mornin he wis up at five, inspectin the three traps he'd set. There wis a deid moose in the first yin richt eneuch, hadna had mair nor a wee bit smacher at the cheese afore its craig had been snackit. A drap o bricht-reid bluid bloomed frae its lug. Throu in the kitchen there were corpses in the ither yins an aw. He tuimed them intae the bucket an reset the traps. Three in the ae nicht. It was mair o a problem nor he'd thocht.

He had tae gie a lassie her jotters that day. For bein late again. She'd had fair warnin. But he didna feel guid aboot it because he kent she had some kinna faimly bother, kent she needit the wage. But he cudna mak an exception, juist cudna dae it. If he let the wan awa wi't they'd aw be swannin in at ten-tae-nine. Ay an Mrs McGibbon tae nae dout, the frosty luik she gied him efter the lassie gaed oot greitin, wi a week's wage in her pocket in lieu o notice. Gilchrist had mair drink nor his usual in the pub that nicht.

Sune as he wis hame, the first thing that hit him wis a thick, fousty kinna smell. He smelt it e'en throu the whisky he'd been cowpin, sax drams yin efter anither, an chasers tae. He cudna place the smell, it wis like somethin auld-farrant, frae his bairnheid. He'd brocht back anither trap he'd fun in the shop sae he set that yin in the kitchen tae. There cudna be mony mair o the craturs, shairly.

In the mornin he woke an for the first time he cud mind in years his heid wis dirlin. If he hadna been drinkin his lane he'd sweir somebody had laced his gless. He cudna mind comin tae bed, he cudna mind onythin efter settin the new trap.

There wisna a moose corpse in the bedroom. He gaed ben tae the kitchen. Nae a corpse in sicht. Syne he luikit aboot for the third trap. He fun it, on the tither side o the room, sprung an restin on its side hard up agin the waa as if it had been flung there. He maun hae kickit it on his wey tae his bed. An the first trap had nae cheese in it. Nae wunner he wisna catchin onythin.

Syne he saw the paper poke he'd brung hame the loaf o breid in. A haill new white loaf it had been, sclicit in the machine afore he left. He wis shair o it. He mindit sayin tae himsel, tak thon last loaf hame for yer breakfast, an he mindit sclicin it. Smellin thon foustiness when he wan hame an kennin it wisna the breid he had in his oxter. Did he no? Na, it maun hae been the nicht afore. Or mebbe he'd had some toast last nicht. He wis that fou he cud hae dune onythin. Weill, either it wis him, or it wis a haill army o mice, for fient a sclice o breid wis left, juist a wheen crumbs skailt aboot on the flair. He maun hae knockit the breid aff the coonter when he kickit the trap. If he'd kickit the trap. Jesus. A haill loaf. He wud need tae watch the drinkin, he cudna afford tae loss his licence.

He cam hame straucht frae the shop that nicht, he wis that knackert. Wisna hungry, juist wantit his bed. He'd been oot in a sweat aw day, gettin the alcohol oot o his bluid. His heid wis sair yet.

Nae evidence o mice at aw. Nae corpses, nae shite, naethin. He stude in the middle o his bedroom wi his shune aff, listenin for the skelterin noise ower his heid. Naethin. Thank Christ, he thocht. He fell intae his bed an wis asleep in an instant.

Somethin woke him the first time an oor later. The room wis black as pitch. He had a memory o a terrible crashin noise up in the roof, as if a couple o sclates had cam aff in the wind. He listened. There wis nae wind at aw.

A dream. He wis haein bad dreams. That wis it, he wis cuttin oot the whisky for guid.

He dreamed again, an this time he dreamed o his mither. But no as she wis afore she dee'd, an him no as he wis nou either. He wis juist a wee laddie, his mither had him gruppit by the craig an wis forcin his heid doun, bendin him ower the big kitchen table in their auld hoose. An she had the belt oot, his faither's belt, the only thing o his she'd no thrawn oot when he'd upped an left. An she wis leatherin him wi't, bringin it doun on the backs o his legs, skreichin abune anither vyce that wis skreichin tae, a vyce that he kent in the dream wis his ain. He cudna hear whit she wis skreichin or whit he wis skreichin but he kent she wis lairnin him. Lairnin him guid, lairnin him a lesson he'd niver forget.

He shot up in the bed, the backs o his legs were burnin. He wis droukit in sweat. There'd been anither awfu crash, it seemed as tho it had been richt there in the room. He luikit oot but he cud see naethin. The image o his mither fadit awa an he wis left breathin like an auld man wha's juist sclimmed a fifty-fuit lether, pechin awa an gruppin the sides o the bed in the terrible mirkness. His heid wis gowpin.

He wis no weill. He'd niver been no weill in his life but somethin wis faur wrang nou. He'd hae tae see the doctor the morn.

As he breathed, he wis aware o that smell again, that lourd, fousty, stoury kinna smell. Kinna like the back o the shop, but no like. Like a horse, or a steadin.

He wis feart.

Syne somethin muved. Whitiver it wis, somethin shiftit in the faur corner o the room. The derk refused tae disperse, but nou Gilchrist cud feel stour in his nostrils, the smell o plaister an wuid. An the thing muved again. A rat? When it muved the flairbuirds creakit wi't. Bigger nor a rat.

He raxed oot slawly for the lamp-switch, but his haun wis shakkin that muckle he cudna fin it. His haill airm wis jumpin as if it had a separate life frae the rest o him. Wi a crash the lamp cam aff the table an landit on the linoleum.

Across the room, as if the noise attractit it, the thing shiftit again, a wee bittie closer. An the terrible smell o stour awmaist gart Gilchrist fent. But he didna. He daurna fent. An nou he heard it, its braith, comin in wee pechs but tho they were wee they seemed louder nor his ain braith. He pressed himsel back up agin the heidbuird, ettlin no tae breathe at aw, ettlin no tae shak, an prayin for licht.

Mazzard's Coop

Dilys Rose

The dead shall live. The living die,
And Music shall untune the sky.

Rabbits again. Outside the gate, on either side of the street. Could be roadkill, could have been thrown up by the wheels of a passing car and landed there, just so, heads pointing north and south. But you know those eternal burrowers are not roadkill. You know how they got there, why they're there, know they mean Della's been by, hexing the place.

As if a tinker's curse could bring you worse luck than you've had already – or anybody else around here.

But you're a gambling man, Mazzard. You, Jack and Willie were all gambling men. A gambling man pays heed to signs, doesn't underestimate Della's dirty tricks.

The day's been warm and sunny, grand for the kiddies' gala. Wild garlic seasoned the breeze. The bunting draped between the tight huddle of miners' rows fluttered and flapped. No miners left in the rows now, of course. Even those, especially those, who hung on till the bitter, bankrupt end of the pit's history couldn't begin to afford the inflated prices of the renovated dwellings. And how many who turned out to cheer the brass band as it paraded through the streets, trumpets and trombones flashing in the sun, would have had a clue what the fanfare signified? Incomers every one, with work elsewhere. Had to be elsewhere. Nothing left here. In two minds about going anywhere near the gala but after a week of rain you'd felt restless, cooped up like your blasted birds. You needed to get out. The smell of wet birdshit hung over your house like a hooped net. You slapped the bunnet on the old head. Smooth as bone now. No more curls to charm the girls. You cleaned out the cage, changed the water, filled the food trays and set off on the walk you could do with your eyes shut, your personal stations of the cross: under the viaduct, along the riverbank where the water runs fast and high, across the bridge and down the concrete path which leads past the powerhouse, the pit-head, the visitors' carpark. Even as a museum, a showcase for Tilley lamps, embroidered union banners and the smiling black-faced camaraderie of yesteryear, the place once again is on the verge of going under. When it does, when the vast, grimy anachronism is eventually demolished and replaced by clusters of commuter homes in quaintly named cul-de-sacs, when the last traces of coal dust have been sluiced away, what will be left of it all, Mazzard? What will be left of that hellish quest for black diamonds?

Not always enough birds to go round, so some days you had to take a chance. Willie knew the odds. So did you.

Even before you reached the street party you knew it was a waste of time, knew your ties with the rows had been severed long ago. Jack O'Lantern, from next door, was there in the thick of it all, sat on a bench, dandling somebody's bairn on his knee. Jack's a familiar face, as familiar as could be, but you'd be lucky to get as much as a nod. Instead of edging into the sunny crush of folk enjoying themselves, you turned away from the brass band, the bunting, the bouncy castle and took the main road home. None of the partygoers noticed you pass by. But you could feel the cardboard men at your back, all the way to your gate.

You could leave the rabbits for nature to take its course, for that buzzard circling high above your head to tear apart. Or next door's cats. But you can't be sure they're clean kill, can you? Can't be sure Della hasn't tampered with the carcasses. She knows her herbs and potions, knows what can be sprinkled on what and still taste safe. Even though there's no love lost between you and next door's cats, even if they're forever sniffing around the coop or crouching in the long grass by the burn, waiting for the chance to do their own killing, you wouldn't want them getting sick from something they found by your gate, would you, Mazzard? You wouldn't want Jack-o-Lantern chapping the door of an evening because his beloved mogs had copped it from some tainted meat they found outside your place.

You and Jack go back a long way. You, Jack and Willie went back a long way. The pub on payday: bright-eyed from beer and freedom from work. The *Morning Star* in your pockets and rosy-tinted talk of the glories of Moscow, Beijing, Havana. The marches: hand-painted placards held aloft between you, linked arms as you trekked south, a united front, a wall against greed and injustice. The strikes: the divvying-up of food, fags, fire-wood, when there was any to go round. Gala days – the real thing: the three of you scrubbed and shaved and gleaming in starched white shirts. Jack with his battered whistle, you with your granddad's wheezy old squeeze-box, Willie with his sweet bass voice belting out everybody's favourite airs – while he still had puff in his lungs. The good times.

You fetch the shovel, scrape the rabbits off the tarmac, tip the mess of mashed fur, blood and bones into the wheelie bin, close the gate, look down the road. A big mistake moving into a place where you could still see the pithead and the overhead walkway from your own gate. You should have made a clean break, tried your luck elsewhere. A big mistake, but not your biggest, eh, Mazzard? The cardboard men are gazing out of the windowed corridor, taking one last look at the day before they descend into the dark, one last glance at the cankered skin of the earth before they slip inside it, before the doors of the cage clang shut and the canaries, in their own cramped enclosures, twitter and fling themselves at the bars.

In spite of the sunshine, you can feel the coming storm in your bones. Your head buzzes like an overloaded fuse box. Your veins sizzle as you stand amidst oxe-eye daisies, scruffy willowherb and knee-high grass. In the coop, the canaries twist and turn in panicky loops. It's a diversionary tactic, an attempt to bamboozle a predator with fancy wingwork. Like you, the birds are jangled. Which way to fly? How to escape?

Della won't be diverted. You're old and slow and ache all the time, but that's not enough. Nothing's ever enough for Della. She's not far away. On you in no time. No time at all. Soon you will count the seconds between the rumble and the flash. Any time now the first heavy drops will hit your head, you will look up at the sky and see the dark, massed cloud pressing down on the viaduct and, like the canaries, you will panic. You will run inside, bolt the door and leave the coop to mind for itself, let the birds fly madly in every direction, rattling the wire. Though you draw the curtains, turn off the lights, it's no good. A blanket over your head, fingers pressed into your eyes, Willie is still there, his eyes like lamps, following your every movement, never letting you out of his sight. Willie is still there, on the overpass, with the cardboard men, crossing the road forever.

You will sweat and shiver, sweat and shiver. Thick ropes of rain will stream down from the pocked stones of the viaduct high above your little house, stream down and lash the roof, walls, windows and doors. Your house sits at the bottom of a rounded valley, a valley like a deep bowl, a chalice set where it will catch whatever comes its way.

The rabbits are in the bin. The coop is locked up. The cardboard men are just cardboard. Replicas, tokens, stand-ins. Nothing more. They have no faces. No features at all. Just pinkish painted ovals beneath cardboard safety helmets. No eyes, no mouths. No bristles push through a shift's deposit of coal dust. No sweat beads on painted brows. No breath stirs in cardboard chests. No songs pour from ruined lungs, no curses either. No curses. But Della will more than make up for that.

You are trying your best to forget, to push it away, but the more you try, the more it flies back in your face: those cold dripping walls, the flooded tunnels, Willie wading into an immensity of darkness . . .

They sang to you. All of you lucky ones. Sang their sweet little songs. Sang their little hearts out. Every one a diva. Every one a twittering star in the dark, a trill of comfort, a match-flame of melody, saving you again and again. And now, the redundant descendants of those pit canaries are in your yard, in the fancy coop you tore up your hands building for them. As far as life in a cage goes, they have it good, better than then. Then, those subterranean songbirds had the odds stacked against them.

The sky flares with storm light. Della's at hand. Doesn't come by for nothing. Doesn't like to see things slip, has no truck with time filing down rough edges, bridging gaps, patching up old wounds. Della doesn't go along with forgive and forget. Oh no, Mazzard, Della doesn't do forgive and forget. Not her style.

Not just chance, Mazzard, not just chance Della came by. Not just roadkill outside your gate. As you very well know. Nothing accidental about the rabbits.

* * *

Around here, around pits, every day's a day of the dead. And this one's Willie's.

Come outside, Mazzard. Come out and open up that damned coop. Let those canaries fight it out with Jack O'Lantern's cats. They won't stand a chance, of course, but without his wee yellow soprano, neither did Willie. You knew that. Everybody knew that. Come out, Mazzard, go to your gate, look down the road, at the cardboard men on the overpass, trudging towards the crumbling, impotent pithead. There's Willie, empty-handed. And you, you're up there too, with Willie's bird swinging on its perch. Let those birds out. Let them sing a requiem, before the heavens open.

Dream Lover

Magi Gibson

Maxwell picked up the photo from his desk and Fionnuala smiled at him from behind the glass. She stood by the edge of the loch, her white dress, swan-bright, almost luminous, glowing against the gunmetal grey of water. The blustery wind had snatched her long veil and train, had lifted them into the air behind her like great white wings. Maxwell fogged the glass with his breath, then rubbed until she reappeared like magic.

He opened his diary, glanced at the entries for the day, then snapped it shut.

She had been on the phone for almost an hour the night before, but with the radio in the kitchen blaring he had been unable to make out the conversation, only the low murmur of her voice. After a while he'd wandered in on the pretext of fetching a beer from the fridge, but while he was there she'd fallen all but silent. At last, the phone call finished, she poked her head round the door and announced she was going over to Hannah's. I'll come too, he'd offered. No point, she'd replied, her voice trailing like wash from a speedboat, the door slamming a full stop on his protest.

At midnight he'd tossed the remote control aside and dragged himself to bed, his head a pigswill of suspicion and concern, self-pity and anger. Of course, he could have waited up, could have confronted her, but he had no evidence. It would be too easy for her to accuse him of paranoia, of being an over-possessive husband. He had to be careful not to jump the gun.

It was after two when he heard the car door slam, the key click in the lock. He listened to the soft rustle of her clothes as she undressed in the bathroom, then felt her slip in beside him, her skin cold from the night air, her hair smelling of stale cigarette smoke. He coughed and turned uneasily away from her. He longed for her to spoon herself into his back as once she would have done, but after a few moments her breathing steadied and he knew that she was asleep.

Maxwell had suspected for some time. Had Andy not warned him of the danger signs? The older man knew so much: how to track deer, to take note of the broken twigs along the way, the tuft of fur caught on the low branch, to see what the untrained eye could not, to be patient and wait for the right moment to take aim, to squeeze the trigger. Andy had learned through bitter experience of the tell-tale signs, the tiny carelessnesses that trail behind an adulterous woman like spoor behind a deer.

From his breast-pocket Maxwell took a piece of paper. While she had been out he had scribbled down the names of all the men she knew. He opened a new file on the computer and secured it with a password. He quickly punched the names in and fed the paper to the sharp blades of the shredder.

He thought of phoning her, just a quick call to check whether or not she was at home, whether or not the line was engaged, but the buzzing intercom forced him to push Fionnuala to the back of his mind. The first client of the day had arrived.

That night when Maxwell came home Fionnuala led him excitedly up to their bedroom. She stood back, her arms folded, a smile playing at the corner of her lips. Well, what do you think? she asked. Maxwell stared at their bed, transformed from a riot of overblown roses to a cool sea of cream frothed with lace, topped with soft pillows puffed up like fat marshmallows.

She had changed the pictures on the walls too. Down had come two little Victorian girls playing by the side of a brook, to be replaced by a sketch of Michelangelo's David, naked as the morning sun. And above the bed she had hung another painting, which looked at first glance like a patchwork quilt in golds and browns, but which on closer inspection revealed a man and woman in a passionate embrace, her gown slipped from one shoulder, the rosy nipple of one breast just visible.

That's a waste of money, he'd chided. *Who's going to see our bedroom anyway?* And immediately after he asked the question, the words seemed to flap like a banner in the air, taunting him for his naivety.

Maxwell lay awake in the dark, uneasy with the strange covers, the naked David, the half-dressed woman and her lover sharing the room.

At last tiredness sucked him into a dark sleep. The crack of gunshot, the stink of cordite woke him with a start. He almost called out, then understood – the gunshot had been in a dream, a dream still so sharp and real that he lay trembling, the sweat chilling on his skin, as it rewound, replayed . . .

He arrives home early from a shoot with Andy on a still and cloudless night, mist seeping up from the earth swirling eerily in the fields. He puts the gundogs in their pen, then, from the boot of the car, he gathers the dead rabbits. He lugs them into the shed and hangs them by the hind legs from hooks screwed into the rafter. Their twelve bulging eyes stare blindly as they pendulum slowly. He goes back to the car to fetch his rifle, but like an animal catching the scent of danger long before it sees the hunter, he senses – what? Only that something is amiss.

Sitting in the open tailgate of the car he removes his boots, while in the half-light the dogs' eyes glint as they watch his every move. Somewhere in the woods a cat screeches. Then the sudden crackling of twigs breaking in the undergrowth. Maxwell feels his muscles tense. He hears his own breathing, deep and steady. Slowly he picks his rifle up, loosens the safety catch. A swift glance to check it's still loaded. He is acting on instinct now, his brain switched off, every fibre of his body adrenalin-filled, alert. Nearby, an owl calls softly. The stars prick the sky like peppershot holes in a blackout cloth, a hundred-thousand eyes watching. He slips into the house and in his stocking soles, makes his way softly up the stairs, lightfooted as a cat closing in on its prey. Even before he reaches the bedroom he hears the low moans, the animal grunts. The door opens with the quietest of clicks and he stands watching them, her hair tangled on the pillow, her legs splayed, his buttocks rising and falling, the lace covers in a heap on the floor. The crack of the gun. The momentary silence. The screams, the smell of cordite, the gundogs baying, leaping against the gate of their pen.

Maxwell took to turning up at home more often. At odd times. Suddenly. He explained to his boss that his wife was poorly and he was worried about her; he needed to keep an eye on her. He developed the slight stoop, the faint frown of the concerned husband – and binned the flowers and cards his colleagues gave him for Fionnuala.

Their house was set on the edge of the village, surrounded by woodland, with only the one way in and out. Sometimes he parked his car in a layby half hidden by trees a short distance from their driveway. There he sat, his binoculars in his lap, his rifle on the back seat, under a blanket. Against the law, he realised, but laws were for civilised people, for civilised times.

He kept the computer file at his office updated. He noted the increase in the number of phone calls she was making and the sudden and lengthy visits to her girlfriends. He noted the new tight-fitting skipants, white and slightly see-through, that attracted the eyes of men as surely as the white rump of a doe in flight draws a hunter's sights. He noted the way she sometimes seemed a million miles away when he spoke to her, the resentful edge on her voice when she replied. He noted the number of times she encouraged him to go to the pub and her sudden enthusiasm for his hunting trips with Andy. (Once she would have moaned, once she would have whined, *not again.*) He noted the number of times he called her at home and she was not there. But most of all he noted the small dark hair he'd found curled on the bedsheet. Darker than could have come from either of them.

One day Maxwell came home unexpectedly from work (on Andy's advice) and found Fionnuala, naked in front of the bedroom mirror, frowning at her reflection.

'I don't want to grow old,' she said, as if it was a simple question of refusal, as if like Canute she really believed she could hold up her hands and command the waves to stop flowing to the shore.

He said nothing. Just stood and stared like an awestruck schoolboy. How long was it since he'd seen her naked? When had she started jumping quickly into long cotton nightdresses and fleecy pyjamas? As he ran his eyes over the smooth curves, the proud nipples, the flat stomach, the golden V, he felt the old desire stir.

He moved towards her, slid his hands down her sides and pulled her to him. For a moment she seemed to hesitate, then she tilted her head up, parted her lips, waited for his kiss. 'It's been a long time,' she murmured, and in that second she seemed again to be the Fionnuala from the photograph on his desk, the Fionnuala who had promised to love, honour and obey. But when he placed his mouth on hers, her kiss was cold and mechanical, the kiss of a whore for a customer.

'I should be at work,' he said sharply, pushing her away. She sprawled awkwardly back on the bed, a woman with tousled hair, her breasts lolling, her legs slightly parted, a woman playacting desire for a man she did not love.

'I have an appointment. A client.' he muttered, smoothing his hair and straightening his tie in the mirror.

'The client can wait. This is more important.' Her voice seemed urgent, pleading. Doubt flitted through his mind like a bat through the dusk, a trace, a shadow, there and then gone.

Andy's wife hadn't even tried to playact. Maxwell could recall (with a clarity that alarmed him) the first time Andy had spoken of his wife's adultery. The two men were lying on the hillside at dawn, the valley a sea of shifting mist, the tip of a pink sun licking the horizon.

First she'd gone off sex. He'd given her a few days, then a few weeks, but no matter what he tried – romantic meals by candlelight, surprise flowers, weekends away – she wanted nothing to do with him. Finally he asked what was wrong, was relieved when she said it was her hormones.

Maxwell took out his hunting knife and started to polish the blade.

Then, of course, there were all the little things that he hadn't noticed at the time: the phone calls, the nights out with the girls, the new underwear, the sudden addiction to sunbeds. It had been going on for a year, a whole bloody year, behind his back; had Maxwell known? Maxwell lifted his eyes from the blade and stared at the horizon. The sun, higher now, gaped back, a pink and liquid wound in a yellow skin of sky.

'I didn't suspect a thing,' Andy said quietly. 'Not once.'

The dozing gundogs pricked their ears as Andy's voice wavered.

'I thought of ending it all,' he said suddenly. Maxwell looked him in the face. 'Seriously. I didn't see how I could go on. It wasn't just losing her. It was the shame. With everyone knowing for all those months, when I didn't. Talking behind my back . . . laughing . . .'

Maxwell rubbed harder at the blade, then held it up and scowled at his reflection. One enlarged eye, dark and distorted, stared back. For a moment he didn't recognise it as his own, as though the eye belonged to the knife, as though a dark spirit dwelt within the steel. He tightened his grip on the heft and felt a sensation of pleasure at the way it fitted snug in his palm, so familiar it felt like an extension of his own arm.

'You just don't think it'll happen to you,' Andy blurted. 'You always think it's something that happens to some other bugger, some sad bastard . . .'

His voice collapsed and a wail rose from his throat, long and thin and high. Maxwell had heard a wail like that before, a wail that set your heart battering like a bull trapped in a cage. In the woods a few miles from his house he had found Fionnuala's dog caught in a gin trap. The more it had struggled, the tighter the wire had pulled around its hind leg. It had struggled until the wire had sliced into the flesh, severed the tendons, sawed half-through the bone, till it hung – a dirty ribbon of fur and sinew caked with blood-soaked earth.

Maxwell looked at the mist shifting slow and ghostly across the valley floor. He turned the knife over and over in his hand. He had known what he needed to do for the dog. He had sunk the blade deep into its throat, had twisted it and let the blood and pain spurt hot and red on to the forest floor.

He was interviewing a client the first time Fionnuala burst in on him at his office. He heard his own voice falter mid-sentence.

She came striding in without knocking and stood facing him. He almost didn't recognise her – her breasts high and curved in a black push-up bra, the flesh at the top of each leg pale against black suspenders and lacy stocking tops. The knee-high stiletto boots. For a moment he thought she was a strip-o-gram.

But it was her face, his wife's face, brown eyes flashing behind long dark lashes, magenta lips smiling wickedly.

The room rocked and swayed like a boat in a storm and he gripped the edge of his desk.

'You were saying . . .' the client cleared his throat.

And she was gone. Dissolved into the grey walls.

It happened a few times a day after that. He'd be staring at a spreadsheet or talking on the phone and she'd appear. Sometimes in black. Sometimes in white cotton panties, bra and kneesocks, her hair bunched like a schoolgirl's, her lips pink and pouting. But no one else ever seemed to see her.

Once she appeared on the computer screen in a diaphanous negligée, and he heard her laughing, a mocking laugh, that grew to a frenzied cackle, as she started to whirl around the screen like the company logo, faster and faster, until he felt dizzy, his mouth dried – and he vomited in the wastepaper bin.

Another time he was driving home from a conference in the city. He had called home four or five times, but there had been no answer. The urban motorway was scalextric, five lanes of traffic jostling for space, the young bucks cutting and carving as if they were hurtling dodgems at the shows. Maxwell was strictly a rural driver. He scoured the overhead gantries for directions and his heart sank, his stomach tightened. He needed to cross to the right-hand lane or miss his exit. A juggernaut roared on his outside, its huge wheels spinning level with his face. He indicated right and tried to hang back to fall in behind it, but the white van klaxoned long and hard and bullied him forward.

And in that moment she appeared. Standing in the road before him in scarlet leather, legs spread, red whip in hand, laughing. His foot slammed on the brake and the car skewed on to the hard shoulder, the tyres screeching. The van behind swerved around him, clipped his wing mirror. The stench of burning rubber filled his head. His hands shook uncontrollably on the steering wheel. He glanced at the wing mirror, swinging loose like a broken limb, its glass shattered.

That night he found new perfume on her dressing table, a tiny bottle in a velvet pouch. The next day he checked it out at Boots, told the girl he was looking for a wedding anniversary gift for his wife. How many years? the girl asked. Nine, he smiled, and the girl looked all dewy-eyed. I think that's lovely, she said. You hear of so many marriages breaking up these days. Congratulations. You're a lucky man. Maxwell said he'd think about the perfume. It cost forty pounds.

'*You're* spoiling yourself,' he said next morning, fingering the bottle while she lay in bed, her back to him.

'Someone has to,' she mumbled, her voice muffled beneath the froth of lacy covers.

And someone was, he thought. Otherwise where had all the glamorous underwear come from? The black-silk panties, the clingy satin body, the red-leather basque?

He waited until she'd gone out, then searched the house for the lingerie, the sex clothes she kept hidden for her lover. He would find them, confront her, force her to confess, force her to beg his forgiveness.

'What are you doing?' she asked when she came back and found him on his knees, surrounded by small piles of her underwear, a pair of lacy panties in his hand. Maxwell stared up at her and felt the blood drain from his face. For a moment he was twelve years old, kneeling before his mother who had come home early from shopping and found him crouched on the bedroom floor, his flies undone, clutching a pair of his sister's panties. He felt again the sharp pain as she slapped him. He felt again the sting of her words like vinegar sprayed in an open wound.

'I think you need help,' Fionnuala said, her voice unnaturally low and slow, the voice of a nurse to a disturbed patient. 'I've spoken to the doctor. He says you should go and see him. You could get treatment. Therapy.'

She bent down and started to pick up the clothes and put them back in the drawers.

Maxwell left the room silently. Ashamed and dirty.

He sat up late that night drinking whisky. She had gone to bed without saying a word. She didn't need to: her eyes bored into him, accused him, reproached him, just as his mother's had. He went for a long walk with the dogs in the moonlight, sat on the cold heather by the edge of the loch, and watched a pair of swans, luminous angels gliding on water black as sin. Swans mate for life. Where had he read that? He watched one dip its neck and disappear down into the black, then reappear, white and glistening. *Treatment and therapy*, she'd said, as if he was the one with the problem.

He pushed the whisky bottle across the table. It rocked noisily on its heel like a drunk. Maxwell gripped his fist tight around its slender neck and stilled it; it was empty, yet he'd never felt more sober in his life. He stared into the bottom of his glass, as if he might find some guidance there. Maybe if she was still awake, maybe he could explain that they were like swans; they were paired for life, for better or for worse.

He opened the door to the bedroom. The lights were out, but through a gap in the curtains a half-moon, unnaturally bright, cast silver on her smooth skin. She turned in her sleep, her hair dragging across the pillow. He stood silently, listening to her breathing soft and steady. He crossed the room and bent over her face. It was hard to believe that she had been deceiving him. He kissed her neck and tasted the perfume, the perfume her lover had given her, bitter as venom on his tongue. He stroked a few strands of hair from her forehead and she wriggled lightly at his touch. He wondered if she wriggled like that for him and the thought pierced him like a stab wound in his chest.

'It's too late,' she murmured sleepily.

He stood staring at her face. Sleep softened the hardness that had edged her mouth these last few months, her hair spread like a golden aureole around her face and shoulders. The creamy covers flowed over her like robes. Maxwell stood and stared and saw again the young woman he had married, the young bride who smiled at him every day from the photograph on his desk, untainted, unsullied. He wanted to lie down beside her, to hug her, to hold her close, but there was a gulf between them now, a cold space that had appeared, when? He struggled to reach across it, but it was too wide. And it was filled with hurt and pain and deceit.

For a moment a cloud floated across the moon and the room was dark; her face was gone. He felt something block his throat. A ball of grief bulged against his windpipe and he feared his chest would explode with the pain. She was beautiful. So beautiful. And he had lost her.

Out in the shed he found a rope. The deer he'd shot last week hung in the corner, lashed by its splayed forelegs to a rafter. Maxwell had sliced it open from throat to tail, had tugged out its steaming innards and slung them to the baying dogs. Now its head lolled forward on to its gaping chest. Its mouth, specked with mucus and blood, grinned. Its brown eyes, fringed by long dark lashes, strangely feminine, watched as he slung the rope over the rafter. He accidentally knocked the bare lightbulb and it swung crazily, sending shadows swirling round the cold brick walls.

His thoughts flickered unsteady as the light. He tied a firm knot. On Andy's farm he'd learned to tie a knot strong enough to hold a straining bullock or a bucking horse.

He went back to the house, climbed the stairs slowly. The bedroom door opened with the quietest of clicks and he stood in the doorway. In the distance he could hear someone night shooting; the dull thwack of shot as some creature met death in the darkness.

He moved closer to the side of the bed and gazed down at her sleeping face. The ball of grief had dissolved. He felt a new calmness.

Her eyes opened wide as the blade kissed her throat.

Kiss of Life

Linda Cracknell

Four kisses got me here. A pocketful of kisses. A plague of them.

The first was an exploration probing new places with tangling tongues. A tightrope of saliva glinted in the sun as we stretched apart. It was maybe where I got it, what my mother calls the 'kissing disease' and the doctor called Glandular Fever. I don't care about the name, just that I've spent the last month swimming through treacle.

Then Mum's kiss on my cheek, dispatching me to recover at Anne and Bill's hotel. Sending me far away from my discoveries with Simon. She's a good girl, I heard her say on the phone. She'll be no bother, I promise.

The third, you could describe as a kiss. Lips meeting red-ripe skin, teeth piercing, juice bursting on my tongue. The back of my hand wiping away sugar crystals and fluorescent stains. Strawberries, kissed under the evening sky, leaving seeds to swell dark inside me.

And of course the one I refused. Watching her body heavy and motionless in the sun, keeping my distance, spellbound by the white legs straight and still. She was waiting for a kiss I didn't want to give; a kiss that would be red and blue and icy as the mountain stream.

Too busy with meals and rooms, Anne gives me a pink-jacketed map. Walking's the pathway back to health, she says. I try to please, following dotted lines on the map in spider's legs from the hotel, as each day circulates with no clear beginning or end. I feel the weight of mountains towering above me. The spaces between things are so big; there are so few houses, not a single shop. I never seem to get far before my legs waver, and I need the shelter of my bedroom again. I return with hanging limbs to let my body doze while my mind clambers on to some kind of roundabout. I've got used to it these days – the thoughts that unravel in slow motion in a curtained room. Each one turns on an unoiled cog, labouring its way through a backwards logic, being overtaken by the next.

I pull the curtains across my window but they don't meet in the middle. Or if I make them, they leave a gap at the side, a vertical slot through which dark forests, mountains and daylight glare in at me. The world outside won't quite leave me alone. My hotel room should be a sanctuary, but it's not peaceful. A faint scratching shudders against the walls, and the shrieks of something soaring in the sky outside pierce walls, doors, windows. I peer upwards through the slot in the curtains and trace the shrieks to the arrow-shaped birds which swoop and flicker in circles, greedy for midges and flying ants. They chase each other in arcs into the eaves above my window.

They're swifts, Bill told me. They can't land on the ground, you know.

I hear them late at night, long after birds should be in their nests, whistling so high over the night air. I imagine them circling and shrieking all through the night, never resting, till presumably they die of exhaustion, in flight.

Anne bustles in and out of the breakfast room, a glimmer of familiarity among silver teapots, deer's heads on the wall, porridge on the menu, different guests every day. Toast – that's all I want. I push away the bowl of jam. A wasp settles in it, legs scrabbling in the red. It's in wasp-heaven, feasting stickily, until it becomes too entangled in its own pleasure. Stuck. In too deep to escape.

You must eat a bit more, Anne says. You're here to get strong. I can't let your mum down. By the end of the week you'll be running as strong as that river out there, you'll see. Anne bobs down to window level and points at the silver thread which cuts through the land. Even from here I'm dazzled by the sun colliding off the leaps and dashes of water as the river pursues its descent.

There's nothing wrong with me now. No sore throat anymore, I say. I'm just tired; I need to sleep. But it doesn't seem to be that easy.

One morning early in the week the daylight wakes me, gets me out of bed, calls me to the window. I don't want to upset Anne by being late for breakfast. The usual view greets me – the hills backing the flat sheet of floodplain, the standing stone guarding the river, the phone box red at the end of the road. My watch says four thirty am – it's not breakfast time at all. But there's a day already underway out there, one we know nothing of, getting on without us while we sleep. At first I can't make out what makes it so still, but as I watch I realise it's because there are no people. I feel like an intruder in a world I'm not supposed to see, like a child peering from the stair-landing on to an adult party, trying to fathom the laughter which swells and skips between guests with no apparent reason.

I'm ready to retreat but with a lurch I realise my mistake. There *is* someone, standing by the phone box. She's so still I hadn't noticed her. A girl with long orange hair who stares up at me. The swifts swoop over her, greedy for the air around her head, daring to sweep closer and closer. Her only movement is the chewing of her mouth at something as she stares. I snap the connection of our gaze, pull back the curtain, and return to bed, protecting myself from the eyes of this other day, trying to dispose of the image of the girl. Maybe I just imagined her. In this daylight night anything seems possible.

I continue to explore the local area, the strength in my legs dictating how far I go. In the field opposite the hotel, I skirt around a grassy mound left ragged and wild among the cultivation. 'The mound of the dead', a sign tells me. Bodies were brought here after the plague in the fourteenth century, pulled by an old lady with a white horse. How would it be to die of the plague – did they catch it from kissing too? Did they waste away, not wanting to eat, walking shorter distances each day? Did the bony fingers of midsummer prod their eyelids open, not allowing them to rest? I imagine, under the thin soil of the mound, a pit holding the tight embraces of arms and legs, necks coupling, heads buried under the weight of limbs, fingers caught in one another's hair. I feel the press of Simon's arms around my ribs and back, his weight on me, heat passing from skin to skin. But their embraces would be cold and clammy, and the weight of so many bodies too much to bear.

A faint path entices me towards the river to catch the shade under the trees. In the next field the bent backs of berry-pickers are pressed down by the sun. I've seen their produce in plastic tubs at the end of the track, the red letters on a white board signalling 'Strawberries, Raspberries'. They're sold to passing tourists with pots of cream, and to locals for making jam. Maybe to spread on toast, maybe just to trap the wasps.

In the gaps between trees, white light sparks off the river as it spills over rocks. It stabs at my eyes, punctuating the leafy gloom. Tree-shade, river-light, tree-shade, too bright. Mesmerised by the strobe show, I feel sick.

Then, through the trees, above the crackling of water on rocks, a scream rushes at me, stops the pulse of my steps. Through trembling leaves I see snatches of arm, leg, shoulder. A group of women and girls are in the river, their jackets and skirts thrown off to expose skin to sun and water. They must be taking time away from the berry fields. Laughter follows the scream. They are ankle deep in the water, just off a shingle bank. The girl with orange hair is there too. She stands deeper than the others, green dress tucked into her knickers, her thighs ash-white. She scoops the river into her hands, throws it at the paddlers. Her laughter sweeps and swoops around the group, tumbles through her loose hair with the sunlight. She falls backwards, letting the river close over her head, then springs back to her feet with snorts of water and laughter. I guess she's my sort of age, shrieking with life, so unlike the motionless figure she was the other night. I retreat into the shadows before the women should see me, before the effort of speech.

The scene reminds me of lying on a riverbank with Simon, a wider river than this, without rocks. A friendly sun, tickling grass, the crawl and nip of ants across bare legs, the whisper of his eyelashes against my cheek. There was a smell of something, like a kind of pollen, but it made me think of garden plants in the street at home, not the wild sort you get here. We turned to devour each other in the moments between passing pleasure boats. I wiped away our mingled saliva with the back of my hand.

Simon, so far away. Missing him. You'll meet people there, Mum had said. Maybe there'll be folk your own age in the village you can get friendly with. I don't think so, Mum. There's just a gap where Simon was. His kisses sent a tickle into parts of me quite distant from my mouth. A tickle I want more of. Am I getting in too deep, like the wasp stuck in its own jam feast?

We never went in the water like the berry-pickers. Even though I love to swim; I'm a strong swimmer, have a life-saving certificate. Simon said there might be things in the water – bacteria or bugs, and it was dangerous anyway, almost as if he was afraid. Perhaps the river here is a different beast, cleaner water straight from the mountains, with more shallows and pools to protect the heat-dazed. I'm not sure though. I have a feeling it's just disguising its anger, acting demure as it seeps slow through the floodplain. I've seen the dark ravine it tumbles out of just a little upstream – a torrent that could catch you up, entangle you in its tendrils of current, seizing the muscles in your arms and legs.

Later, I find the orange-haired girl standing by the phone box when I want to talk to Simon. It's as if she's waiting for the phone, but no one's using it. She stares at me, unsmiling, winding her hair around one hand. She has wide lips, fattened further by a red stain. Her eyes stay on me through the glass.

As I come out of the phone box, she holds out to me strawberries in a plastic tub. With the other hand she feeds herself one, its brightness blending with her own vivid mouth. I think of her unwashed hands all over the strawberries, her sneezes even. But I take one because I don't want to seem unfriendly. I'm close enough to her now to see a strawberry seed dried on to her chin. She pulls a paper bag from her dress pocket and holds it open. Sugar. She nods my hand into the bag. It clothes the strawberry in a gritty white coat which crackles on my lips as I bite in. Juice squirts into my mouth. The craft of the strawberry. It coils around my tongue with its sweetness so that I can't think for a moment. Boss-eyed. Drugged. She watches me; it's as if she is watching me in the intimacy of a kiss.

Thanks.

She sits down on the ground, back to the wall, hunches over cigarette papers and tobacco, rubbing something into the open paper, concentrating.

Where do you stay? I ask, trying to like her.

She points a red-stained finger across the field to the cluster of vans and trailers beyond the mound of the dead, near the river. People are standing in the open doorways, sitting on warm evening steps among children and bicycles.

Tinks, Bill had said. They come for the berry-picking every year. Always have done. Always will, I guess.

I wonder if they are the plague survivors.

She doesn't withdraw the cigarette when I tell her I don't

smoke. It's long and lumpy; not like one from a packet. I take a puff. I already know I don't like it. And anyway I'm a good girl. Another puff so she won't think me dull, then I give it back. Shiver. Crumpling legs. I sit down next to her. Everything drifts sideways, going blank like it does for the Hollywood spy whose drink has been spiked. A chain of her words process past me. First their meaning, then their tune fades, until I just watch the red lips chewing them out. She mouths a story that seems to hold me down for hours, a day, a night. I hear nothing. All I know is that I must get back to my room. I claw myself back towards her words, grasp at the moment, push the nausea down. She blows smoke, thrusts more strawberries at me.

Eat one. Sweet.

No. I have to go.

I stagger to my feet, propelled by the need to stretch a distance between us. I feel her eyes pursue me as I focus hard on the line to the hotel. The image of her red mouth works on in my mind until I seal her out with the door.

On my back, the curtains gape at me. My ears close down, heart thudding into them. Amplified in my right ear, something nibbles, scratches, crunches. It doesn't stop when I move my leaden head. I search the shell of the room from the bed and then pull myself upright to circle it with probing fingers. I find a wasp, mauling at bare wood on the doorframe. Its front legs act as a brace, as it pumps its mouth backward and forward against the wood, gnawing a furrow. It's so loud for so small a thing. But when I fall back on the bed, the nibbling noise continues in my ear, burrowing its way through my brain, drowning in the sticky jam of my thoughts.

As I fall towards sleep, the room fills with water and I slide into the cold gasp of it from the edge of my bed, letting it hold me, seep into me, filling up the empty parts of me.

* * *

I don't walk the next day. I avoid the phone box, abandon Simon to be free of her shadow, stay in my room. My throat feels constricted; my face prickles.

I hear Anne on the phone to my mother:

A bit of a relapse today, I think. I can't get her to eat much. No, no bother at all, she says. Very quiet.

And I want to ask, how long can one week be?

Anne brings me a bowl of strawberries at lunch time.

Sweet. So sweet. Eat.

But I don't trust them. They turned my night upside down. Or was it the sugar, the cigarette, something else she did to me, the orange-haired girl? She made this chaos emerge out of me like a creature that's hatched from an egg, and is now finding its wings.

That night I see her again, at ease in the other day, the daynight. She bends over something, near the standing stone. I try to stretch the curtains across her but the image remains, burnt into my eye. The glint of orange hair, and the shock of the red-stained mouth, even from a distance.

Then something starts to eat away in my imagination. Lying on my bed, I picture her ill in her caravan, unable to work in the berry fields, tossing and restless, trickling tears. She wouldn't trouble me then. I let the idea grow. She becomes a plague victim: dress tucked into knickers, her limbs matching white with the horse who drags her to the pit. Something unfastens in my throat, loosens its grip. A flourish of energy seeps through my body. It's quieter than the energy I had before I was ill, moving in unfamiliar currents. As I lie behind the protection of curtains, I feel the charm begin to work – my visualisations creeping into life, becoming possible. I become stronger and she more feeble. It raises a smirk behind my hand. I allow my imagination to delve deeper. How many other ways might there be to stifle her hold on me?

You're lucky, Anne insists. This is our heatwave. Take a book to the river. Some strawberries maybe.

Blasted with sunlight, the mountains vibrate behind the floodplain haze of river, the mound of the dead, the backs bent in the berryfields. The orange hair isn't visible, not yet. I drop my blanket, my book. I'll stop here, stay well away from the pickers. I plunge on to the blanket, into a pool of heat and shade. I half read, half sleep, in a shimmer of leaves and grass, until footsteps jar the ground under my ear, urgent and fast.

A child bursts through the trees near me, runs toward the pickers. He stumbles, head turned over his shoulder, slaps chest to thigh into the man picking in the first raspberry row. The man straightens, listens. His bellow shakes the air, jolts the surrounding mountains. He runs towards me, his mouth transforming into a square hole as he gets closer, the rasps of breath louder, and then louder. He turns before he reaches me, splashes into the river, pulls something on to the bank. A mound with a green sodden dress, orange hair saturated black, white legs straight and still. Up from my blanket, I creep closer. Sunbathing on the bank, her face looms at me, blue with red-stained lips. In too deep. She was in way too deep.

The man kisses at her lips, raises his head to shout, tries again. He looks up at me, his face swimming.

You do it. Do you know how?

I shake my head. I don't want to kiss her taste of strawberries, sugar, and her mountain-cold breathless mouth. I shake my head and watch him kiss and blow. His eyes plead up at the gathering faces. He strives for her life but doesn't tip her head back far enough to clear the windpipe.

The berry field empties people on to the river bank. The air fills with screams and sobs. Someone runs to the phone box. I sink down, crouch in the grass, watching. They hold her body, turn her over. Her hair and dress come alive with stolen river water, streaming. But the limbs remain stagnant. I imagine the paper bag soggy in her pocket, the sugar crystals dissolved, their mischief diluted, mingling sweet with the river water as it twists away downstream.

The ambulance siren and the sobs ebb away, leave me alone in the field as the day softens to dusk. I lie on my back on the mound of the dead, my arms and legs seeping into the shared bed. The hills and sky lurch over me in a protective arch. Swifts shriek, scooping the air inches from my head. My hand strays into a pocket. I place a strawberry against my lips and kiss its flesh entirely away from the spidery stalk. Sweet. So sweet. The best sort of kiss.

At the Time

Sophie Cooke

Out of the darkness came the girl, kind of dancing, just next to him, glowing like amber. A rush of dark hair obscured her face, but Dan could see her eyes and they were looking at him. She had said her name was Gina. She danced devastatingly in the heaving music, curving herself around it like ivy. She was looking at him hard. She was looking hot, Dan thought. He liked her orange dress; it was dark orange and tight, with little zip pockets. There was a zip down the front and she had it half undone. Her neck and her breastbone gleamed sporadically in the lights. The lights were only accentuating the darkness, making it something solid by their perforations. He wanted to touch her through it.

Dan thought of Kelly. Drugs and strangers could make her redundant. It was a shame she didn't care. He tried not to scan for her blonde ponytail as he danced, wanting her to see him having a ball.

Over and over again Kelly left them, freely and without thinking, like melting ice-cream. This evening, she had left them almost as soon as they'd arrived at the club. 'Let's go to Tribal Funktion,' she'd said, and then she had just flitted off and left them standing, Dan and Susie, hating her. And Barry, not minding because he thought himself so dull that her friendship was a freak gift. The three of them had stood together wordlessly, swigging their pills with bubbling water from the Alps.

Dan's head jerked round; he thought he had heard Kelly shout. He saw her face, then the boy's lazy hand on her hip. Her long fingers rested on his naked torso, all seen through a sliding screen of other bodies. Dan didn't say anything. The moment dragged like a glitch on a record and then suddenly it sprang free again. Dan fell back to appreciating the amber girl next to him.

'Let's go,' Gina said. She was talking in his ear and the loud beat of the music fanned out around the touch of her breath. 'Let's fly,' she said.

Yeah, thought Dan, you are pretty fantastic. Kelly can fuck off. 'Yeah,' he said coolly, 'let's go.'

Susie was dancing on her own, feeling good. Sweat trickled down her back as she moved in a noisy surge of sound and half-bare boys.

Dan banged on Susie's shoulder. 'We're going,' he said. Susie stopped moving and looked at the new girl beside him. She flicked her wrist, viewed her watch. It was quarter to. Susie hated being there when the lights came up. She hated those harsh lights, the way they showed you'd just been dancing in a room. They made you feel like such a prat. 'Me too,' she said, grabbing Barry's dopey wrist and bringing him with her.

They pushed their way out to the cloakroom; Susie leaned over the counter and giggled at the guy who took her raffle ticket. They all shrugged their coats on. Dan was being a gentleman and helping Gina into her sleeves when his gaze tilted over her shoulder and caught Kelly, ahead of them at the exit. She was strolling up the steps with the vacant boy. She heard their voices and turned.

'Hi,' called Kelly, and laughed. 'I'm going home with Dimitri.'

Susie stared at Kelly, and suddenly felt lost.

'Dimitri,' said Dan tartly. 'Aye right, I bet his real name's Colin.'

'Fuck off, Dan,' said Kelly cheerfully. 'See you later.'

She went.

Gina took control. She walked up the steps and stood looking at Dan, strangely. There was a bright light around her, but the funny thing was that she was in the dark. You could just see the breeze of a smile around her lips. She stood looking at him like that for about five seconds. The beat of Dan's blood slowed through every second of her smile, back to a gently yearning thud.

'Come on!' said Gina, and they all heard it like something beautiful and thrilling. It was the way she said it.

They followed Gina up on to the street. They walked around her, up under the gargantuan arch of the road overhead. They were small underneath its high stone. They walked along Princes Street and the brightly-lit, closed-up Burger King made them feel happy and smug. They felt like they were doing something different.

'Look at the castle,' said Gina. 'It's beautiful.' It was. 'The night is alive,' she said, 'and people sleep. But not us!' You would never have guessed that she hadn't taken anything, hadn't even had a drink.

Dan looked at her, luminous with darkness like a wet coal. She was magnificent. A feeling like a sheet of hot ice sliced through him.

'We should do something,' said Gina.

'Yes,' said Susie, 'let's do something.'

'Like what?' said Barry, swinging his arms.

'Anything!' said Dan. 'We could do anything.'

'I'm hungry,' said Gina. 'Maybe we could get something to eat.'

There was a slow deflated silence.

'Yeah,' said Dan, 'let's get something to eat.' He looked away, feeling tragic now. The night was so particularly beautiful that it seemed a terrible crime not to pay it some more suitable homage than getting a pakora.

The sky stretched over them on a slant, like it was a flat plane, propped open somewhere up ahead. They could feel the new air rushing in. Clouds bloomed like fractal algae, soft flowers drifting across the stars. Every second popped outside their ears, gently. Pop pop pop. Like bubbles floating to the surface. The fresh new air came to their heads, and the dead, closed shops only heightened it. They turned up the Mound past the big Greek-looking museums.

'It's funny,' said Susie, 'how museum sounds like mausoleum.'

'Or linoleum,' said Barry, and they started laughing.

Gina was smiling.

'Let's do something,' said Susie. She looked delighted.

They were up by Bedlam, the old church that the students used for staging plays. A drunk man wavered on the wall. The shadows made wings for him. He's an angel, thought Susie, an angel thought Dan and Barry. They all saw it.

'Ah!' he said as they approached, feeling afraid of his wings and white light eyes. 'And darkness covered the Earth,' he said. 'Are you my friends?'

'Are you my friends?' he called after them. Gina turned round.

'Ssh,' she said.

'Ssh,' he echoed after them. 'Ssh, ssh,' like a snake swishing through the grass.

Trees danced ahead like seaweed. It was only a light breeze. They were just flexing their fingers really, in the current of air.

Gina gripped Dan's arm. 'What's that?' she said. They all stopped dead still.

'Someone in the hospital?' said Dan.

'No,' she whispered, shaking her head.

'It sounds like a baby,' said Susie.

'No,' Gina urged. 'It sounds like an animal, doesn't it?' She looked at Susie, her eyes strong like inky stamps.

'Yeah,' said Susie, 'maybe.'

'Listen,' said Gina.

'Oh yeah,' said Barry.

They kept on walking. The noise guttered in the wind. There were just occasional whimpers now.

'It's coming from over by the wall,' said Gina. She swivelled round to face them all. 'I think it might be a puppy!'

Great, thought Dan. He watched her racing towards it, legs like white spillikins. He stared and moved after her, his breathing loud in his head. The trees and the buildings were grown into each other. By the high wall, the night was black like an underground chamber. Gina's shape shifted somewhere inside it. Dan touched her back and her face appeared just below him, weakly opalescent, like it was constructed from moonlight or breastmilk and not flesh and bone.

'Look,' she said.

'I can't see,' said Dan.

'Look,' she said again, as they emerged from the shadows of the wall. 'A baby dog.'

He glanced at the bundle inside her coat.

'It looks weird,' he said.

'Ugh,' said Susie, 'it's revolting.'

They carried on across the Meadows, between trees that were joined to the sky now, Dan noticed.

Susie span round and round and ran off ahead. Lights were streaking across the city, red purple green. She saw them, pretty, pretty lights. She stopped, turned round and bent towards the others with her hands on her thighs. She was smiling and her eyes were black and wide. They had grown into the sky.

Dan took Gina's hand. She smiled and withdrew it, using it to stroke the dog's head. Stupid dog, thought Dan. Kelly, in the back of his mind, was laughing at him from behind a tree. Ousted by a dog!

Barry wasn't much interested in the puppy. He was just

ambling along behind them all, thinking how nice the sky looked, flickering with all those purple fireflies. And Susie, with fireflies in her eyes, she was really beautiful, Barry thought. She was still standing at the end of the Walk, far away. Barry stared at his shoes. He looked up at Dan and the girl Gina; the pair of them were walking just ahead.

Barry frowned. He could swear Gina was turning feline. She seemed clothed in a sleek, dark fur. In the shadows, her ears looked longer. He could see them grow. Barry had never witnessed his flatmate being romantic with a cat before. It was unnerving for him. He touched his own ears, stroking their cartilage, checking. Orange lamplight fell when they moved out of the avenue of skeletal cherry trees, fell plainly on Gina's skin, but still . . . No, not a cat. Maybe just the way she was moving, it was cattish. She was walking a fine line with ease.

The faux-baronial turrets of Marchmont were hard above. Stepping up into something. Into that rush of peculiar air perhaps, standing on the buildings below to grab purer gulps, dribbling bits of light on to the pavement there.

They turned up their street. Susie yanked her keys out, and stopped. Gina looked like she would live forever. Susie wanted to.

'I want to do something,' she said, wriggling.

'Yeah,' said Barry shyly, 'So do I.'

Susie gazed at him, twirling her keys, and looked at the other two.

'We'll do something,' said Gina, with gorgeous promise.

Susie seemed happy. She opened the door and they climbed the stairs, Dan saying, 'Gina is a really nice name, you know, Gina,' Susie and Dan both knowing somewhere in their brains that Kelly had left them and was away making origami with a strange boy's limbs. Barry didn't care about that, he was just watching Gina, keeping an eye on her ears.

'Where's the bathroom?' asked Gina, and she went in and

locked the door. The others went into the kitchen. Susie and Dan were restless; you could see it in their hands. It was imperative that they have a good time. They badly needed to impress themselves. Dan switched on a lamp with a very soft light. It was just a glow in the corner. Susie put on some music, fast and loud. She started waving her head from side to side in time to the beat. Kelly was off with someone else; Susie couldn't forget. Kelly had left them again.

Gina came in.

'Hi, Gina!' said Susie, loudly through the music. She had a new friend. 'What shall we do?' she asked.

Gina grinned. 'Let's play with the puppy,' she said.

Whoopee, thought Dan.

She laid it on the table, laid it on its back with its feet in the air. It wriggled.

'What's wrong with it?' said Barry. 'Where's its hair?'

Apart from a thin tuft on its crown, the animal was smooth like neoprene.

'Mexican Hairless,' said Gina. 'A foreign breed. They're all bald.'

'Who'd want a bald dog?' said Susie.

'Fucking horrible,' said Dan.

The dog squirmed, pawing at the air. Its flesh hung in fatty folds around its joints.

'Let's kill it,' said Gina. They all looked at her. 'Hairless dogs can be pretty vicious,' she noted. 'But more importantly, I think we all agree that they're ugly little bastards.'

Dan started laughing. 'Brilliant!' he said. 'Yeah, yeah,' he was wiping tears of laughter from his cheek.

'We don't like ugly dogs,' said Susie. 'No foreign baldies in this house.' She grinned.

'No,' said Dan. 'This is a house of beauty.'

Barry started laughing too.

Susie fumbled in the cupboard and brought out a little saucepan. It was heavy on her wrist because it was made of cast iron. She smiled as she approached the table, doing a little dance to the speeding music. The dance was a bit lopsided, with one arm being dragged down by the pan. She handed it to Dan. He stood up. His chair scraped under the drumbeat.

'Barry, get the back legs,' said Susie. She had rolled the dog on to its side and was leaning forward, pinning its two front legs down on to the table top. She had watched *Vets in Practice.* Gina was grinning as she held its torso steady, her long hair touching its soft belly.

Susie glanced at its head. 'Oh!' she said. The boys paused and looked at her. She had seen its eyes. Its eyes looked so human, that was all. The others were smiling at her though, so she smiled too. 'What?' she said.

Dan laughed and raised the pan over his shoulder like a fairground mallet. He brought it down. You couldn't hear anything above the music, but the arms and legs squirmed in their hands. Dan did it again, and a shudder of finality reverberated through.

They stood there for a bit afterwards. Dan couldn't stop laughing. Susie was laughing as well. She slapped its belly.

'Hey mate,' she said, 'aren't you playing?'

Barry laughed and she looked at him and they were laughing together. Barry felt happy now.

They sat down and Susie breathed out loudly.

'What shall we do now?' asked Dan, spread proudly on his chair.

Gina smiled up at him from her curtains of thick brown hair.

'I'm still hungry,' she said slowly. Barry stared at her, faintly appalled. Susie looked at her too. Her eyes were fixed on Dan.

'Go on then,' said Dan. "Let me get you some cutlery."

He stumbled out of his seat and pulled the cutlery rack from out of the top drawer. Gina picked through it. "Thank you," she said, as she selected her knives, and Susie started laughing again, and shaking her head. She thought Gina was great, really wild.

'You're very professional,' said Dan.

'Oh,' she said, 'I used to work at the meats counter.'

It was quite slow, though, because the knives weren't Sabatier or anything, and also the thing was half in the dark. They couldn't really see that well.

Gina ate it off the fork, bloody and wet. She put it in her mouth very calmly and just sat there chewing. 'Mmm,' she said, when she'd finished her mouthful. She had another. She was cutting from the thigh.

'Want some?' Gina held the fork out to Dan, a shiny lump on its prongs. Dan took it and ate it. He pulled a bit of a face. Then he went: 'It's all right.' Barry was tapping his hand against his leg, thinking the night was turning rather peculiar.

She was onto the ribs now.

'I want some!' said Susie with her face tense. It flopped into a smile. 'I want some,' she said quietly.

'Okay,' said Gina, giving her what she wanted.

Dan was tired of waiting his turn, so he laid into the shoulder by himself. He was quite messy. He hacked it up a bit.

'Aren't you having any?' said Gina to Barry.

Barry shook his head, still tapping his leg.

"Why not?" she asked with sweet concern.

He looked at her.

'Raw dog! No way.'

'Don't be so bourgeois,' said Susie.

'No, but – I mean – you guys go ahead,' he said. He nodded.

'It's just like sushi,' Gina explained. 'It's no different, is it? Raw fish, raw dog.' She shrugged happily. 'You've got to try everything once, Barry.'

'Yeah,' said Dan, talking with his mouth full.

Susie was nodding fervently.

'But,' Barry looked confused, 'it's a dog.'

'So?' said Gina. 'They eat dogs in China.'

Barry thought of something.

'So,' he smiled, 'like, if you went to somewhere between China and Japan, right – if you went to Korea – they would all be eating raw dog.'

'Oh Barry,' said Susie, she was smiling and laughing with shining eyes. 'That's great!'

'Barry!' Gina shouted, proffering a piece of meat. 'Would you care for some Korean sushi? A little canine canapé?' He smiled bashfully and took the food. He grimaced, but it didn't taste so bad. Just very wet.

They sat round the table, the four of them, underneath a poster of red poppies done in black and white, which Dan had got from Habitat. They laughed and made jokes about having dog breath in the morning and sometimes they stopped to change the compact disc.

Dan leaned back with his hands on his taut stomach, stretched flat under the black cloth of his T-shirt.

'I'm full,' he said.

Gina piled her hair up on top of her head with her hands. 'Let's go to bed,' she said. 'Good night.'

Her hair fell down and she and Dan slipped out of the room.

Susie sat on her chair, but it was making her feel lonely, sitting on stalks on the floor and half the other chairs empty, so she got up. Barry followed her as she went into the hall. He felt afraid. 'I feel sick,' said Barry to Susie. 'Susie, can I sleep in your bed?'

Susie shook her head. 'No, Baz. You'll feel better in the morning.' She kissed his cheek, stumbling a little.

Dan watched Gina lurching over him, looking foxy. He could see her face quite clearly now. There were grey freckles over her nose and under her eyes, and her eyes had a rich upward curve to them. Her eyelids were rising and falling with the rest of her. She opened her mouth and a high whine whistled out from between her teeth.

She was biting her lip. Blood trickled down her rocking chin. Just a little. Dan put his hand up to touch her face. Maybe he wanted to wipe it away. She ducked her chin and bit his thumb with sharp little teeth. 'Fuck!' he said, but maybe he kind of liked the pain because when she smiled, he smiled back.

She was gone when he woke. He lay under the duvet for a while, and then he heard Barry's footfall in the hall. He swung out of bed and pulled on his jeans.

Barry was in the kitchen when Dan slouched in.

'Hi,' he said. 'I need a coffee before I do anything.'

'Yeah,' said Barry.

Dan put the kettle on and they sat down.

'That Gina girl was really weird,' said Barry.

Dan ignored him. The carcass had gone. 'Did you clear up last night?' he asked.

'No,' said Barry. 'Maybe she took it.' Dan was gazing out the window. "It was her idea," said Barry.

'Aye, aye,' said Dan quickly. He got up and went to the kettle. It was nowhere near boiling. He sat down again.

There was just one thing left on the table. You couldn't help but see it. There was just one thing. Dan looked out of the window. He looked back at it. He looked away. Dan stared at the kettle like it was going to save his life, and then after a few seconds he had to look at the thing again. A pale keratinous circle was embedded in a little lump of soft pink skin.

'What's that?' said Barry.

Dan was shaking a little.

'I don't know,' he snapped.

'What's that!' said Barry, shouting.

'Gristle!' said Dan. 'It's just gristle.'

Barry and Dan both looked at it.

Susie was up. She came in wearing her dressing gown, pale

blue with a rabbit on it. 'Thanks for clearing up,' she said. She started making coffees, placing the mugs on the table. She looked at the tiny fingernail lying there, the fresh round rose of it and the white arc of its tip. The clean flesh was torn off, like a ripped-up root. She looked at it and then she looked some more. She looked at the others.

'What's that?' she asked.

It was her, it was that girl, howled Barry's soul. She'd made them all act funny, they hadn't been themselves. She was evil, it was her, she'd bewitched them all.

'I'm,' said Susie. 'I'm going to get dressed.' She went out of the room and they heard her feet going quickly up the stairs.

Dan took a fork and a spoon. He pincered it, picked it up like a tricky piece of salad and dropped it into the bin. It wasn't really real, he knew that. It couldn't be real, and anyway, it was in the bin now. It hadn't been real. He wiped down the table. Barry watched him.

Susie was getting dressed under cover of her dressing gown. She didn't want to see her body. She put it in trousers and a long-sleeved T-shirt. Oh God. What had they done. But they hadn't known, that was the thing. She'd seen its eyes, baby blue and human-wide, but she hadn't known, not really. Half known. Half a second. No. Not really. We are very sorry but we did not know. It was not our fault. Oh God.

Dan went and called up the stairs. 'Do you want some toast?'

There was a long pause.

'Yeah,' she called. When she came down she was fully dressed and her hair was done.

They were spreading butter on the toast when Kelly flared through the front door, her cheeks blazing with oxygen from the world outside. 'Hi,' she called, but they were silent like their coffee. She appeared in the kitchen.

'Hi, Kelly,' said Barry, wanting her to protect him with her life.

'Hey, Baz,' she replied, smiling. She looked at Dan and Susie. 'You two are very *sotto voce*,' she said, in her strong and carefree voice. There was a laugh at the edge of it.

She picked up a piece of toast. They all watched her. She was innocent by default and it wasn't fair. She would have done it, she would have done it, if she'd been there. They didn't know. They'd done it, and it wasn't fair. Kelly took a huge bite out of the corner.

'Anyway,' she said, through the crumbs and bits of blonde hair, 'I had a great night.'

The Land of Urd

Chris Dolan

The castle, where my quarters were, is closed now, gates all padlocked up, barbwired. They've not even tried to maintain the structure, so the walls and turrets are crumbling and melting in the rain. It's strange, being the only person on the island – I'm so used to seeing it packed, thronging with knights and knaves and visitors. But somehow, in this state of disrepair, and in the dark and smir, it seems more real than ever. They've closed up all the bridges and entrances from either bank, but I managed to scramble over the makeshift barricades with only a graze or two. Now that I've broken in, standing looking up at the turrets and strange mouldings that rise up into the darkening sky – I'd forgotten the sheer scale of the place! – I don't know why I've come back. The need to mourn, I suppose. Stand by my own grave, come to terms with my loss.

Walking along the central esplanade, weeds sprouting in the cracks, drawbridge pulled up tight and the moat switched off, I decide to take the long way round to the Parthenon. Maybe I won't go down into the interior after all. The entire structure feels pretty insecure, and anyway the dark is closing in earlier than I expected – I don't fancy renegotiating the barbed wire when it's completely pitch. When I set out this afternoon from the *pensión*, the sun was quite high, and I felt confident about the expedition. But winter nights descend a sight quicker in the high meseta than I realised. There are ghosts everywhere.

Echoes of kids screaming, grown men yelling, all the hullabaloo of the pageants and the machinery. The waterfalls and fountains roar and gush louder than ever in their lifelessness.

Heading due west the castle ramparts suddenly transform themselves into the sheer sides of the Egyptian Pyramid. The sarcophagus boats are stacked up at the top, their painted plastic as indestructibly garish as ever. At night, when the tourists had gone, the staff got to play on all of the attractions, free of charge. A policy that lead, catastrophically, to the demise of Euromyth. Quite apart from the tragic deaths, the amount of money that must have been lost on this place! Several billion dollars, they say. Trillions of pesetas, once you add the zeros. All because of the madness of one man, Josef Aznavorian. Even today, alone on a fake deserted island in the middle of a vast man-made lake, I find myself trying to catch glimpses of him. Rumour had it that he never came up from his control room – an entire sealed level, they said, directly beneath the staff quarters – watching everyone on CCTV. We know now that that was true, but also that he dressed up in the costume of minor roles and wandered around the complex, getting involved in the workers' romps himself.

The staff games weren't part of the original plan, but nobody made any objections. After all, it was hard and tedious work during the day and we were all young students, taking time out, having a high old time to ourselves and making a spot of holiday cash while we were at it. Six hundred in all. Scores of leading roles – Odin, Redbeard, Ulysses, Cleopatra, Zeus and, in my case, Orpheus. Hundreds of non-speaking and non-public contact parts – gladiators, mummies, vampires, Gauls, Celts. No doubt the papers are right – it was a recipe for disaster. To us, it had the makings of a heaven on earth.

When the centre closed down for the night and the tourists were gone, the whole place became one wild, extravagant party. Even the most inhibited and refined of the young staff, once they were disguised and had their faces painted with substitute wode and kohl, their hair dyed, they were tempted. Once they had worked for a few days in that heat and had toned up, none of them could resist the fun of the fair.

Linda and I arrived as a couple, but no relationship survived long in that atmosphere. She had landed the role of Mary Queen of Scots, thanks, mainly, to the pleasing Gaelic quiver in her Scots accent. Authenticity wasn't Euromyth's strong point. On the contrary, Management went out of its way to avoid it. In press briefings, Aznavorian stressed that the park dealt in dreams, not history. He made no apologies for the name, Euromyth, even though half the protagonists were real historical figures. Caesar and Cleopatra and Tut'ankhamun and Rob Roy, he declared, were possessed of a mythological stature.

Aznavorian was no lightweight. He commands – commanded – a huge respect in this country. An authority on classical history, writer of a seminal book on the human need for the fabulous, he had already successfully revitalised the Bacchanalia Festivals in Mérida and Carcasonne. With Euromyth he set out to surpass the limitations of a roller-coaster fun-park. The limitations, even, of history and legend. His vision was to create a new Saturnalia.

– A totally transformative experience – he told the press – to put ordinary people in touch again with their mythic selves. Only thus, will we escape the boredom of modern, corporate life and find a truer happiness.

The only sackable offence in the park was clever-dickery. So long as you turned up on time, dressed correctly, repeated, word for word, your few lines of script, you could do as you liked. Aznavorian's internal police – huge Viking bouncers, wrongly kitted with horned helmets and hard plastic batons to keep overenthusiastic visitors at bay – only ever exiled improvising actors. Students who knew their stuff and tried to throw in a bit of Latin or Greek, or used real quotes from Sophocles or Shakespeare, adapted their dress to be more realistic, were dismissed on the spot, driven off the island.

Linda was a quiet Oban girl. Well cast, too, pacing her tall Fotheringay tower with long blonde tresses attached to her hair (Management had fused Queen Mary with Rapunzel). Her job was more tiring than it might seem. All she had to do was walk sadly to and fro, to a strict timetable, in front of her barred window, declaiming every five minutes (there was a clock above the window which the public couldn't see) 'My heart is in the highlands.' On the quarter of every hour she had to select one of the children who mounted the ramp to file past her window, pick it up and plant a tearful kiss on its cheek. Without fail, the brat would burst out crying every time. Mary Queen of Scots was a popular attraction.

I played my part in Linda's change of personality – I recognise that now. Keener on the freetime games than she was, I argued that it was one summer of our lives, we all have to live a bit. I started going out on the escapades. At first just to watch, and report back to Linda in our shared dormitory. It spiced us up a bit and put us in the mood for sex. Then I started to get involved, on the periphery, no more, just the odd bit of touching. Linda still liked to hear about it and she would get more excited than before. It was me who encouraged her to surrender to requests for Queen Mary to return to her cell at night for some private parading. Asterix, an Afro-Caribbean guy from London, and Helen of Troy, a Minnesota law student, both said that, as they went about their daily duties, it turned them on glimpsing the beautiful slender Mary, her chemise damp with sweat, caged in her tower. I dressed Linda up in her 100 per cent polyamid shift – market research shows it gives a truer impression of silk than silk itself – and I sat, unseen, in a corner behind the door, so that Asterix, Helen and a couple of others could watch her, uninhibited.

She looked so tragic in the gas flambeaux, and soon learned how to excite her watchers. The humidity of the Castillian evenings created dark pools of perspiration on the clinging material, which dried up just as quickly when not in contact with her body. With her watchers behind her, at the barred cell door, Linda walked slowly and bent forlornly out of her window. When she twisted slightly to the left, her right buttock was clearly defined in her chemise; then she would turn in the other direction, let the dampness of her body pick out her left thigh. From the first night, it was evident she was enjoying herself. Her nipples hardened and clung to her dress. She began to lift her hem, as if to inspect a bite or a bruise, and Asterix and Helen would moan, pleasuring themselves on each other without taking their eyes off Mary Queen of Scots for a single moment.

On the third night, she asked me not to accompany her, that she would be fine. We agreed to go our own ways in the evenings, and then come back and report in detail everything we had seen and done. For that first month we made love wonderfully, Linda describing who was watching her, what they asked her to do, how she had treated her audience to glimpses of her naked breasts in the lamplight, allowed her dress to tighten round her sex, highlighting her damp pubic hair. In return, I told her about the sarcophagi. How I had seen the dare of making love in a *montaña rusa* at 100 miles an hour with a complete stranger while plunging into the dark depths of the Tut'ankhamun's Tomb, thrash metal music screaming over the sound system. About who did what to whom in Cyclops's Cave – a twist of bodies in the softer light and subtler sounds of Mano Chau. About the increasingly violent games in the Gladiators' Arena.

We even took the potions that the Vikings made, free of charge, for all staff. They were supposed to be powerful aphrodisiacs containing traces of urine from the bulls in the Minotaurs' Labyrinth, liquidised oysters and even, in the final weeks, menstrual blood from some of the extras in Valhalla. No one really believed that, of course. We assumed they were just *cubalibres* with tequila and exotic fruit juices. Now the media is claiming that Aznavorian spiked them with drugs.

Although I had been up to much more than I admitted to Linda – far more involved in the tangle of bodies in each of the park's different sections – it hadn't occurred to me that Linda too had been understating her activities. When the whole affair came to its dreadful end, I found out that Linda had been a main player, a setter of dares, among the most hedonistic of the staff. From what I've heard, she has been moving around Europe's visitor attractions ever since, even getting herself sacked from Eurodisney for gross indecency.

Tonight, though, looking up at the vast, inaccurate Corinthian pillars of the Parthenon – surely taller and more impressive than the originals – it's not Linda that's on my mind, but Ayesha. The woman who stood over my grave and pronounced me dead. The woman I truly loved. I'm getting used to the dark now, can make out the vast sky-tunnels that form part of Odin's Cosmic Tree, split in two – the Lands of Urd and Skuld, Past and Future. I'm getting over the feeling that I'm not alone tonight in Euromyth. All I'm hearing is the breeze rattling the props – the chains and sails and flagpoles and discarded spears and assegaia still lying around. I'm not sure how I'm going to get down into the Styx without the aid of the lift, but if I've come this far I might as well give it a try.

It was a lucky stroke, me getting the part of Orpheus. For the first few days I was a mere elephant rider in Alexander's Army. The original post-holder, a particularly beautiful guy from Ghana, took an aversion to being pawed by tourists and then at night by the entire staff. When he quit, Orpheus was transformed overnight from a tall, ebony black African, to a peach-white Ulsterman. They couldn't find anyone else, at a moment's notice, who could play the lute. Nor could I, but I can pick out a jig or two on the mandolin, and Management decided that would do nicely.

My job was to cross the Styx thrice daily, calling on Eurydice, play a romantic tune (in fact 'The Kerry Reel' *allegro ma non troppo*), attempt to bring her back from a virtual reality Hades, surrounded by shifting water-holograms of dragons and furious Thracian women. Then, with as much melodrama as I could muster, look back at the wrong time, lose her forever. My leading lady was a pretty local girl. (Management, in a sop to the Government, had agreed to a minimum of 10 per cent national staff. Most of them were deployed in The Inquisition section, but some – the Antonio Banderas and Penelope Cruz lookalikes – got themselves positions elsewhere in the park.) We sometimes went to the sarcophagi together, but there was never really a spark to our relationship. Inma, I got the impression, ultimately preferred the other women in the camp.

Ayesha and I had eyed each other during working hours, and had found ourselves, quite literally, thrown together during the evening games. She was one of Cleopatra's maids, a Romanian I found out later, and she had a liking for thin, delicate, white-skinned boys with curly hair, even if it was only a wig. What happened between us was the reverse of what happened with Linda. We got to know each other amidst the orgiastic games but then gradually became more private in our activities. We both liked Valhalla, Ayesha swapping her Egyptian costume for the virginal uniform of the Valkyrie. Along with a few of her friends she went around anointing whoever turned up with potions and unguents (actually, Cream E45 with colourants). Increasingly, though, she anointed only me, covering my body thickly with cream, slowly undressing me, and with special care and tenderness massaging my thighs, abdomen and sex.

Without having to say it to one another, we privately removed ourselves from Valhalla to my quarters. Linda seldom came back at night anymore. On the odd occasion that she did turn up, she watched us listlessly for a few moments, touched herself, then gave up, caught up on some sleep. Ayesha revealed herself slowly to me over a month. From the very start she had me stripped naked, and immediately erect. But I had never seen her body in the light and only gradually did she tantalisingly expose herself. Her back, calves, arms, loosening her virginal

Valkyrie gown to the rise of her breasts. She promised that, by the end of the season, I would see her completely naked, but that we would only make love properly once we had left Euromyth and had returned to normal life. I was in love with her. If I hadn't been, I couldn't have tolerated the teasing, the taking me to near-climax and then, laughing, backing off, forbidding me to touch myself. I gave up going to Cyclops's Cave or any of the other sexual amphitheatres, even on the odd night when Ayesha stayed in her quarters to sleep.

The belief in the camp that Josef Aznavorian was watching us all the time grew as the summer progressed. Previously, Linda and I had searched our small bedroom for a hidden camera and found no trace, so I didn't think he could violate our privacy. I know now that he saw, and recorded, everything. Ayesha liked the idea of it. Although I never got to see her most intimate parts, she would contort herself while bending over me and, her eyes witch-bright, say

– Do you think he can see me Orpheus? Is his camera focused on my gown?

The idea that there was another man devouring with his eyes what I could only imagine increased the sexual tension almost unbearably. I honestly thought that was what Ayesha had in mind – to tease and tempt me to the limit, adding the spice of jealousy to my desire.

We planned our escape for the close of Euromyth's season – the night, as it turned out, of the horrific tragedy. Management should have realised that on the last day the games would get out of hand. We had all been paid, the tourists had gone, all rules and restraint thrown to the wind. The out-of-control Viking police dished out what was left of Aznavorian's barrels of potion, and 600 youngsters readied themselves for a final, frenzied night of demented orgy. Crowds gathered at the Gladiators' Arena, Cyclops's Cave, the lands of Urd and Skuld wherever there was a chance of drink, sex, adventure. The boldest and wildest headed for the Pyramid's daredevil roller-coaster.

Each sarcophagus carriage was designed to hold 8 adults, but on that lawless, manic night 15 joyriders – Romans in mail, armoured nights, naked men and women, threw themselves, or were thrown, inside. Ayesha and I knew nothing of what was happening until the next day, when I finally got up out of my grave. We heard the screams and yells, but thought nothing of it, so used to the uproar of kids and tourists, and knowing that our colleagues were determined to have the night of their lives. We wanted away from all of that, conduct our escape from the inferno of Euromyth far from the speed garage and nu-metal music and the insanity growing around us.

The Vikings sent the carriage down the railed waterfall at its highest possible speed. The passengers thrashed around inside, grabbing at one another's bodies, three or four of them sitting – against all safety regulations – astride the sides of the boat, increasing the splashing from the waterfall by urinating inwards. Others rocked the sarcophagus from side to side as it sped down towards Tut'ankhamun's Tomb.

I'm standing now at the grave Ayesha made for me. I've had to scramble over gates and fences and bricked-up sections of the park to get here. The glass-walled lift that used to take the tourists into Hades still isn't functioning, but I found the emergency staircase again, as I did that night, and now I'm sitting where I last saw her. Remembering her precisely, that night less than a year ago, standing there on the other side of the River Styx, perfumed water soaking the hem of her gown, a contented smile on her face. I knew that at last I would enjoy my precious Ayesha, untouched, unseen by anyone but me, and perfectly bare.

We weren't completely alone that night in here. At the back there were a few girls, one or two young men, all of them tearful, fearing the worst for what was happening elsewhere in

Euromyth. They sat in a dark corner, caressing one another, Belle and Sebastian playing quietly over the speakers. They took no notice of us, nor we of them. I cared only for Ayesha. My Eurydice.

– Tonight, my Orpheus, I will be yours.

She placed herself between two spotlights, one red, the other green. I could see her move gently and sway as she took off her gown, loosened her hair. By her silhouette I knew she was naked. Could make out the straight, curt lines of her calves and thighs, her skin and hair glowing darkly, the gentle swell of her breast, the blackness of her sex. I crossed the stream in her wake, strumming softly and calling out to her. I could smell her skin. Fresh mermaid tang; waft of sepia-ink. I could hear her whispering softly, until another voice shattered the moment.

– Remember the script, young Orpheus. You're on contract yet.

His voice is well known to me now, after so many TV interviews. Nowadays he's always dressed in an impeccable suit, but that night Aznavorian was Hercules. In his books and lectures he had spoken of his personal devotion to the Herculean myth. Central to our European psyche, he claimed. The Greek rendering, Heracles, becomes Kalisto. Karisto, Cristos. Sacrificed to redeem us from our banality, our mediocrity.

– You mustn't look at Eurydice. Not until you have conducted her safely across the river of Death.

At the time, I assumed this Hercules was just some staff-member getting in on our act, and his intrusion angered me. But there was no doubt he was correct. Not just academically, but in the plans Ayesha and I had made for our final union and escape. So I did as he said, and turned around, headed back towards the Styx. I listened hard for her footsteps behind me. But none came. Reaching the other bank – where I am sitting now, tears welling uninvited in my eyes – I remained facing away from my naked lover and the solitary man who was refereeing our union.

Then I heard her. Not her footsteps. But other movements. Skin against skin, a deep whispering, an ominous moan. I withstood it as long as I could, trying to overcome my suspicions, until at last I couldn't bear it any longer. I turned.

Was that the moment that I heard the crash and thunder from above? Or was it later, while I was lying alone in my open grave? I can't remember. Yet it rings in my ear still, that awful grind and rip. I can feel again, sitting here alone, the tremor that growled through the park structure, rocking the entire man-made island. The snapping of chains and cables sounded like whipcracks, then that distant unearthly screech, like the death-cry of Icarus too close to the sun. I took it all to be part of my own drama with Ayesha, never thought nor cared for a moment of other lives, elsewhere.

Ayesha hid her nakedness from me, covered herself with Hercules's lion skin. He held her gown for her and looked at me, not harshly, it seemed to me – paternally. Ayesha's eyes were moist and – I'm sure of it – a little hesitant. But the expression on that bearded, Slavic face of his, condemned ever since on the front page of a thousand newspapers, struck me as almost compassionate.

– You failed, Orpheus. Such a simple task. Eurydice comes back with me over the river. You live; she dies.

I looked pleadingly at my lover, still hiding herself from me. She didn't move. She glanced from me to him, and her eyes remained with him. At the time, I thought I understood. He was so powerful, so placid, possessed of an authority beyond my reach. I was shaking, wet with tears, small and scared.

My life, Aznavorian said, is, of course, the truer death, and so it seemed to me too. They crossed the stream, and I knew what I had to do. The tremors from the accident still shivered around us, and a low groan grew horribly close. The loss of Ayesha was more than I could bear, and it was as if the whole world knew that the end had come for me. I lay down. They crossed the perfumed river, a tide forming in its flow from the shake of the earth. Together, silently, they gathered the light plastic stones and rocks of this fake Hades, placed them around me. Hercules took the gold amulet in the shape of an upside-down tree from around his neck, placed it on my breast. Ayesha kneeled to kiss my closed eyes. I could feel her head turn sadly, her hair brushing my face from cheek to cheek. She didn't have to explain that she was building a grave for our love. I lay there – here – for a few minutes, perhaps ten. When I opened my eyes, I was alone.

As alone I am now. The amulet and stones still as I left them last August. I've decided to stay here until dawn comes. It'd be too dangerous to clamber over the barricades so late at night. It's warmer down here at any rate, the night air outside several degrees below zero. Inside my pocket I have last week's front page. A photograph of Josef Aznavorian and his wife, who the media have uncovered as the Club Queen of Ibiza, entering the court in Madrid.

I lay still until I thought it was morning. When I got up, feeling like a ghost of myself, empty, I tried to take the lift back up to the park's surface. The electricity had failed. There was a little dun light from the gas torches and an eerie silence, save for a few far-off sobs, the odd creak. The youngsters, huddled earlier, had gone. I found the emergency steps and made my wearily up. It was darker above ground than it had been below. A crowd of people, faces as white as fading moons, stood deathly quiet at the Egyptian Pyramid.

I never witnessed the horror of the scene below. Like everyone else, I only saw the pictures, days later, of the pointless rescue attempt. The fated sarcophagus had come loose from the rails, plummeted down hundreds of feet, through cables and chains and machinery and shattered into the hard stone altar below of Tut'ankhamun's Tomb. All fifteen passengers were killed. They had to gather up limbs and piece them together, like a gory classical jigsaw.

I rip Ayesha's photograph away from Aznavorian and the text listing the accusations against them. Second-degree murder; manslaughter; negligence; pedalling illegal pornography; filming without consent; drug trafficking. I scrunch up and throw aside the mad Hercules's quote that he does not recognise this court. He and his wife have answered to a higher authority, are satisfied their mission was pure. Bending over the circle of plastic stones, as she once bowed over me, I place Ayesha's face in the centre of my grave.

There's no rush to get out of here. No rush back to Edinburgh – I'm mucking up my degree anyway. It feels appropriate to be here, in this unnatural place. Nothing in the world seems real to me any more. Not my impulsive trek back to Spain, nor any part of my ordinary life at home. Not the stories I hear about Linda, nor the ever more scandalous facts emerging daily about fated Euromyth. Lying down to rest in this crumbling tomb of a place, I'm not sure if I'm alive or dead. Death doesn't feel real now. And love, certainly not love.

Stifelio

Christopher Whyte

Florence 1546

I rarely feel pity for the people I kill. I am familiar with an infinitude of ways of killing, using poison or gunpowder, a dagger for stabbing or a cord for strangling, or else a heavy pillow which can suffocate at one and the same time the cries and the life that animated them. Whatever method I use, I prefer not to have to touch them while they are alive, far less once they are dead. I am sure you could kill a man with fear alone, although I have never attempted to prove it. Once I was asked to set fire to a bedchamber so as to kill the couple who were sleeping there. If you had heard the way the deceived husband who enlisted my services laughed when it was done! Another time a rather odd nobleman asked me to use a poisoned spider he had had brought back from the Americas. I was worried the creature might kill other people besides the ones who were our target. But he insisted it was a special breed, and would die in the very act of releasing its poison.

I cannot explain why I am telling you this, you of all people. You have a grim air about you, though you look sensitive, too. With those slender, delicate fingers, you could be a poet or a musician. But your eyes are troubled, as if you had been shown the door by a high-ranking family or else, who knows, had yourself killed a man. In any case, you must be ruined. Otherwise you would not be drinking in this tavern.

I'm rich enough myself. I don't come here because I cannot afford to pay higher prices to have more agreeable surroundings. Degradation attracts me, that is the reason. And I need to talk to someone. Not just to anyone. To someone whom the world has brushed aside, as if he were a piece of litter which has no reason to exist. I stopped going to confession long ago. You are going to be my confessor tonight. I will pay for our food and drink in return for whatever absolution you are able to offer me. But do not imagine you will stay alive for long if you breathe a word of what I say to other ears. Your face is already imprinted on my memory. I will track you down in whatever corner of the city you choose for your hiding place. It would be a pity to have to watch the blood dripping down from those shapely lips of yours.

Her name was Margarita. A servant came to my lodgings three days ago to tell me the Rucellai were looking for me. To be more precise, my client was that old hag of a grandmother who lives on the top floor of their town house. The one who is rotten inside with ill will and viciousness. I wasn't looking for work. I have enough money to last me till the end of the year. Recently I bought a small piece of land near Carmignano, with olives and a vineyard and a fruit orchard. There is a house in the middle of it I want to have rebuilt. It already gives me all the oil and wine and fruit I need for use at home here in the city. I don't have much of an establishment. Just a couple of rooms that get plenty of air and sunlight, with a woman who cooks and cleans for me and washes my clothes. I am rich, though, and will be richer still in time. But I am not enough of a fool, or bold enough, to ignore a summons from the Rucellai hag. We have known each other for many years now. I don't employ polite or flattering words in dealing with her. She knows I consider her to be a repellent, cruel witch, and that I could not care whatever she thinks about me. She is a cancer in the body of that family, ruling it still and sucking their vigour from the men. They are all afraid of her. None of them would dare to contradict her wishes or show her a discourtesy.

She kept me waiting a fair while at the top of the stairs, as is her custom. She is afraid I will forget that I am a man beyond the law, a mere instrument in the hands of those who are richer and more powerful than me. My calling is to personify their hatred and ill wishes, to give them physical embodiment. Standing there, I toyed with the idea of turning back and sending the old crone and her plans for me to the devil. But a large tapestry was hanging on the wall opposite, rocking to and fro in the draught coming up the stairs. Its embroidery was exceptionally fine, with trees and meadows and gallant riders urging on their dogs to hunt the deer. It made me think of the little casket I had seen two days before in the shop of Righello the goldsmith. It was delicately carved, with emeralds and carbuncles set into the lid. I love jewellery of all kinds and have quite a collection of different objects at home. They are things I can stroke and caress and set in order, when a long day stretches ahead of me with nothing to fill it, or when my brain is troubled by thoughts I do not wish to offer shelter to. And I decided that it would be worth my while after all to find out what the old hag wanted from me, to fulfil her wishes and take her gold, for with it I could buy the little casket, and it would be a pastime for me to examine it closely and wonder at the virtues of its workmanship.

Come now, finish off your glass and let me fill it again from the new flask which has just arrived. You're not in the habit of drinking so much? Well, you had better get into it, for you will need to fortify yourself if you are going to cope with all I have to tell you. From your eyes I would guess you could make a confession still more devastating than my own. But the roles we are going to play have been staked out already. I do not wish to hear a word about your past, or about the future that awaits you, if you have one. I do not even want to find out whether the prospect of opening your eyes tomorrow morning excites or terrifies you, or merely fills you with a loathing from which there is no escape.

Now your attention is wandering. You have been distracted by that pair who just came through the door. Two women, one of them short and fat, the other tall and fine looking, but with a gait that is just a little too energetic and virile. Yes, I said virile. You look shocked. Am I to believe that you never paid a prostitute to give you satisfaction? What kind of a Christian are you, young fellow? Where is your charity? What would happen to those poor wretches if men like you and me did not bring to them desires we have no lawfully wedded wives to satisfy, and pay them richly for their services? You are wrinkling your nose in disgust. Truly, you must have fallen from a very great height in a short time, to end up in a hole like this and still preserve a degree of fastidiousness.

The smaller one is Letizia. Though she is no beauty, she performs a certain function with a skill and effectiveness that has made her name a byword in all the stews of the city. With the money she earns she could have given up the trade long ago. But the fool has a soft heart she is determined to indulge. She fell in love with a good for nothing, a youth with hair as blonde as the whitening corn the day before they take the sickle to it, and every penny she can spare goes to satisfy his caprices, be it for a new suit of clothes or for a pair of roast partridges when none are to be had from one gate of the city to the next.

The taller one's name is Giuliana. But it might be more honest to call her Giuliano. How you raise your eyebrows at the suggestion! You gulp in horror and surprise. I can see your Adam's apple bobbing like a small boat on the Arno when a freak wind stirs the waters up. If you listen to me attentively, and drain your glass as I request, who knows but I might give you a bag of silver at the end of the night to reward your patience. You can use it to taste venal pleasures for the first time. And I will even advise you about which prostitute to ask for.

What kind of a renegade can you be, if you have never paid for pleasure?

When I first trod the streets of Florence I was younger still than you are. Seventeen years old, if I was a day. All that I wanted was to be a painter. I was ready to take on the most menial tasks if they could only help me draw closer to my objective. Cleaning out latrines, burnishing old pewter, tending to the horses' stables, nothing would have been too base for me. But wherever I went, they rejected me. One innkeeper, more honest and outspoken than the rest, told me I had a look in my eyes that would frighten his guests away, as if I could have brought ill luck on them with a glance or a mere flicker of my lashes. By the end of the week I was close to starvation, sitting in a tavern just like this, one they have closed now. A man approached me offering me a kind of work I had never thought about before that day. Though I said yes, the real nature of what he proposed did not dawn on me until I had gone so far in his employment that a word to the authorities would have been sufficient to get me locked away for years. Before I had started, he gave me money which I used to eat and find a lodging, and to pay for pleasures of the kind I have been describing to you. His generosity ensnared me.

That was when I met Margarita. She was as inexperienced in the ways of the city as I myself had been till shortly before. And, I swear to you, she was a virgin. Wipe that look of disbelief off your face, or I will put an end to your existence this very minute! There, I have refilled my glass, and drunk from it, and will drink from it again before continuing with my tale. Wine dulls and calms me at one and the same time. I admit that what I said sounds incredible. But it was true. And because she was pure, and kind, and helpless, I promised I would keep her to myself, paying what was needed to the owner of the house she dwelled in to make sure that no other client should get access to her. And for a while at least, the promises they made to me were kept.

It meant I needed money, and this drove me further and further into the trap set for me by the man who had approached when it looked as if I was going to starve. In his service, I undertook a task which meant I had to leave the city for ten days. When I returned, Margarita was no longer to be found. I beat the mistress of the place and threatened her with worse, until she broke down and confessed she had sold the girl on to a solider, a mercenary returning from the wars in Germany. But she would not tell me the man's name or where the two had set up residence.

What has this to do with the Rucellai hag and her commission to me? I can read in your features the puzzlement and the boredom you are trying hard to hide. You think you have fallen into the hands of a maniac, a fool who recounts disconnected incidents, who makes up tales about his life and loves that do not even hang together. There are fewer years between us than you think. Though my beard is as black as it ever was, I know the hair at the sides of my head is dappled with grey. Yet as few as fifteen autumns have gone by since I lost Margarita. Listen to what I have to tell you.

The Rucellai woman told me a story which was dismal in its predictability. Gianfranco, the eldest son of her third daughter, had fallen in love with a prostitute, an older woman of unusual beauty and sophistication, who could scan his verses with him, play on the viol and read to him when melancholy overtook his soul. Not content with maintaining her in an establishment of her own, not far from the church of Santa Maria Novella, he was now determined to make an honest woman of her. That involved bringing her in front of a priest and swearing vows of fidelity which would bind the two of them together for the rest of their days. Vows which, moreover, would make her a member of the family whose presiding spirit was that old crone at the top of the stairs. And she wanted none of it.

Need I tell you what she asked me to do? Because I had not felt like working for her, I agreed all the more readily to the cruel plan she had drawn up, as if acquiescing in all her wickedness could help me be revenged on her for troubling me. She wanted to allow the church ceremony to take its course, not putting an end to the woman until the wedding feast was in full swing. That way both my employer and I would have the satisfaction of watching her death throes and Gianfranco's reaction to seeing the thing he loved most in the world shrivel and collapse before his eyes.

We agreed that I would be dressed in the livery of the house and would pose as one of the extra stewards taken on for the occasion. The normal thing would have been for Gianfranco's majordomo to serve both food and drink to the chief banqueters, at the centre of the top table. But the old woman said she could arrange easily enough for him to be decoyed to the countryside on a false errand. She had offered to pay for the feast herself, a show of generosity intended to camouflaged her role in what was going to happen. That made it easy for me to be assigned the task of bringing Gianfranco and his newly wedded wife their meat and drink. It also gave me the chance to slip a small black pill into the fresh goblet from which she was to drink the dessert wine, a pill that no sooner came into contact with the sweet, syrupy liquid than it dissolved, leaving no trace.

You can guess what happened next. I made my way to the back of the chamber, close to the doorway, as if to get a breath of air, but in reality in order to escape more quickly. I had served everything to the guests from behind their backs, and had not been able to get a good look at their faces. Maybe I ought to have foreseen the trick that fate would play on me. When the young woman at Gianfranco Rucellai's side took her first draught of the dessert wine, then removed the goblet from in front of her face, I saw that she was Margarita.

Something broke inside me then. A dream I had had and retained, a thing of wonder which I had lost and could never regain but which, nonetheless, existed somewhere in the world, was shattered. For as long as it existed, everything in me could not be destroyed. And it left the world with my connivance.

Everything I have told you is true, but I may have deceived you in one particular. I have not killed since that day. Two weeks have gone by now. I am obsessed with the compulsion to speak, to tell my crime, to proclaim Margarita's death, and what it meant for me, to the four winds. Until this evening I resisted it. Now that I have confessed, I feel I cannot stop. I want to talk and talk and talk, as if my words were flowing water which, moving through and out of me, could in the end cleanse me and allow me to continue living. Will you stay with me? Will you forget my threats and taunts and stay at my side for as long as it takes? Will you hear everything I have to say and lodge it inside you, without betraying me? And without allowing it to contaminate you? For that would mean that the rottenness I am seeking to expunge would merely take root in another man. Can you help me be free of it without yourself succumbing? Will you do this for me?

The House Outside the Kitchen

Raymond Soltysek

It was strange, the house my uncle died in. I spent Thursday lunch times there, in the stone-flagged kitchen with work surfaces worn and bleached like driftwood and bone, light channelling through the narrow window over the deep porcelain sink. The table joggled under my elbows on the uneven floor and spilled bright-red, perfectly round droplets of the Cream of Tomato soup my aunt left for me, her little note always reminding me to be careful of lighting the cooker.

I'd never been in a room before which hadn't any wallpaper or plaster, and the misshapen stonework leaned out at me like the blank faces of dead owners, struggling back into the real world. I tried to speak to them, now and again, ask them what they wanted. 'Is there anybody there?' I whispered, just like ghost hunters on the TV, and I waited for one of them to reach out and touch me, a stony, grey, cold finger pushing towards my forehead. They never did, and, being a rational child, I knew deep down they never would. But I had an imagination too, and I stared at the wall, picking out the hollows of eyes, a mouth slightly twisted.

I gave them histories. The Victorian father frightened me most. He had a moustache that he twirled, and he'd murdered his wife and child – they peered out from behind him, submissive and terrified – because he suspected the boy wasn't his. He'd dismembered their bodies on the chopping block and fed them to his dogs, then scrubbed and scrubbed until all the blood was wiped away. Finally, unaccountably, he'd hung himself, in the attic, where I'd never been and definitely didn't want to go.

I rarely stepped outside the kitchen: it was the only room the dead owners tolerated me being in, provided I kept the back door open, even in rain, so that I could escape if they found their faces or voices and suddenly told me to go. I would sit, buttoned in my blazer, zipped in my anorak, soup chilling rapidly and the wind whipping the steam from my spoon and the breath from my mouth.

'Go to your Aunt Sylvia's for lunch on Thursdays from now on,' my mother had said. 'She'll leave a key under her back doormat.'

My insides lurched and froze, and a sliver of spaghetti slipped off the fork and ran down my school shirt. 'Why?'

'So you can get in, daftie,' she said. 'You don't expect her to leave the door open do you?'

I was lost for a second, then realised that she was deliberately avoiding the question. 'No, that's not what I mean. Why do I have to go? Why can't I come home?'

'I've been offered an extra shift,' she said, dabbing my front with a damp cloth. 'At the laundry.'

'So? I can see to my own lunch.'

'You can't. By the time you get back, it's almost time for you to leave. When I'm here, I can have your lunch ready for you. But I'll be at work.'

'But Mum . . .' I pleaded. I couldn't tell her, couldn't put the fear into words, but surely she would feel it, sense it?

'Go to your aunt's. I'm not telling you again.' She lifted my plate and stuck the knife in. 'Or get school dinners.'

That won the argument. An extra hour among boys who hard-fisted me across the ear until I found somewhere to hide. Once, one of them had launched a table-tennis bat at another, arguing over a point. It axed his mouth. Blood spattered onlookers as his head flung back. I found a tooth, red and white, slimy meat at the root, sticking to my blazer sleeve. If I couldn't go home, I wasn't staying in school. So I went for lunch to my aunt's and my dying uncle's.

He wasn't my real uncle. Not really. According to the boys at school, I was a mongrel because my mum was from Wales and my dad was from God Knew Where. I never had a relative within a thousand miles and my mother didn't like travelling. But he was an uncle nonetheless, adopted from the flat next door, a family shoved and squeezed like we were into a tiny flat. When I was five, I would take his hand, we would stand on the back green and I would point at the night sky, trace out constellations, and he would tell my mother what a boy I was, so bright, even though he knew I made most of them up. I would look at him, craning my neck, and the glowing tip of his cigarette melted into the sky and he told me how the Merchant Navy had taught him to navigate by the stars.

They moved away from the flat next door. They looked for somewhere bigger, and the house outside the kitchen echoed up and down a staircase my aunt and uncle wanted for their daughter. Her train spilled like milk from step to step on her wedding day. A last conceit for a dying man.

Sometimes I had to venture deep into the territory of the dead owners to use their toilet. I peered out behind the kitchen door, waited for the soughing and sighing of the air in the rest of the house to hold its breath, then dashed along the hall, past the sitting room and the front room where my uncle lay, up to the top of the wedding stairs and along a balcony. I had to turn my back to the landing and the gloomy corridor which led to the upstairs bedrooms, and I could feel the dead owners hurrying at my back, inches behind me, laughing at my panic, reaching out close enough to draw the hairs on the back of my neck towards their fingertips without ever touching.

They did odd things in that house. They would skew the floors on a whim, and I would find myself accelerating down the balcony towards the toilet door, in danger of crumpling against it. Sometimes they would pitch the hallway floor upwards and I would feel like Doug Hasson, grizzled and frosty-bearded and reckless, a real rebel, climbing the last incline to a summit. My mother said the floors were like that because of mine workings beneath the house: she mentioned subsidence and that the house hadn't been worth buying in the first place. I wondered about the tunnels beneath, and if the tired old house longed to sink into them, slowly tilt on to its side and gracefully slip beneath its weedy flower beds and overgrown lawns, leaving no trace. I asked her about this, if we were in danger of suffocating underground, of being buried alive, wet clumps of earth filling our mouths and noses and ears, of being eaten by worms: she said not to be so silly, that an explosion was more likely because the shafts were filled with gases.

I stood at the stairhead one day and looked down the corridor towards the bedrooms, daring myself to face whatever it was I knew was there: after all, I was eleven and a half. The lines of the corridor, the ceiling, the dado rail, the frames of the doorways, funnelled to a small gloomy oblong sapped of light. As I looked, all the vapours of the mine shafts and the spirits of the dead owners and the steam from my soup spoon and the breath from my mouth swirled and gathered, made visible by my being there to watch them.

I ran, of course, hurtling down the wedding stairs three, four, five at a time, bouncing off the wall and landing with a thump loud enough to waken the dead. Which was the last thing I wanted. I squatted there, my bowels churning, my heart about to burst through my chest, just waiting for the crack of the floorboards that would send me tumbling into the mine shafts below.

Instead, the stained glass of the entrance door billowed and rattled a little, and I heard a tortured groan from the front room where my uncle lay dying.

I hadn't seen him for almost eight months, not since he'd

been confined there after his daughter's wedding. She kissed him goodbye, with the man she would divorce within two years smarmy on her arm, and the next day my uncle disappeared into that room. When my mother visited I was left in the sitting room until she came back with my aunt. In the taxi on the way home my mother shook her head, said 'Don't ever disturb your Uncle Jim, he needs his rest;' and I felt glad and guilty.

I pushed the door open, half expecting shadow and candle-light and a four-poster bed. Instead, I had the impression of water: the smell and the light made me think of a swimming pool, but that wasn't quite right. The bay windows were huge, dazzling the room in shimmering blue puddles. The walls were light, the cornicing pale blue. A dark-green picture rail. Two arm-chairs, carved wood arms with gold leaf from the captain's cabin of a pirate ship. A massive, dark veneered cabinet hid the television set like treasure.

The bed was set against the near wall, and I had to lean around the door to see. The two huge, black torpedo shapes stood upright behind the door, blocking my view. They hissed slightly, and I wondered if the mine shafts were leaking up into the real world.

I edged round them and found my uncle. He had shrunk so much. The sheets were pink, and he was propped up against a dozen pink cushions. He wore cream-coloured pyjamas. Plastic tubes connected him to the black canisters, feeding him oxygen, and his face was indistinct behind a translucent mask.

He opened his eyes and swivelled his head to look at me. A reedy finger beckoned me over and feebly patted the quilt. I couldn't sit on the bed. He growled something beneath the mask.

'Pardon?' I said.

His eyes widened with the effort of trying to concentrate. He was only half conscious, and I wasn't sure if he recognised me.

'Uncle Jim, I'm sorry. I can't hear what you're saying.'

He breathed in, the sound somewhere between a kettle

whistling and a drain. His hand reached towards me, but I couldn't extend my own to meet his. He leaned back, his lower jaw slack and exhausted. Then he coughed, a huge sound from the depths of the caverns of his wasted chest. A bright red, perfectly round droplet spat on to the inside of the mask.

I stared at it, trying not to see his eyelids flutter closed. Instinct and my mother's training told me to rush and find a cloth to wipe it off. I went to the kitchen and ran the warm water from the tap over the corner of a dish towel. Then I realised I would have to lift the mask, hook my fingers under the elastic around his head, and touch his face. It would be old and dry and papery, so instead I rinsed my plate and went back to school.

We got the call later that night to tell her he'd died: I watched Mum speak into the heavy, black receiver, her face going hard, a sympathetic noise crooning at the back of her throat. She'd be straight round, she said, she'd ask Marjorie next door to stop in to look after me.

As she put on her coat and fussed over her handbag, I tried to ask her, to find out when he'd died. Aunt Sylvia found him when she came back from work, that's all she knew. 'Why are you asking?' she said, not thinking that I might have been frightened at having had lunch with a dead man.

But I hadn't. I'd just watched him die. Maybe.

What did he look like? I could hardly remember: all that came to mind was the wizened fingers and the dim eyes focusing on something far away. And the red stain on the inside of the mask, dribbling gently, smearing the plastic.

I hadn't cleaned it up. I went to my room and cried underneath the blankets, said sorry to him again and again, and dreamt about fingers reaching out to me, pointing at me, blaming me. I was a bad boy for not cleaning it up. A thoughtless, careless, dirty boy. Why hadn't I cleaned it up? Why?

I wasn't allowed at the funeral: I was too young to go. But my mother said that he looked so well in his casket, and there were lots of flowers. His daughter cried and kissed him goodbye: her husband couldn't be there because of business.

I didn't go back on Thursday lunch times, took my chances with the bullies, joined a club to keep out of the way. I left the house to my aunt. She sold it a year later to a builder who modernised the whole place.

I often passed it on the way to school. It was soon unrecognisable, with its new windows and double garage. An extension sprouted from its side, housing a cheery, yellow-flowered kitchen. I saw the family regularly, sitting round a pine table spooning cereal into their mouths, happy and at ease.

I wondered about the dead owners, their faces plastered over and wallpapered like the twentieth century. I felt their frustration, pushing out into a world they didn't recognise and found too sophisticated, too bright, to terrify.

And I thought of my uncle, and if he had joined them, only to find that times had changed and the past was superfluous and the freedom of their mischief had come to an end.

The Final Weight of all that Disappears

John Burnside

When Sally Hamill sleeps, she always has the same dream. It never changes; yet when she wakes, she feels the promise of something still to come, something new. She probably has other dreams, but this is the one she remembers, waking in the small hours with Tommy asleep beside her, safely remote in his own dreamed world. Knowing him, she imagines that world as tidy and strange, but her own dream is very simple. She has been having it ever since she found the dead girl, gradually refining it to its purest form, like an alchemist in search of a healing elixir. When it begins, she is a spectator: a girl of fifteen or so at the circus. There are clowns and ballerinas; there are horses and jugglers. At the centre of the ring, a man in a black coat and a tall hat stands like a Master of Ceremonies, looking out across the audience with a knowing half-smile; beside him is a large box covered in stars and crescent moons, the black-and-silver lacquer dusted with moonshine. The man is scanning the audience, looking for someone; when he finds Sally, he raises his hand and, with a flourish, draws her towards him, clearing a path through the dancers and the circus animals, while the lights go down, and the audience falls silent. Finally, there is a long, quiet drum-roll, and the man lifts the lid of the box, which seems to grow larger and darker as she draws near. Even the other performers – the dancers, the clowns, the bareback riders – have stopped what they were doing and have turned to watch, as the man takes Sally's hand and she steps inside. Now, for the first time, she realises what is about to happen: that the Master of Ceremonies is really a magician, and she is to be his beautiful assistant. The audience has known this all along, and probably think that they understand this trick; that, after the lid descends, the magician will wave his wand above the box, concealing it, for a moment, in a cloud of smoke, before throwing it open with a flourish, to reveal an astonishing emptiness. They are not quite sure, but they think they know how it is done: a false bottom, a trapdoor, something of that order allows the girl to slip away, to perform a quick change, and prepare herself to be revealed, in a sparkling ball-gown, or a shimmering trapeze-artist's costume, next time the lid is raised. What they cannot know, however, is that there is no trapdoor; there is no way out. The walls of the box are smooth and firm, yet Sally really does vanish in that dark, quiet space, for all the long minutes till the trick is concluded and she reappears in a shiny blue frock, smiling and waving, identical in every way to the girl she was when the dream began, but also – for a handful of moments, at least, between sleeping and waking – different, in every way, to the woman who had fallen asleep, in her ordinary bedroom, only a few hours before.

She found the girl in Tommy's shed. There was nothing special or different about the place; you could find similar huts on allotments all over the country: dark, somewhat musty wooden rooms, with a crate of old plant pots in one corner and a pile of John Innes No. 1 in the other. There might be a shelf lined with squat brown jars of insecticide or paraquat, the lids crusted with salt or rust, which would account for the faint chemical smell; yet there is always something else, some vegetal undertone, part-tuber, part-new-mown grass, that clings to your fingers and clothes long after the more pungent odour has disappeared. It's as if something live is there, something that might breed in the creases of your coat, or between your toes, if you didn't wash it off right away, and it was this, more than anything else, that Sally noticed, when she found Kerry Mitchell's body, late one Saturday afternoon, in Christmas week.

It had begun to snow that morning. Tommy had gone out at eleven o'clock, pausing at the kitchen door to say he would be back around three – his usual routine, in other words. Sally knew he would stop at the bookies, then go on to the club and have three or four drinks before wandering home with some chocolates, or a pot plant from the greengrocer's, to keep her sweet. This time of year, he wouldn't have any work to do on the allotment – there was no reason, once it was all dug over and left to weather in – but when the clock struck five and he still wasn't home, Sally thought she would take a walk out, to see where he was. It was an excuse, mostly, to go out in the snow; she was like a big kid when the weather changed, taking any chance she got to walk to the end of the road under the orange street lamps, listening to that soft, creaking sound her boots made, and feeling the cool, blown flakes against her cheeks and eyes. She went as far as the shops, but she didn't see any sign of him, so she walked home the back way, just in case he had gone to check the allotment and had forgotten the time. She knew Tommy liked the allotments best when there was nobody else around; sometimes, when the earth was bare, with nothing save cabbage stalks and the odd shrubby plant standing naked in the cold, he would come down here and stand at the shed door, smoking a cigarette, and staring off into space. There were days when he seemed to come home haunted by the place, and he would be quiet and thoughtful for hours afterwards, detached and aloof and far away from her. It made her happy, then, to know that there was something more to him, something he knew or felt, but couldn't talk about. He felt more like a husband to her, with this mystery about him.

The girl was suspended from the crossbeam of the roof, among the plastic bags full of charcoal and roots that Tommy kept there, out of the wet. Sally knew who it was right away, though when they asked about it afterwards, she had no idea why: the face was covered in blood and grime and there were thin creases in the dirt on her cheeks, where the girl must have cried, for as long as it had taken, or for as long as she had stayed conscious – maybe for hours, Sally thought – while her killer worked. There was no doubt in her mind that Kerry was dead. The blood on the floor, the blurred whiteness of the skin, the smell she knew from the time she had been at the hospital: it all added up to a slow, miserable end. Yet it wasn't the fact of death that mattered so much as the obvious traces of the man's presence that struck her, when she walked into that dark chamber. Later she would recall the sadness she had felt – the sadness, and the sudden grief that had struck her like a blow in the dark – when she saw what that man had done. It was nothing like the murder films she had seen on television; she didn't scream, she didn't even cry out, or hurry away to fetch help, hysterical with fright. Instead, she waited, stock-still, drained of will, fixed by the horror of it all, yet absorbing it piecemeal, lingering over the details. When they questioned her, afterwards, she worked out that she had stood there for five, maybe ten minutes at most; yet it had seemed much longer – or rather, it had seemed like forever, as if nothing else would ever happen to her, as if her life would end if she were to look away, or cry out, or run.

When the news broke, the papers said the girl had been tortured, but that wasn't how Sally would have told it. What she saw in the shed would stay in her mind forever, but she didn't think of it as torture, or even murder. Kerry's hands were bound together with rope; her mouth was hidden by a length of insulation tape, which had been wound around her head several times, and her clothes had been removed, leaving her so thin and naked she looked more like a child than a girl of eighteen. Her skin was very white, in the unmarked areas between the cuts and burns; but what struck Sally most forcibly was the look in

Kerry's eyes. It took her a moment to work it out, but when she did, she understood that what she was witnessing wasn't torture, it was something much worse. Sally remembered seeing it on television: how, when the Aztecs performed a human sacrifice, they would cut the heart from the still living body, and she had shuddered at the programme's suggestion that a whole people, an entire community, could believe that this was the only way to protect their crops, or ensure victory in battle. To believe in human sacrifice, not as a secret, ugly thing, but as something glorious; to accord the highest honour to the priests who scooped out those living hearts and raised them to the sun seemed to her obscene beyond belief. It also seemed mercifully remote: the horrible, absurd practice of a primitive, warlike race. Now, as she stared into Kerry's eyes, she understood that the girl's slow death had meant something to her killer, something religious, something mystical. She didn't know how she knew, but she did. It wasn't the cuts, or the bruising, or the agonies Kerry had obviously suffered that told her what the man had felt; it wasn't anything rational and it was certainly nothing she could have repeated to anyone, when they came to question her. It was just something about the arrangement and position of the body that struck her as significant, an arrangement in which she sensed the reverence of that last moment. No matter how strange it seemed, she knew that, for the murderer, there had been a tenderness here, an almost religious regard for whatever it was that disappears at the moment of death, something exact, something equal to the presence of a living creature: the measured weight of a small bird or a rodent – a field mouse, say; or perhaps some kind of finch.

Afterwards, she thought they would find the man but, even though they kept the investigation open for a long time, the trail went cold. They had to check Tommy out, because it was his shed, but he was easily eliminated; he had an alibi and anyway, according to the police, the killer had left some of his

DNA at the scene. Sally had to think for a minute before she understood what this meant. It was all oddly familiar: the policemen who did the interviews acted and spoke just like the policemen on television, so there were times when she began to think it wasn't altogether real, that the investigation was nothing more than a test, or a rehearsal of some kind. After a while, though, she realised they were putting it on – though she couldn't decide if it was for her sake, to make it easier for her, or because they weren't really murder detectives, and they didn't quite know how to behave. Sally thought they were decent enough men, for the best part. She got to like them, especially Michael Cunningham, the young sergeant who wasn't quite tall enough for a policeman, but had a kindly manner and a way of coming into the house that vaguely reminded her of someone else. The funny thing was that, even while the police were carrying out their business, even while they seemed at a loss as to what to do, Sally couldn't quite shake off the suspicion that they had already guessed who the killer was, that they were in league with him all along, and were only going through the motions of the investigation. It was a ridiculous idea, she knew that, but she still felt at the back of her mind that they couldn't be trusted, not even the young man with the kind smile who seemed so familiar, like a long-lost nephew, or an old schoolmate that she couldn't quite place.

After the first couple of days, Tommy was no use to her at all. He made the tea, and asked several times if she was all right, then he switched back into the old routine, and got on with things. That was what he said, when they brought him back from the station: you just have to put it out of your mind and get on with things. But Sally couldn't. She kept thinking about Kerry and that thought would lead to something else: to the idea of death, and then on to a vague, almost unformed notion about everything she knew, everything she could see and touch, everything and everyone that lived and breathed. It had something to do with the way things disappeared: how, even while you were alive, pieces of your body were flaking away – strands of hair, broken fingernails, scrubbed skin. Memories that had once been vivid and clear melted down to nothing. When she looked at Tommy, she knew there had been a time when she had really loved him. When they were first married, they had been close. There had been some wonderful holidays in Spain and the Kyles of Bute. Yet now, though she knew those days were real, she just couldn't remember them clearly enough. The truth was, she hadn't so much stopped loving him as given up thinking about it. It wasn't better that way; it was just easier.

Eventually the police stopped coming. This upset her a little; it was as if they didn't think she mattered any more. She also saw that she had been dreading not having their visits to look forward to. She hadn't left the house for days; Tommy had done the shopping, the way he had done in the past when she was ill, or that time she had the miscarriage. Now he started getting at her, to go out, to get on with things, to stop brooding. He would invent reasons for her to be afraid – that the killer might still be in town, for example – then explain patiently why there was no danger. In the end, she put on her coat and headscarf and headed off to the shops, just to shut him up.

As soon as she was outside, she sensed the looks. It wasn't anything obvious, but she could tell that people were paying that little bit more attention, watching her as she went around the supermarket, stopping when they saw her in the greengrocer's or the paper shop and trying not to seem too curious. It didn't bother her at first – she even felt a little apologetic about finding Kerry; by the end of the day, however, she was tired of the discreet glances, of the way people would look then turn aside, pretending to be totally enthralled by the label on a packet of chicken breasts. Even people she thought of as friends, people she had known all her life, seemed awkward, even unhappy to see her. She kept telling herself she was imagining it, but she knew she wasn't; they really were staring, they really did look as if they wanted to turn and run when they saw her coming. As she walked home, in the slushy aftermath of the previous week's snow, Sally realised what she had lost. She had never understood, till that day, how invisible, how unremarkable she had been; now, all of a sudden, life had singled her out and made her too visible, as if she had been going about the place with blood on her hands, or talking to herself like a mad woman.

That night, or some time early the next morning, the dream began. It was very simple, at first, but slowly it became more elaborate and, though she was sure she didn't remember ever having had it before, it seemed familiar, as if it was a dream she had been having all her life, and had always forgotten till now. In the dream, there are clowns and ballerinas. Someone is riding a horse around the ring. At the centre, a Master of Ceremonies is looking out across the audience with a knowing half-smile; beside him stands a large box covered in stars and crescent moons, the black-and-silver lacquer dusted with blue moonshine. The MC is scanning his audience, looking for someone: when his eyes find Sally, he raises his hand and, with a flourish, he clears a path through the dancers and the circus animals, while the lights go down, and the audience falls silent. The girl in the dream knows what is coming now, and she steps up, happy and confident. In the dream, she understands everything, not just the disappearing act, but every one of life's secrets: the origin, the vanishing point, the final weight of all that disappears. One of these nights, she will sleep deeply, more deeply than she has ever slept before, and everything will fall into place. It isn't a trick, she tells herself, it's a secret. There are no real deaths in this circus, there is only the magician's box, which changes everything it contains into something new, different in appearance and form to what went in, but exactly the same, in weight, as what disappeared.

Mons Meg

A Fluid Fairytale

Janice Galloway

Once there was a city with a castle on a hill. The castle was built on a strong rock but still it did not render the people of the city invulnerable, for they needed water. Not any water, but water clear and clean enough to keep the hearts of the city-folk hale and the roses in the cheeks of their children. So they sent a pack of ten strong men and three women to the top of the hill where the castle gates stood to dig into the hard flint and earth they found there. Rain and spring-water collected from distant hills would come to this place, they thought, and here they would keep it safe, guarded and wholesome in a pit deep enough to drown a behemoth. They dug with picks and axes, pikes and hammers, and before long found a floor. The floor was made of stone, worn thin with the passing of feet and heavily cracked. Under this, a chamber some two men long and two men wide, with space enough for children between. And within this chamber they found many things. They found 1) a carved white figure of The Queen of Heaven with stars in her hair and a white bird at her feet, the whole unsoiled by burial; 2) a pair of candlesticks in heavy brass, stumps of beeswax still visible within the twin, crusted, cups; 3) four Scottish coins depicting a King and a Lion-head and four French of ancient denomination depicting a fox couchant; 4) charred paper, molten sealing wax, burned wood and pottery; 5) two boulders taken to be cannon shot and a lapis figurine of a flying owl. These they put aside. By nightfall, they had dug through a thick bed of clay to an equal depth of moss, with a coin of the Emperor Constantine embedded therein. Immediately under that, as work was closing for the day, their spades struck wood. Carefully, the diggers levered two coffins from the still, caked earth, each a hollowed oak cavity with clearly-marked spaces for head and feet, enclosing a single, entire, picked-clean skeleton. Closer to, one set of bones proved male, the other female, the heads, it was observed, pointing due West. Between them, a set of massive antlers had been placed, intricately carved with dogs, hares and fish; nearby, a fragment of hunting spear made of sharpened horn. These things looked so pitiful that some of the men shed tears and all made silent prayer. They waited four minutes in silence. But the pile of stones for the reservoir was clamouring at their backs, the people in the city beneath the rock were waiting. Lest the havoc they had made with their digging should provoke foul luck, they hid the artifacts, skeletons, coins and charms under what earth, peat-shavings and dung they could muster and scattered their crime with lime. Next morning, fearing the number of their party to be inauspicious, they killed the smallest and most pious of the women and settled her body into the simmering lime-slurry at the bottom of the pit, a peewit feather in her bluing hand. Twelve now, a godly number, they spoke amen and turned away from the hissing which had already started. They ate a hearty breakfast of grease and oat groats and resumed their work, saying nothing more. They built the reservoir reverently, however, and thought of it as a shrine. And since, they say, Meg's nourishment has kept the waters of the Castlegate fair. Her bones have given minerals, her melted tissues a softness of texture, her veins and their former content the rosy tint of health for which the city's water is justly famed.

* * *

Picture her under the city slabs and engine noise, good citizens.

The animals that visit her.

How blessed in us she must surely be.

Cloven Tongues

A Gothic Bibliography

Below is a finite list of Gothic novels by Scots (though the first is a poem; it would have been a dreadful omission). I have also included one work of non-fiction, and while it may be troublesome to brand journalism with terms usually reserved for fiction, the work certainly seems to me Gothic in its effects and implications. While I have not included short stories or plays, I feel, however, that there should be a mention at least once in this book of Robert Louis Stevenson's masterful tale of demonic possession, 'Thrawn Janet' (1891), and also of Shakespeare's *Macbeth* (1606), which, while not written by a Scot, is perhaps about as Scottish as can Gothic be.

This, of course, like any list (or any definition of Gothic for that matter) is purely subjective, and I feel sure that there are some texts on it which may be disputed by readers, likewise some which it is felt should be added. There are a higher concentration of books from recent years, perhaps due to some strange upsurge of pre-millennial fear, perhaps simply because there are more books in print/living memory than in previous years. I apologise for any shortcomings or omissions, but hope you find the guide useful nonetheless.

A.B.

1790	Robert Burns	'Tam o' Shanter'
1814	Sir Walter Scott	*Waverley*
1815	Sir Walter Scott	*Guy Mannering*
1822	James Hogg	*The Three Perils of Man*
1824	James Hogg	*The Private Memoirs and Confessions of a Justified Sinner*
	Sir Walter Scott	*Redgauntlet*
1886	R. L. Stevenson	*The Strange Case of Dr Jekyll and Mr Hyde*
1901	George Douglas Brown	*The House with the Green Shutters*
1927	John Buchan	*Witch Wood*
1955	Robin Jenkins	*The Cone Gatherers*
1960	Muriel Spark	*The Ballad of Peckham Rye*
1978	Emma Tennant	*The Bad Sister*
1981	Alasdair Gray	*Lanark: A Life in Four Books*
1984	Iain Banks	*The Wasp Factory*
1986	Iain Banks	*The Bridge*
1987	Iain M. Banks	*Consider Phlebas*
1989	Janice Galloway	*The Trick is to keep Breathing*
	Emma Tennant	*The Two Women of London*
1990	Brian McCabe	*The Other McCoy*
1991	Elspeth Barker	*O Caledonia*
	Janice Galloway	*Blood*
	Ian Rankin	*Hide and Seek*
1992	Ian Rankin	*Tooth and Nail*
1993	Irvine Welsh	*Trainspotting*
1994	Iain M. Banks	*Feersum Endjin*
	James Kelman	*How Late it was, how Late*
1995	A. L. Kennedy	*So I am Glad*
	Duncan McLean	*Bunker Man*
	Alan Warner	*Morvern Callar*
	Irvine Welsh	*Marabou Stork Nightmares*

1996	John Burnside	*The Dumb House*
	Andrew O'Hagan	*The Missing* (non-fiction)
	John Herdman	*Ghost Writing*
1997	Ian Rankin	*Black and Blue*
	Christopher Whyte	*The Warlock of Strathearn*
1998	Dilys Rose	*Pest Maiden*
	Alice Thompson	*Pandora's Box*
	Irvine Welsh	*Filth*
1999	Toni Davidson	*Scar Culture*
	Ian Rankin	*Dead Souls*
	Christopher Wallace	*The Resurrection Club*
2000	Michel Faber	*Under the Skin*
	Maggie O'Farrell	*After You'd Gone*
	James Robertson	*The Fanatic*

ABOUT THE AUTHORS

Alison Armstrong has written a number of short stories. Her friends have described them as weird, or even unpleasant. Alison finds them cathartic.

Alan Bissett was born in 1975. He is an English Studies research student at the University of Stirling. He has had stories published in a variety of Scottish magazines, and was shortlisted for the Macallan/*Scotland on Sunday* short-story competition 2000. He has recently completed his first novel (the non-Gothic) *Boy Racers.*

John Burnside has published seven books of poetry, of which the most recent is *The Asylum Dance* (which has been shortlisted for the Whitbread Poetry Prize, the Forward Poetry Prize and the T. S. Eliot Prize for Poetry), two novels, and a book of short stories, entitled *Burning Elvis* (Jonathan Cape 2000). He is currently working on a book of essays and a new novel, *The Locust Room*, to appear in May 2001. He lives in Fife, where he teaches creative writing at the University of St Andrews.

Sophie Cooke is 24. She read Anthropology at Edinburgh University and now lives in Glasgow. She was the runner-up in the Macallan Award 2000 with her short story 'Why You Should Not Put Your Hand Through The Ice' and is currently working on a clutch of other stories, as well as the beginnings of a novel. A qualified journalist, she writes freelance travel articles for various national newspapers.

Linda Cracknell moved to Scotland from Devon ten years ago and now lives and works in Highland Perthshire. She won the Macallan/*Scotland on Sunday* short-story competition in 1998 with her first published piece of fiction, and her short-story collection *Life Drawing* was published in October 2000.

Toni Davidson was born in 1965, and is the editor of two collections of fiction: *And Thus Will I Freely Sing* (Polygon 1989) and *Intoxication* (Serpents Tail 1998). He is the author of *Scar Culture* (Rebel Inc) which was published in 1999. The novel was shortlisted for the 1999 Saltire Society First Book Award and has been published in nine countries. He is currently working on a screenplay entitled *The Tower of Babel* and his second novel, *Wild Justice.*

Chris Dolan returned to Glasgow after living abroad. He writes for page, stage and screen. *Ascension Day* (Headline Review 1999) won the McKitterick Prize; he received the Macallan for a story in the collection *Poor Angels* (Polygon 1996). His play *Sabina* (Faber & Faber 98) won a Fringe first. His latest play, *The Reader*, is an adaptation of Bernard Schlink's novel. Winner also of the 1999 R. L. Stevenson Award, he is currently working on a second novel and another collection of shorts.

Michel Faber was born in Holland, nowadays the least Gothic country in Europe (but what about Hieronymus Bosch, eh?). Since winning the Macallan in 1996, Faber's work, published by Canongate, has continued to win prizes, including the Saltire for the collection *Some Rain Must Fall*. His novel, *Under the Skin*, which has been shortlisted for the Whitbread First Novel Award, has been sold to fifteen countries. He likes touching fur.

Janice Galloway's work includes novels (*The Trick is to keep Breathing*, *Foreign Parts*), short stories (*Blood*, *Where You Find It*), collaborative poetry texts (with visual artists) and music texts (for Sally Beamish and Alasdair Nicholson). Her literary prizes include the American Academy's E. M. Forster Award, the McVitie's and MIND/Allan Lane Awards. She is currently completing a third novel.

Magi Gibson's third volume of poetry, *Wild Women of a Certain Age*, is published by Chapman. Her first book, *Kicking Back*, was nominated for a Saltire award. Her work has appeared in many magazines and anthologies. She has held Scottish Arts Council Writing Fellowships in Renfrew and Aberdeenshire. She lives near Stirling.

Laura Hird was born and lives in Edinburgh. *Nail and other Stories*, her first book, was shortlisted for the Saltire Award. Her first novel, *Born Free*, was *The Face* Book of the Year 1999 and has been shortlisted for the Whitbread First Novel Award. Two other novellas appeared in the anthologies *Children of Albion Rovers* and *Rover's Return* (Rebel Inc.) Her short stories have been published in *The Face*, *Blvd.* (Netherlands), *Barcelona Review* (Spain), *Bang* (Sweden), *Grand Street* and *Story* (USA).

Jackie Kay was born and brought up in Scotland. Her first collection of poetry, *The Adoption Papers*, won a Forward Prize, a Saltire First Book Award and a Scottish Arts Council Award. Her first novel, *Trumpet*, won the Guardian Fiction Prize and the Authors Club first novel award. Her latest collection of poetry for children, *The Frog who Dreamed she was an Opera Singer* won the Signal Prize. She lives in Manchester.

Helen Lamb is a poet and fiction writer. Her work has been widely published in anthologies and magazines and broadcast on BBC Radio 4, Radio Scotland and RTE. Poetry collection *Strange Fish* (with Magi Gibson) published by Duende, 1997. Her first short-story collection, *Superior Bedsits*, will be published by Polygon this autumn.

Brian McCabe was born in Easthouses, near Edinburgh. He has lived as a freelance writer since 1980, and has held various writing fellowships, most recently as Novelist in Residence at St Andrews University. He has published three collections of poetry, two collections of short stories, plays for radio and television, and a novel, *The Other McCoy* (Mainstream 1990/Penguin 1991). He lives with his family in Edinburgh.

Maggie O'Farrell was born in Northern Ireland in 1972 and grew up in East Lothian, Scotland. Her first novel, *After You'd Gone*, was published last year.

About the Authors

James Robertson was born in 1958. He studied history at Edinburgh University, worked in various jobs, returned to do a Ph.D. on Sir Walter Scott, and has been a full-time writer since 1993. Publications include two books of short stories, *Close* (1991) and *The Ragged Man's Complaint* (1993), two collections of poetry, a book of *Scottish Ghost Stories* (1996) and a novel, *The Fanatic* (2000).

Dilys Rose has published two collections of poems, three of short stories, most recently *War Dolls*, and a novel, *Pest Maiden*. Currently working on a second novel, as well as short fiction and poetry. She lives in Edinburgh.

Andrew Murray Scott's novel, *Tumulus*, won the inaugural Dundee Book Prize in 1999. A second novel, *Estuary Blue*, will appear in 2001, also from Polygon. As well as a number of short stories, Andrew is the author of non-fiction books, including work on Alexander Trocchi, and is presently involved in setting up a literary magazine, *Riverrun*.

Ali Smith was born in Inverness in 1962. She has published two collections of stories, *Free Love and other stories* and *Other Stories and other stories*, and a novel, *Like*. Her new novel, *Hotel World*, is due out in 2001. She lives in Cambridge.

Raymond Soltysek was born in Barrhead. His stories have appeared on Radio 4 and in several literary magazines and anthologies, including *Flamingo New Scottish Writing* 1997, Shorts 1998, and *Something Wicked: New Scottish Crime Writing* (1999). His first collection, *Occasional Demons*, was published by 11:9 in October 2000. He teaches and runs internet creative writing groups for young writers.

Christopher Whyte was born to a mixed Scottish-Irish, Catholic family in the West End of Glasgow and educated by the Jesuits there, then at Cambridge and Perugia (Italy). He lived in Rome from 1975 to 1985, began publishing Gaelic poetry in 1987 and has so far written four novels: *Euphemia MacFarrigle and the Laughing Virgin*, *The Warlock of Strathearn*, *The Gay Decameron*, and *The Cloud Machinery*. He is currently working on a fifth, *The House on Rue St Jacques Street.*